3vE

Other Books by Jason DeGray

RE: World

Blaze Against the Machine

Family Matters

The Ruined Man

The Dark Goddess

Absolutely True Retellings: The Saga of Shamus

A Hollow Monk's Dreams

3vE

by Jason DeGray

To the sleeping masses. May you awaken before it's too late.

3vE

Suppose that there does actually exist a force which can be mastered and by which the miracles of Nature are made subservient to the will of Man. Tell us, in such case, whether the secrets of wealth and the bonds of sympathy can be entrusted to brutal greed; the art of fascination to libertines; the supremacy over other wills to those who cannot attain government of their proper selves. It is terrifying to reflect upon the disorders which would follow from such profanation; some cataclysm is needed to efface the crimes of earth when all are steeped in slime and blood.

--Eliphas Levi

1

I have been in many shapes before
I gained a congenial form.
What if we're wrong, Cathar?
During the 12th century, the
Kabbalah was transcribed by
Rabbi Isaac the Blind in Provence
in the south of France.
We aren't wrong, Bogomil. Or at
the very least, we're close enough
to right that it doesn't matter.

Air, thick with smog, hung in a shroud over the technological wonder that was Corporate Denver. It was a city of disparity—of dizzying heights and dense, oppressive lows. The pinnacle of human achievement, it and the other corporate city-states, were made possible at the expense of the earth itself. Humanity's monuments to its hubris existed because of its reckless ambition and desire for progress. Skyscrapers, like fingers made of metal and glass, reached to the heavens, the tops of the tallest piercing the veil of gloom and breaking free into the clear blue sky. A sky dotted with skycars, zipping and zooming, carrying frenetic people who were constantly busy to keep their minds off the truth of their depressive reality. Down below, at street level, a colorful assortment of common folk milled around the streets with apathetic purpose. They saw the writing on the wall—they knew they lived in a world in decline. There was nothing left; they stared into the abyss of the certainty of their annihilation. Thus, the only freedom that remained was found in acts of complete and utter societal rejection. There were no cohesive groups, just morose and sardonic people lost in their own personal delusions. Delusions they projected outward with the help of immersive technology, but it wasn't only outlandish fashion and extreme depravity. Man had merged with machine and varying examples of this union could be seen in the eclectic proletariat who their betters lovingly dubbed 'noobs.' It was the worst among them that Jacob Riley hunted.

Riley screwed the lid on the cylindrical glass case; the severed head inside floated weightlessly, its eyes staring into nothing and mouth slightly agape. The body at his feet jerked and writhed around in an expanding pool of blood. He donned a plastic poncho and face shield, pulled rubber gloves over his hands, and took out a cleaver. Then he rolled the body over and buried the blade in the headless corpse's back. He hacked at it a few times, ignoring the blood splatter on his faceguard, and pried open the ribcage, exposing the spinal column. Wrapped around it was a shimmering blue cord. Riley pulled out clippers and snipped the cord at the top and bottom of the spine and carefully pulled it free, depositing his loot in a clear plastic bag. He tore off the plastic poncho he wore and pulled off his rubber gloves, throwing both on the mutilated remains of his bounty. He picked up the head case and strolled out into the streets of Corporate Denver, smoking a cigarette and heading for his favorite diner. Clouds were gathering on the horizon; there was a storm rolling in from the badlands soon. Time enough for a cup of Feen and a bite to eat before he turned in his bounty.

He awoke with a sharp, desperate inhale as if he'd been drowning and finally broke the surface. He had escaped the shadow. The hiss of steam expelling from the cryopod broke the still silence of the pristine room, and its occupant fell to the ground, staring at his fuzzy reflection in the polished floor before climbing unsteadily to his feet and shuffling toward the door. His vision blurry, he could hardly make out the vague and shadowy shapes that were the other cryopods filling the room. The thick fog over his physical brain parted slightly.

How slow it is, he thought, *the body tethers everything, weighs it down. Even the mind. No, especially the mind.*

CharWang Industries's HyLyfe Tower. That's where he was. That's where they put his body—all their bodies. This was one of the most secure facilities in the world. He would be safe if he could find help, but the cryopod chamber he was in appeared empty. He'd have to get to people. He knew he wouldn't make it far with his quivering body weak from Resuscitation Sickness. But he had to. Lives depended on him; the lives of each and every one of his sleeping comrades. He had to find help and warn the others.

He tumbled into the hallway, leaning heavily on the wall trying to catch his breath and convince his mutinous body to move. He still couldn't make out much, but he saw darkened offices on the opposite side.

"Help!" he croaked. "Someone. Anyone. Help!" He reached out his hand and a quiet stranger clasped it. His throat was parched and he could only wheeze, "Help. I need help."

He noticed the stranger nod, the head--a fuzzy oblong shape, bobbing in assent. The kind stranger helped him to his feet, ushered him into a dark side office, and eased him into a chair.

He was just about to ask for water when the stranger jerked his head back and, drawing a gleaming metal blade across his neck, opened his throat up from ear to ear. He felt the blood splashing over his flimsy cryosuit even as the shadows crept in at the fringes of his hazy vision. He hadn't escaped the shadow after all. He managed a choked sob. Darkness overwhelmed his vision and snuffed out the last of his life.

The kind stranger jammed the knife into its victim's eye socket and quietly left as the first alarms began to sound.

2

I have been the slender blade of a
sword...
Lives depend on him and us. We
have one chance left. If we fail
we're all dead.
For the first time in its six
thousand-year history, the ancient
magic techniques were put down on
paper.
That's a chance we have to take.
Gnosis was never achieved by men
afraid to take chances.

Beautiful vistas of Corporate Denver paraded across the screen while CharWang Industries CEO, Dr. Elijah Gold, narrated.

"It's a wonder we made it as far as we did. Face it. We were headed straight for a brick wall at 200 miles per hour. And, for some inexplicable reason, we constantly invented new ways and gadgets to make us get there faster. Like we couldn't take the insanity anymore and wanted it to be over as much as the universe did. And when we hit that wall we slammed right into it, smashing everything we'd created, worked for, and built into fucking dust. Dust. Ashes to ashes, dust to dust—that's how the old saying goes. And boy was it spot on. We had a good thing going, though, didn't we? I mean, it wasn't all bad. We made beautiful things, we created. We expanded. We sought to crack open the very Mystery behind the universe and steal its secrets for ourselves. Pretty bold, right? Pretty daring? Pretty stupid. But we are tenacious. That's what drives us on and on until we have nothing left to give. It's what forces us to progress when we hit that wall and all that remains is dust and tears. Something always rises from those ashes. That's what makes us triumphant. That's our gift—our

superpower. And I know that we will rise once again. Be brave. Be fierce. Be tenacious. Stare the Abyss right in its dark, unfathomable eye and spit in its face. Never flinch. Never give in. Never quit. You're alive. You survived. That's something. You know what the alternative to something is? Nothing. Nobody really wants that. Be honest. Now, look outside. Find something good and say, "See? The world really is a beautiful place."

The video ended with the CharWang logo fading off the screen.

Dr. Gold stared hard at the young man in front of him. Jimmy Lee Gold seemed to be making a point of aimlessly scrolling through his wrist computer. "What's the lesson here, Jimmy Lee?"

"Huh?" Jimmy Lee looked up from the screen grafted into his forearm. "Lesson from what? That stupid video you made me sit through? I don't know. Maybe the lesson is that you severely overestimate your role in fixing the mess we're all in." He stared hard, right back into his father's eyes, unflinching.

"Wrong. The lesson is that we haven't accomplished all we have by pointless idealism. There's no room for that in the world. Not anymore. We have no choice but to make the hard decisions to get us all to a better place. Project Ed3n is that better place."

"Look around, Dr. Gold," Jimmy Lee sneered, "None of this is natural. Not one thing in this whole damn city comes from the earth. And your little project is just as unnatural. That's not idealism. That's fact."

Gold slammed his fist down on his desk, sending a web of cracks in all directions. "I didn't pull you away from those psychotic Rainbow Children only to have you develop some warped case of Stockholm Syndrome! You get your shit together! You are going to be a vice president soon."

"No. I'm done with this," he motioned around the room, "All of it. I'm getting Lola and my child and we're out of here. Back to the Heart."

"You're not going anywhere. As a matter of fact, as of now, you aren't authorized to leave the HyLyfe Tower premises. I've already scheduled your first meeting with the company shrink. So forget about that Burbanite slut and the bastard you put inside her! She will never have Status. And neither will her spawn. Do your part or I'll make it harder for everyone. Yours wouldn't be the first bastard we had to KiSS." Elijah took a deep breath and pulled out a cigar from a box on his desk. "Now get out of my sight. Some of us actually have to work around here."

Jimmy Lee quivered in impotent rage, his eyes full of hatred. Dr. Gold ignored him and made a show of lighting his cigar. The door to his office opened and two Suits entered.

"You're going to have to come with us," the first one spoke.

"There's a 45% chance you will be fatally injured if you resist. We'd rather not have that kind of damage done to so valuable an asset."

"Yeah. I was done here anyway." Jimmy Lee straightened his leather jacket and turned around. He swaggered out of the office with his head held high.

Gold watched him go with a soft smile. He was unbreakable, his son. He had to be proud of that much. Come what may.

Dr. Gold took his smoking cigar and strolled down to R&D. Labcoats hustled to and fro, busy with their various tasks. He ignored them all as if they were ants scurrying beneath him and walked up to the supervisor.

The man stood on a platform in the center of the room wearing a huge helmet connected to a tangle of wires funneling into a cylinder that disappeared into the ceiling. His head was tipped back, eyes rolled to the whites. When Dr. Gold stepped in front of him his head snapped up, his eyes cleared and all the Labcoats froze in mid-action.

"Dr. Gold. Pleasure. What can I do for you, sir?"

"Checking the progress on 4D4M and 3vE."

"Ah, yes. As it stands, both models are in excellent condition. We just finished the alpha testing. We have calculated that it had a 76.2% success rate with the noted exception of one minor flaw."

"Which is?"

"That of the nanobots. As it stands, they replicate too fast and end up destroying the body. As is the case with our live subject."

"But the models aren't fully organic. They're hybrids," Gold argued, "The nanobots were supposed to account for that and self-correct."

"That was the hypothesis. However, the results proved otherwise. As it stands, Project Ed3n's first couple isn't likely to live as long as anticipated. That is until the issue is resolved. At which point we project success in the high 90 percentile range," the supervisor added quickly.

"How can it be resolved?" Gold blew smoke in the supervisor's face. "And you better dazzle me with an idea. Your job depends on it."

The supervisor shifted uncomfortably. Just a few weeks ago he had been another faceless Labcoat until his predecessor gave Dr. Gold unfavorable test results. He was fired on the spot. The horror of that day was so unforgettable it often bubbled to the surface despite the overwhelming white noise of the Hivemind. It is what motivated him to succeed where those before him failed.

"We have discovered an option with a 72% probability of success. That of finding the subject's spawn. We hypothesize that some of the nanobots were attached to his sperm. These would have been introduced to the fetus as a result of insemination. If this is the case, then the nanobots developing inside the womb would have self-corrected to become part of the new organism. They would be more docile and easily assimilated. If we could get a culture of those nanobots we could replicate them."

"What do we need for that?"

"The spawn's head, sir. We'd need to collect a sample directly from the brain tissue. Thus, we need it cold capped. We could employ an Integration Technology consultant to get the job done discreetly."

"Whatever you need, it's authorized. Just get it done," Gold said, and then his earpiece chimed. He held up a finger and turned around. "Yes? Another one? I'm on my way." He turned back to the supervisor. "Something's come up. Carry on."

"Very good. Thank you for stopping by, Dr. Gold," the supervisor said and his head lolled back once more. Labcoats immediately resumed their tasks.

Nate sat in the community school's virtual construct only half-listening to the digital avatar of his teacher drone on about basic VR functions. He was lucky just to be there, he understood that. The community schools were all run on a lottery system. Not all children in the Burbs got the chance to attend. That they had access to eSpace netsets was a miracle in and of itself and Nate, who was 10 going on 11, wanted nothing more than to leap off into eSpace and explore. But oh no, not for him, not today. Today he was stuck in another boring lesson learning simple commands he had been using since before he could walk. Nate never considered himself a savant, a genius, or special in any way, but that's exactly what he was.

"Nate?" the teacher's avatar called out to him, "Are you still with us?"

"Yes," he replied dryly.

"I asked how you executed a file search on eSpace."

Nate pointed at the space in front of him and pulled down the options menu. He selected 'Search.' "Anything else?"

"Wow, who taught you how to access the holographic functions like that? The dropdown menu alone is an expensive avatar add-on. Where did you get it?" His teacher glared at him sternly and the rest of the class turned toward him.

"What are you talking about? I thought everybody had them."

"No, Nate. Very few people without Status have them, actually. And no one in the Burbs, to my knowledge. So again, where did you get it?"

"I don't know," Nate said, his heart racing.

"Nate's a swiper!" said Angela Finster, her cartoonish avatar glaring at him with comical anger.

"I am not!" Nate yelled, "I didn't get it from anywhere! I made it, alright? I made it!"

The teacher opened her mouth to respond and then froze. Nate looked around. Everything had frozen. The other students, the background effects—everything. He looked at the door leading into the hallway (which was really a loading room to prepare an avatar to be uploaded to the classroom construct) and saw a flicker of something— like a gray robe and wisps of long, white hair fluttering past. Nate looked around to make sure nothing else had changed. It hadn't. The scene was still frozen. He walked to the door and out into the hallway where another door suddenly appeared. Only this door was very small. On a table next to the door sat a vial of blue liquid. Tied to the stem was a note that read "Drink Me." He looked around and picked up the vial. He uncorked it and swirled it around. It sloshed exactly like real water. The realistic graphics of eSpace always amazed Nate and as a small child, he had some difficulty distinguishing eSpace from the real. Before long, city shrinks started using words like 'schizoid' and 'dissociative identity disorder' when talking about Nate, which is why his mother and father left the city to live among the Rainbow Children. They had to ground him, to give him an understanding of and connection to the real. A flash of movement caused him to start and look up from the hypnotizing liquid of the blue vial. The tiny door closed shut and without another moment's hesitation, Nate uncorked the vial and swallowed its contents. He was immediately beset by vertigo that was followed by the pull of an inescapable vortex. The closest feeling he knew to associate it with was the experience of disconnecting from eSpace, so that's what he assumed was happening. But once the feeling passed, Nate stood before a door exactly his height.

"Curiouser and curiouser," he said aloud and, opening the door, stepped through into worlds unknown.

3

*I have been a drop in the
air... insignificant...
What detrimental dreamscapes! If
we tread dark paths we will find
shadowed treasures.
The Kabbalistic writings of Isaac
the Blind were obtained by nine
French noblemen.
Stop quoting poetry. You know I
hate it.*

Riley sat in his favorite diner sipping Feen from a Styrofoam cup and staring out at the city drenched in rain. The streets were empty just like they were every time it rained for the past 150 years. He'd seen the old movies, read some of the old books; the ones that talked about the earth before—in the old times when life still flourished and the land wasn't poisoned. "Singing in the Rain" was impossible now unless you wanted third-degree burns and to be lethally saturated with heavy metals. He had heard rumors that rain outside the corporate-free cities wasn't deadly, and in some places even caused plant life to flourish again. But those were just rumors. The world was dying and Riley found a morbid comfort in watching it in its death throes.

"See? The world really is a beautiful place," Riley chuckled to himself. He tried to keep his thoughts from drifting back to *her* like they did every time he sat in the diner and wallowed in moroseness. But it never worked. There was too much bad blood and no closure. He never forgave her for leaving after their son got sick. Riley watched helplessly as his boy withered and died while she ran off to that fantasy land she'd been plugged into ever since. HyLyfe—the immersive VR experience for those with enough Status to log in and never come out. He hated the stupid name almost as much as he hated the very thing itself.

His phone chimed and he checked the message. "Randy," he said with obvious distaste. The guy was a good agent. He was a little fruity, but he got him steady and decent contracts. Still though, Riley didn't fully trust him. The world wasn't that kind of place anymore. Trust was a liability.

"Riles, good to see your chipper face," Randy said in his annoyingly too-sweet tone. "How's things been? You check into that vacation in Left Angeles I told you about?"

"Hell no. What do I want with some oil-slicked beaches and hazy sunset views?"

"Oh come on. Don't be stupid. Everyone goes for the raves. You know that. Shit, I didn't see outside for a week straight last time I went."

"I don't care, Randy. What do you want? I've got a case to turn in then I'm heading over to your place. Got some nice gear for you to look at. Next-gen from the look of it. Haven't seen anything like it." Lately, there was an influx of available IT work and he couldn't help but think something dark was stirring in the underbelly of uber-corporate R&D. There was always a spike in hackjobs when the corporations released new Integration Technology. They called it live beta testing. Riley called it Status exploitation. Without Status the only way to come by cutting-edge enhancements was the black market or signing up for beta testing. Didn't take much to guess what the cheaper option was.

"I'll look at it, but I gotta tell you, that's not where the market is going. Buyers right now don't want gear retrieval. They want the corpses intact."

"Intact? What good is a headless body full of corporate gear?"

"That's for the Labcoats to worry about. I'm just telling you how it is. Boys in the underground asking for the same shit. But that's not why I called. I got you something. Something big. Your contact is Mary May. Meeting tomorrow at 9:30 A.M. sharp. Downtown Café."

"That's a corporate joint. How many times have I told you, Randy, I'm done with corporate gigs?"

"It has something to do with HyLyfe. And you told me to call you first if any HyLyfe jobs came up."

"Alright. I'll look into it." He hung up and signaled the waitress for a refill. Outside, the poisoned rain streaked down the filthy glass windows of the diner reminding Riley how deadly beauty can be.

All the Status elite who hadn't logged into HyLyfe congregated in the Downtown Café. It was where real-world policy was made over morning cocktails and more money changed hands than at any bank. But Riley knew it for what it was: a place of deception. This was where the fiddlers on the roof gathered to watch civilization burn to the ground—one last and glorious time. His ex, Shawn, had a membership before she got knocked up by his broke ass and lost Status. Classism, at least, survived the Great Collapses. Some things never went out of style, no matter how cliché they were. As for the café, Riley detested the place—would've rather stuffed his own head in one of his cryo-cases than step foot inside, but business was business. People had lost the luxury of personal integrity a long time ago.

"What's your Status," growled the doorman, barring the way with his massive frame. He distrusted Riley and made it known.

"I'm meeting someone," answered Riley.

"Ain't gonna cut it. I gotta kick a dozen noobs' asses every day who think they can just stroll in and start preaching to the patrons about making a better world. Nobody had time for shit like that." He squared up to Riley, the veins in his neck bulging in anticipation. "Either let me scan your arm or leave."

"My status is fuck off I'm meeting someone." Riley didn't have a personal assistant device grafted into his forearm. He was an oddity in a society that had almost completely merged itself with the technology it created.

"I gotta tell you I'm geared to the tits and have had six martial arts uploaded. If you don't leave I will personally demonstrate all six of them on your pudgy ass." The doorman flexed his muscles to prove his point.

"Fuckin' hackjob," spat Riley and bristled for a fight. People who augmented their bodies with corporate technology, ever seeking perfection in melding man and machine, were abominations in his eyes. He disliked them almost as much as the HyLyfers. "Too poor for the HyLyfe and too weak to live without gear. It's pathetic. You're pathetic."

The look in the doorman's eye shifted from annoyed to insulted the same instant as his face flushed a bright red.

I might have taken that a bit far, Riley thought. He worked as an Integration Technology Consultant and it could be reasoned that his strong resistance to integration had a lot to do with his experiences. Enhancements were not to be trusted. It was never a good idea to prod the hackjobs. They ran a high risk of getting the technocrazies when their upgrades malfunctioned. A hackjob in a technorage was an ugly thing to see. For no apparent reason, they would snap and go berserk on whomever or whatever was around them. Giving them a reason to snap was a death wish. Riley had seen enough of their handiwork to know.

"Now Benjamin, is that any way to treat a guest?"

The doorman instantly deflated when he saw the speaker. She was a gorgeous woman who moved with easy grace, effortlessly flowing from one moment into the next.

"Sorry Miss May. He didn't say he was with you," he shot Riley an accusatory look.

"All a misunderstanding I'm sure. Have a nice day." She smiled at him. Then said, "Shall we, Mr. Riley?"

Riley had seen netvids of the Downtown Café's interior, but nothing could've prepared him for the reality. The entire bottom floor of an old skyscraper had been transformed into a slice of decadent luxury. In a world where everyone had so little, to see a few with so much really grated on his nerves and sense of justice. The whole place was full of plant life—real, actual plants—and the air inside hit Riley with a refreshing blast of sweetness. The center of the room, which once housed massive escalators, had been transformed into a lush mound of grass and clover with a beautiful gurgling brook that collected in a pristine pool at the bottom. Tables were arranged to allow maximum comfort and privacy. High-end shops lined the outer walls selling anything a heart with Status could desire. It was as if he'd been transported back in time. To those hoary days before the greed of a few and complacency of many had ruined the world for everyone.

"So what do you think of our little café?" Mary asked after they were seated and had ordered.

"I think it's a perfect model of exactly what is wrong with society. This is why I don't take corporate jobs."

She looked genuinely puzzled by his response. "But all jobs are corporate jobs anymore. Your file says you're an IT Consultant. You get contracts from your agent. Where do you think the money for those contracts comes from?"

He ignored her and continued, "I mean seriously. Look around. The world has gone to shit. These fucking uber-corporations raped the planet and took everything for themselves. And now, two Great Collapses later, they're holing up in their precious walled 'free cities'. For what? To doom us all to live as serfs so a handful of assholes could claim Status and enjoy what's left. It's bullshit."

"The earth isn't dead. She's just badly hurt. There are still entire tracts of land left pure and untouched."

Riley snorted contemptuously. "Yeah. All controlled by the Rainbow Children."

Nobody expected the hippies to militarize during the Second Great Collapse. No one had even given them a second thought because they were so intent on saving their own asses from the warring between governments and the corporations. Not worrying about the Rainbow Children had been the corporations' one and only mistake in their coup for a New World that resulted in the earth's destruction. The hippies, transients—those living like gypsies—rose up and claimed what remained of the earth's untouched forests and natural areas. Areas now highly coveted by all the uber-corporations because they had strip-mined, polluted, fracked, and buzz-sawed the rest of the planet into a barren wasteland. But try as they might—and they did try—the uber-corporations always failed to oust the Rainbow Children. Turned back each and every time, as if the earth itself was aiding them in its defense.

"They are a minor setback and nothing more. Eventually, they will come to see the need for peaceful coexistence or we will finally find a way to bring them to heel. But enough about them. That's not why we're here."

"Why are we here, exactly? I mean, breakfast was nice and all, but what's the job? Randy said it had something to do with HyLyfe."

"It does." She darted a quick glance around and leaned in, "Somebody has managed to kill two HyLyfers."

Riley couldn't stifle his laugh. "How the hell is that even possible? They're inside a computer."

"Only partially. Their bodies are preserved in a cryogenic state in case they ever decide to log out. Both victims had logged out prior to being murdered."

"If their body dies, do they die in the game?"

"No. In that unlikely event, their consciousness would be completely uploaded into HyLyfe."

"Then why would they log out?"

"Exactly what we need to find out. So will you help us?"

"I still don't know if I care enough about a bunch of Status elites stuck inside a video game to help them find a killer."

"HyLyfers are not just 'a bunch of Status elites stuck inside a video game'." She bristled as if he had insulted her personally. "They don't just lounge around in VR sims all day. They work on solving problems—on bettering humanity while the rest of you trash scurry about your pointless lives just waiting to die from KiSS."

"If you know anything about me, you know that me and my boy got KiSS'd." KiSS, or Kill Switch Syndrome, was a designer virus the uber-corporations infected the entirety of the population with after the Second Great Collapse. "And you probably know why too. It was a deterrent and a punishment—a way to keep us noobs where we belong. Your corporate masters got me with the sustainment meds. I'll be giving myself shots every 12 hours till they cancel my insurance. But my boy, he didn't get that chance. Why? What did he do? What was his crime?" He got up and finished his drink before tossing the glass into the pond. "We're done here. To hell with you and your HyLyfers. I hope whoever is killing them gets them all."

A touch of genuine empathy briefly cracked her cheery, professional façade. "You're right. That was uncalled for. I'm sorry. Please, take a walk with me."

Riley didn't figure he had much of a choice. Everywhere he looked a security guard lurked in the background and a few were starting to look in his direction. "You Status types not worry about having a bunch of gearheads around you all the time?"

"What's to worry about?"

"The technocrazies. They can snap at any moment."

"Ah. Because you work in IT you think all the Enhanced will suffer from Technological Psychosis Syndrome, is that it? That's a conspiracy. TPS only manifests in those with older-generation or experimental gear."

"Yeah sure. Keep telling yourself that." Cognitive dissonance, it seemed, had also survived the Great Collapses.

They walked up a ramp to the upper floors where a myriad of plants grew in hydroponic systems suspended from the ceiling.

"The hanging gardens. A HyLyfe project," Mary said proudly. "All produced and maintained by HyLyfe. The goal is to reintroduce these plants into the wild. In other buildings and in other cities there are menageries doing the same with animals. They've cloned over 43 species already. The Corporate Council knows they screwed up. Pissed where they slept and all that. They're fixing it. Rebuilding a sustainable world from the ground up. Let the Rainbow Children have their forests. We're making our own. Tell me how this is evil or sinister."

Riley couldn't.

"Help us catch whoever is behind this and you will be helping ensure the birth of a new earth. Plus we'll give you Status and a generous stipend. What do you say?"

"If I said no to that, I'd be an asshole."

"So it's settled. Meet me at HyLyfe Tower tomorrow. Nine sharp."

4

I have been a shining star...
And that's why you have no soul,
Cathar. Be glad you still have your
head.
These French noblemen became the
Knights Templar.
Same to you. Be glad you still have
an option. This is what we decided.
Make it happen, supervisor.

Riley looked up at HyLyfe Tower with a mixture of awe and disgust. It was a new structure made of gleaming metal alloys and glass, rising into the sky challenging heaven like the Tower of Babel. The white stone plaza in front was abuzz with hectic activity as corporate drones hurried about on business that was no doubt dictated by their respective Hiveminds. Riley watched with curious disinterest, wondering how people gave up control of their lives in exchange for a false sense of security. The giant digital clock above the entrance rolled over to 9 A.M. and Riley, tossing his cigarette aside, ascended the stairs.

Mary met him halfway, all smiles and chipper—too chipper for 9 A.M. before normal, decent people had their first cup of Feen. "You ready for the grand tour?"

"Not until I have a cup of Feen," Riley grunted. "You corporate types have that? Or have you actually managed to regrow coffee in your hanging gardens and keep it from the rest of us?"

"We have Feen." The chipper edge never left her voice. She began to give him a history of the tower, like some glorified tour guide.

Riley tuned her out and gleaned his own impression of the place. HyLyfe Tower made the Downtown Café look like a dirtshop in the burbs. HyLyfe was a shining testament to the staggering inequality of life created by the corporate ruling class.

Crisp air blew from large vents, carrying with it the oxidized smell of purifying filters. Flora grew out of every nook and cranny and hung from the ceiling, spilling toward the floor as if desperate to reconnect with the earth. Riley noted the furniture made of real wood and wondered how many people lost their lives acquiring it from the Rainbow Children's forests.

"Impressive, right?" Mary said, not without a hint of pride in her voice.

"That's one word for it."

She laughed. "You are just dead set on being a Byronic noob aren't you? C'mon. The Feen stand is over here."

"You know what us noobs call you guys? Trolls. Short for Controllers." He ordered a large cup of Feen with extra Feen. "What's with them?" Riley pointed to one of several animate mannequins performing various basic tasks with slow, stiff motions never speaking or acknowledging anyone or anything around them.

"An experimental android model. We are still working out the kinks."

Riley raised an eyebrow. "I thought artificial intelligence was illegal. Didn't the Corporate Council sign a treaty after the problems it caused during the Second Great Collapse?"

"They aren't AI, so far as I know. They run on basic operating systems. More like walking computers than artificial life."

"Do they speak?"

"Speak? No. That's the point of making them robots. How's the Feen?"

"Tangy and acidic. Like your false sense of privilege."

"My privilege is anything but false. So are you ready to see where the magic happens?" She led him to an elevator and pressed B1.

"We're not going up?"

"Nothing up there but offices, apartments, and low-level labs," she explained. "The real work happens down here."

The elevator door opened on a massive room lit by a sickly blue light emanating from columns of jars stacked in neat rows. Each one of those jars contained a perfectly preserved head.

"What the hell?"

"Some of these might be familiar," Mary joked. "These are the heads of the victims of Technological Psychosis Syndrome."

Riley recognized the work. "I never knew what happened to the hackjobs. Always figured they were destroyed after the bounty was collected. Hard to think this is where they end up after the technocrazies gets them."

"Again with that vulgar word. That's an insensitive term for it."

"Insensitive is hooking them up to this shit in the first place."

"They all volunteered when they signed the Enhancement waivers. And all were well compensated for their participation."

"Yeah. Looks like it from here." Riley leaned in close to examine the nearest head. It didn't look dead, but asleep. Its eyes even flitted behind closed lids. "Are they still alive?" There was an unmistakable tone of revulsion in his voice.

"By the Council, No!" Mary laughed like she was talking to a toddler rambling nonsense. "We aren't barbarians. They are being studied to better improve Enhancement and to find a cure for TPS. Their implants and by extension, their brains, are being stimulated with electric pulses. The rapid eye movement is a side effect of that."

"It's creepy as hell."

"Yeah," she admitted in a loud whisper, "This isn't my favorite room. This way."

She led him to the end of the room where another elevator waited—this one requiring a fingerprint and retinal scan to enter.

"How far down does this place go?" Riley wondered.

"Far enough. But we are only going to B2. Where HyLyfe resides. After you."

Riley stepped into the elevator, Mary following behind. He turned and got one last look at the floating heads seemingly stuck in perpetual REM. The doors closed and he sighed. For a room full of cold-capped hackjobs, he sure felt like he was being watched.

5

I have been a word in a book…
How many have you secured,
Valentinian?
The Templars not only managed
farms and vineyards, but also
engaged in manufacturing, imports,
and even ship-building.
Enough for us all. Twelve hundred
in total.

"Need to see you tomorrow evening. Project Ed3n cluster. Don't be late," Gold's holographic face demanded on the video screen. It clicked off without another word.

Jimmy Lee Gold paced around his penthouse apartment, anger boiling, building pressure like a super-volcano about to erupt. He lashed out at his surroundings, breaking things and wrecking his space like a rock star on a drug binge trashing a hotel room. He hated being a slave to his Status, hated the restrictions his unlimited privilege brought. He tried to escape before, even met a girl and fell in love. But those days ended in fire and blood and it took him weeks to find his girl and their child. And even after he arranged for them to come back to the city, he couldn't see them for fear of what his father would do if he found out. That pain and despair drove him to reckless pleasures. He stopped suddenly and turned to the large video screen hanging on his wall, deciding if he was going to throw the decanter he held into it. Instead, he hacked the vidcall channel with his forearm implant, and securing a private connection, dialed a number.

It rang for a small eternity before Lola's face appeared, a hologram rising from the screen itself. Her big brown eyes widened in amazement and she unconsciously fixed her hair.

"Hey babe," Jimmy Lee said with a smile, "How's it going?"

"Jimmy Lee! What are you doing? I thought it was too dangerous to call."

"Yeah well, forget that. Nothing can keep me from my girl."

"I don't like this. If they trace it…"

"They won't. Stop sweating it. Nothing I can't hack, babe. You know how I roll. So what you up to?" he said, trying to expel the tension from his voice.

"Just about to head to work. Got another double today."

"Is little man there? Can I see him?"

"He's in school. Why did you call, Jimmy Lee?"

"I just…look, I needed someone to talk to. And no way I'm popping off to those idiot shrinks. Not an authentic emotion in a single one of them."

"Ok. I get it. I do. The pressures of Status have always worn you down. Having Elijah Gold as a father certainly doesn't help."

"No shit. Eats at me day in and day out. Makes me feel like a worthless chump."

"Is that what the thing at the club was the other night?"

"How'd you know about that?"

"Give me a break, Johnny. Every time you fart it's all over the social feeds. This has been trending for days."

Fucking social media. It was more of a bane than a boon. "Look, that thing at the club…that was just blowing off steam. Besides, noob had it coming talking to me like that. He's lucky the corporate doctors kept him breathing."

"You got all the Status in the world and you really care what lesser people say? Is your dad really getting to you that bad?"

"I don't know. I mean, sometimes, I just think about my old man and I get so damn angry, you know? Like, I see his face and I want to smash it."

"I read a book when we were at the Heart. A really old book of myths or something. It said there used to be this belief that a son couldn't become a man until his father died."

"Makes sense. Maybe, like, I think of him as a jailor, you know? Like, all I want is to live my life. To go my way and do my thing with you and little man. I don't want none of his world. Hell, I even offered to sign away my shares to my little sisters. But it's not about that, is it? It's about image. It's about what everyone on the outside looking in can see. And forget it if that means cutting me a break. Letting me make my own choices, you know?"

"Yeah. Like when you ran off with me to join the Rainbow Gathering. Didn't last long."

"For real. Not nearly long enough. But we got to take that pilgrimage to the swamps. Saw the commandments. Saw what it was like Outside. Not just the Burbs, but really Outside."

"Yes," agreed Lola, "It really is amazing how much city swine believe whatever lies come across their screens."

"They have to, babe. If they don't, then they're screwed. The real shit's nothing like we been told. I never woulda believed it either unless I saw it. Walked the new Hearts, laid eyes on those huge Guidestones. Can't believe it unless you see it."

Lola's holographic face cracked a soft smile. "You have the heart of a poet. One of the reasons I love you so much. You feeling better? I have to go soon."

"Yeah, babe, thanks. I just, I don't know, needed to hear your voice. Makes me sane in this crazy world, you know?"

"I do, Jimmy. I have to get to work now. I love you."

"Wait! I need to see you."

"Jimmy…you can't leave the towers."

"Nah, I can swing it. I promise. But I need to see you. To hold you."

"How?"

"I'll set it up. Don't sweat it. Be sending you a message soon. Ciao baby." He winked and ended the call.

He took a deep breath and expelled the remainder of his frustration. And that, truth be told, was the reason he loved Lola. She always calmed his inner storms. Pacified his raging emotional waters. He poured himself a drink, and cleaning off his trashed desk, got to planning his escape.

6

I have been a book itself...
Don't question my motives. He has
to be strong enough to win his
prize. It's costing him his life, after
all.
Myths, rumors, and stories swirled
round the Templars like a mist, and
they didn't discourage that...
I understand that, but I still can't
help but think there has to be
another way.

Nate shielded his eyes against the glaring sunlight and tried to turn down the area's default brightness. He couldn't. Frustrated, he tried to open his holographic options menu, again he was denied. Now he was angry and looked around for someone to blame. He found himself in a country of rolling emerald hills beneath a lazy blue sky. Cutting a swath across the landscape was a road made of radiant bricks.

"It's the shining brick road," he said to himself with a giggle, though he wasn't really sure why that should be funny.

He thought he could make out someone walking along the road in the distance so he hurried along, trying to catch up with whoever it may be. He didn't know how long he'd been running. Movement here seemed to mimic the real fairly closely as he was unable to "skip" to different locations. He was stuck walking the old fashioned way. After what seemed like hours along the glowing path he came to a fork in the road.

Both paths looked exactly the same. Both stretched off with consistent monotony into familiar rolling emerald green hills blanketed by lazy blue sky. Like wraparound animation from the primitive cartoons he had access to at the Rainbow Children's camp. That's what this was then—another animation. He hadn't disconnected from eSpace at all. Somehow he had hopped from the school's construct into somewhere else on the Internetwork. Where he was and how he could get back was going to take some digging into. He was just about to step to the right when a voice spoke out of thin air.

"I wouldn't do that if I were you." A pair of lazy blue eyes slid open as if they were lidded from the very fabric of reality. They hovered effortlessly in front of him.

"Who—who are you," said Nate, his voice shaking from being taken by surprise. He tensed, already scanning through his best attack programs.

"I'm me of course," said the eyes scrutinizing Nate as if reading him like a book, a furry snout appeared beneath them, leering with mischief. "That is, unless I happen to be someone else. But today, today I definitely identify as 'me.' Now. At this particular time, I'm me and no one else."

"Do you have a name?"

"Oh sure. Call me Manchester. Manchester the Ferret, if you want to be proper. And what is your name, little one?"

"I'm Nate," said the boy, buffing his avatar with an aggressive glamor that made him look like a bloodthirsty barbarian.

The rest of Manchester appeared, floating in the air before Nate. He appeared as a cartoonish ferret wearing a suit and a fedora. He held up his hands and floated back a few feet. "No need for the mean skins. We're all friends here."

"I don't know you. You just appeared out of nowhere."

"Not 'nowhere,'" said the ferret, wounded, "I was somewhere before I was here. And it's a good thing I got here when I did. You're looking for ol' Baphomet, ain't ya? I know. I can see it in your coding."

"Who's Baphomet?"

"He's who everyone who's anyone is looking for. And I can tell ya, finding him isn't as easy as knowing right from left."

"What's wrong with the right path?" Nate asked.

"Well sometimes the right path is wrong. That's all."

"Fine. Whatever. I'll go left then."

"I wouldn't go that way either."

"Why not?"

"Sometimes the left is bereft. All that direction can lead to a mental infection."

"So which way should I go then?"

"Whichever direction you choose," answered the ferret with a wink, "Or no direction at all."

Nate closed his eyes and took a deep breath, both of them unnecessary actions within eSpace, not to mention completely superfluous avatar addons that only the real purists (or RP'ers) would care to install. Nate had created them organically when he built his avatar as a very young child. At first, his parents had no idea that he was connecting to eSpace. He had barely learned to walk but was already talking better than most preschoolers. His advanced intelligence didn't go unnoticed by his parents, but he was capable of far more than they thought possible. And with his father conspicuously absent, Nate's mother had enough to keep up with, which meant paying attention to her son took a back burner to fighting tooth and nail for their place inside the corporate city's walls. It was a sad story but an old and familiar one.

Nate's first avatar, which he built at 2 years old, had been a mass of primary shapes and colors that slowly took a humanoid form as his self-awareness grew. And his self-awareness progressed rapidly, surprisingly so. Suspiciously so if anyone had cared to notice. No one did, and Nate spent an increasing amount of time in eSpace. Since he had no concept of or desire for commerce, he simply coded anything he wanted from raw eSpace. In this way he developed an intimate understanding of the digital world—a world he began to prefer over the real for its sheer potential. There was nothing he could imagine he couldn't create and for a small child to be aware of that is truly dangerous. His mother discovered him unresponsive lying on the living room floor of their dirty wall-side apartment. After a frantic and hysterical call to Nate's father, they sent him to a round of shrinks. When the answers they got didn't appeal to them, his mother packed and left for the Heart of the Rockies. His father joined them shortly thereafter.

But even with all that innate ability, he was unable to tell if Manchester was a real person or just another digital construct created to facilitate whatever game he'd fallen into.

"Can I get a straight answer?"

"My dear boy, straight answers are an illusion. There are no straight lines in nature. Well, whichever way you may choose, I wish you the best of luck on your journey. He's a hard one to catch. Surprising, really." Manchester the Ferret looked at an antique watch strapped to his wrist and yelped, "Oh! I'm going to be late!" He popped back into invisibility.

"Well this is just great," grumbled Nate. "Can't go right. Can't go left. Might as well go right up the middle." Of course! How could he have missed that? He stepped off the path and walked between the two. In one instant he was in the land of rolling emerald green hills and in the next he was in a jungle thick with greenery and giant mushrooms.

The glowing path was once more beneath his feet and he followed it, gawking at the unreal scenery around him. He passed a large mushroom and heard something say in a drawn-out baritone drawl, "Well hello there."

Nate tensed, attack programs ready, and looked around until he finally saw a giant cockroach sitting on the mushroom's cap smoking out of a hookah. "Who are you?" the boy demanded.

"WHO are you? Who ARE you? Who are YOU?" repeated the cockroach in his lazy slurring tone, "Whoooooo ARE youuuuuuuu?" Its mandibles clicked in what Nate took to mean laughter.

"You aren't much help, you stoned old bug," Nate said and resumed his trek along the path.

"Help? Help? Ah! I can help," the bug called back, "I am of a mind to help. A hive mind. You dig it? Cha, cha, cha?"

"Where does this path lead?"

"All roads lead to Rome my fiery amigo," again the mandibles clacked. "But Rome isn't the Golden City, no matter how much it tries to be. Never let it convince you otherwise, you dig? Cha, cha, cha!"

"I thought you said you could help," Nate said.

"I can," the cockroach replied. "Here's my help: never trust ferrets. They only pretend to help while they're stealing your shinies." The mandibles clacked again and his bottom most leg, the one clutching a red Bic lighter, put flame to the bowl, and started pulling smoke.

Nate stomped off, disgusted.

"One more thing," the cockroach called after him, smoke billowing from its mouth, "You won't find Baphomet in Rome, dude."

Nate followed the glowing brick road and it eventually led him to a city. A flashing neon sign hovering in the air proclaimed this to be 'Rome' in a variety of different languages. All of which Nate could read. The city was a Potompkin village: flashy facades lined the streets pulling avatars just as gaudy into the various bowels of sin and debauchery. Revelers filled the streets indulging in every Bacchanalian fantasy their minds could conjure. And much of what went on in those streets Nate shouldn't have been privy to. He walked in a mechanical daze, gawking at every scene, every building, and every sign proclaiming depravity until he heard a whisper from a nearby alley.

"Pssst! I said, 'hey! Kid'," Manchester the Ferret's beady eyes appeared floating on the darkness.

Nate, glad to see a familiar face, rushed over to him, sputtering and flushed with excitement. "What's up, Manchester? Have you seen this place? Rome is it? They have so much dirty stuff here! People just doing it in the streets! You wouldn't believe it! I just saw—"

Manchester cut him off, his sharp teeth appearing beneath his eyes, "I don't doubt it, kid. Not here in the big city, such as it is. If you can't find your vice in Rome, you're a goddam saint," the ferret materialized and floated lightly to the ground.

He stood eye to eye with Nate, his beady eyes and sharp teeth being his most prominent features. These stood out as if they were altered with an addon. Nate had to admit Manchester had a slick avatar. The rendering alone was astounding. His sleek fur glistened ever so slightly and rippled as if being tussled by a light breeze. Quality work.

"Looks like you solved the old goat's first riddle. How'd it come about?"

"I followed the path right up the middle. Not left or right. Like you said. Then I ended up in a jungle talking to this cockroach."

"Don't believe a word that filthy liar says," Manchester spat and growled.

"He said I shouldn't trust you," Nate admitted. "Said you only wanted to steal my shiny coin. Which I don't even have."

"See? Lies on top of lies! Let me tell you something, there's never been an honest cockroach to walk upright!

The whole lot of 'em aren't even capable of individual thought! How about that for messed up? Every time you deal with one, you're dealing with the whole damn lot! Gotta go in hot and hit 'em in the core, see?" He made a spear thrusting motion, "Sever them at the brain."

"Why do you hate him?"

"Hate's a strong word, kiddo. Let's just say I took his sister to Rome and he hasn't forgiven me for it since." The ferret shrugged. "But enough about me. What are you doing here?"

"Looking for Baphomet, I guess," Nate said. He told Manchester of his journey, how his classroom had frozen and the vial of liquid, of the feeling like being disconnected from the digital. The ferret listened intently, his black eyes never leaving Nate. "So yeah, everyone keeps talking about this guy 'Baphomet'. I played enough RPG's to know that is a clue."

"You're smart, boy-o." He slung his arm around Nate's shoulder and directed him out of the alley, "But not as smart as you need to be." He led the boy up the street, darting through the throng of virtual revelers, his free hand deftly picking their pockets, and stopped in front of a shop. A thick, black drape served as a door and a neon eye blazed above interchanging with the words "Madame Blavatsky's." "First things first, my friend, you gotta see the fortuneteller."

"What? Why? I don't need my fortune told. I need to find Baphomet so this simulation can end."

"What makes you think this is a sim?" the ferret's whiskers twitched, "Real...digital. Is it fake or is it real, what's up with that? What's the deal? It all gets mixed up after a bit. I ain't playing no sim, I can tell ya that."

"It has to be a sim. It's the only way any of this makes sense. My school freezing, the vial and the shrinking bit, the glowing brick road, the cockroach, *you*. I mean, come on. It's all a sim. And I want to run it before I piss myself in the real. It's a thing. A kid at my school did it."

"Well, if you wanna find ol' Baph-meister you gotta talk to Madame Blat. Blat knows where the old goat's at. Simple as that."

"Fine," Nate said with a sigh of disgust and stepped through the thick drape.

Incense smoke thickened the darkness inside and swirled in, out, and about the occult accoutrements that lined the virtual shelves. These were addons for fans of old fantasy stories. Ones about wizards and elves, dragons and fairies. Nate was particularly impressed with the "spell" addons which could give your avatar the ability to shoot fireballs or lightning bolts from its hands. There were also wind addons that gave the visual of walking on air or riding on a cloud.

"Come on back. I've been expecting you," called the fortuneteller from the back room.

Nate stepped through another drape and met Madame Blavatsky. The Madame's avatar looked like something out of one of those old fantasy stories. She was an elfin character—impossibly beautiful with flowing blonde hair, pointy ears, and long, high cheekbones. She wore a low cut dress that seemed to be cut from pure light; it shimmered like the glowing brick road.

"And there you are. Nate is it not?" She sat at a small round table covered with a red cloth. Sitting neatly on the table was a deck of tarot cards.

The boy nodded. "You must be the fortune teller."

"I am."

"Manchester the Ferret said you could help me find Baphomet."

"Ferrets say a lot of things. More lies than truths, to be honest."

"Huh. That's what this smoking cockroach told me."

"Cockroaches lie even more than ferrets," Madame Blat said and picked up the deck of cards. She began shuffling them.

Nate knew the act was unnecessary, that randomization was automatic, but it added a level of legitimacy that he had rarely encountered in the digital worlds. He was becoming increasingly impressed with the detail put into this sim. Whoever was running it knew how to put on a good show. He settled in and watched the fortuneteller lay cards face up in a spread.

The first card she flipped over depicted HyLyfe tower burning and crumbling. "The Corporate Tower," she said sagely, "You have great and violent change ahead. Upheaval. Chaos." She overturned the next card. A reaper sat atop a wall to a corporate city-state lording over countless corpses hung over the edge. "The Great Collapse. The end of an era. Again, violent and unexpected but the end result is a restoration of balance." She flipped over the last card. A sharp-dressed corporate exec stood amidst a cloud of swirling money. "The CEO of Earth. Your father has something to do with all of it."

"I don't really know my father," Nate said.

"You don't have to know your father to be affected by him." Madame Blat looked at Nate, her electric eyes burning into his avatar causing him to shift uncomfortably. "In order to find Baphomet, you must blaze an unknown trail and lose everything that is dear to you. Are you willing to make this sacrifice?"

"Sure," Nate said with childlike nonchalance. It was all a game to him, after all. "I'm not afraid of sacrifice. Just means more experience points."

Madame Blat laughed hysterically at this as she and her shop slowly faded away leaving Nate standing next to Manchester on the street.

The ferret flashed his wicked smile. "I can tell by the look on your face that your meeting was a fantastic success."

"I don't know if I'd call it that. Honestly, it was a low-level encounter. Pretty run of the mill. I didn't even get a quest reward."

"You get to see Baphomet. What better reward could you hope for?"

"I still don't know where he is," said Nate in a huff, "So it's not really good for anything."

"My boy, that's where you are wrong. I know exactly where Baphomet is."

"You do?" Nate eyed the ferret with open distrust. He had come across underhanded NPC's before and was beginning to think Manchester was leading him into a trap. "Where is he then?"

"He's right through that door," Manchester said with a theatrical gesture to a door that appeared in the middle of the street. It towered so high into the virtual sky that Nate couldn't see its end. The doorknob was at least 40 feet above him.

"How do I open it," Nate said, and in response a pastel blue table appeared next to the door. Sitting neatly in the center was a white china plate with a slice of cake on it. Next to the plate was a cardboard tent placard that read "Eat me."

"You want it, you got it," Manchester said and looked at the watch on his wrist. "Well, would you look at the time? I have to go before I'm late. It was a pleasure making your acquaintance. Give my regards to the ol' goat." Before Nate could utter a reply, Manchester the Ferret disappeared into the digital background.

Nate walked over to the table and took the cake. He plopped it in his mouth without a second thought and vertigo suddenly seized him. When the dizziness passed he was looking down on the virtual city of Rome. Avatars scurried along the lighted streets like ants between the shimmering images of the buildings. He had half a thought to break the quest and rampage through the city like a bloodthirsty giant but decided against it. He wanted to find whoever was behind this sim. So he grabbed the doorknob that was now waist-high, and opening the door, stepped through. He immediately fell into blackness and spiraled away into darkness, the light from the doorway shrinking away as he screamed and kicked helplessly.

7

I have traveled as an eagle…
There is no other way, Bogomil.
Your softness is becoming a
liability. Perhaps you need put
back on the shelf?
The Templars were strong warriors
on the one hand, and monks
waging war with vice and demons
on the other.
Of course not, lord! My resolve is
unshakable.

The elevator door opened on a vast subterranean room full of server stacks. Lights blinked and twinkled as if the corporation had pulled the stars from the sky and hid them away in a massive underground bunker.

Riley whistled. "Wow. There must be enough processing power here to run an entire city."

Mary said, "Ten cities actually. And counting."

"State of the art," Riley said impressed. "So how do virtual people get killed? Don't the HyLyfers have a cheat code for infinite lives or something?"

"Funny," Mary replied humorlessly. "Technically, they can't be killed. Not while they're logged in, anyway."

"Then how?"

"The victims' servers were fried. That's why we think someone from the outside is responsible. No one has access to HyLyfe except its Users. And none of them would intentionally upload a virus."

"Are you sure about that?"

"Yes."

"So you mean to tell me that you geniuses with all your processing power didn't think to back up the people you were digitizing?"

"That would take an enormous amount of space and memory. Resources better used elsewhere. That being said, default files of all personas are stored with them in cryo. But—"

"Those are getting fried too," Riley finished for her.

Mary nodded in agreement.

"Wow. Someone is going to a lot of trouble to jack up your little dream world." The more he learned the more he thought they were right to think it was someone from outside the system.

"Exactly. And they are harming progress, impeding humanity's redemption. So will you help us?"

"I dunno. I'm still not convinced it's such a bad thing."

"Come here. There is something else I want to show you." She led him to a huge monitor hanging on the wall that Riley guessed was at least ten feet tall. "One second." She punched a few keys and stood back as a woman's face appeared onscreen. Green eyes and honey blonde hair and a perpetual smirk on her pouty lips—all digitized of course, but the high definition made her look almost lifelike. Almost.

"Shawn."

"Hello, Jacob."

He turned to Mary, "This isn't helping your case."

"Still bitter, I see," said Shawn.

"Still a robot pretending to be human, I see," Riley shot back.

"A robot? Are you calling me emotionally unavailable?"

Riley shrugged. "What else do you call someone who ran away from every difficult thing in her life? Ran away and pretended like nothing happened. And now look at you. Spending all day stuck inside a computer playing games. You don't even have a body anymore; you're just a head on a screen."

It was like every fight they ever had all over again. Twelve years had gone by and the first thing they did when seeing one another was to fall back into the same old patterns. Maybe people didn't learn. Maybe they were who they were and that's all there was to it. Nobody changes for anyone else. Not really. They just act against their nature for as long as they can stand it, resentment building the entire time. Riley and Shawn weren't even fighting like normal couples do. They were having a demonstrative tennis match, bouncing insults and personal attacks back and forth without any emotional investment whatsoever. This wasn't how Riley had pictured their reunion. He at least expected to feel *something* for the object of his anger and depression for all these years.

"HyLyfers have forsaken their fragile and corruptible human bodies," Mary interjected. "They have freed themselves from physical restraints and become entities of pure and unfettered mind. They have become—"

"Soulless," Riley finished. "They aren't human. They are 1's and 0's stored on one of these servers."

"That's unfair, Riley," snapped Shawn. "You think I wanted this? Logging into HyLyfe was the only way—"

The monitor cut out and Shawn's face was replaced with the HyLyfe logo.

Riley mashed keyboard buttons in anger and irritation. "Damn tech. Always works until it doesn't."

"Must be a server restart," Mary said unconvincingly. Then, "What was that?"

"What?"

"I thought I saw something move over there."

Riley squinted, trying to see through the room's poor lighting and expansive shadows. "I don't see anything. It's dark as pitch in here." As soon as he said that, a shadow darted in between the server stacks in front of him. "Hey! Hello?"

He was answered with silence.

"Anyone doing maintenance down here?" he whispered to Mary while creeping in the intruder's direction.

"No. They'd be escorted if they were. By the HyLyfe IRL Admin, which is me."

Riley reached for his weapon and cursed when he remembered leaving it at the lobby's desk. Typical corporate mentality. Expect someone to do a job with nothing. Still, he was no slouch in a fistfight. Growing up without Status either hardened a person into a wicked survival machine or it killed them.

He heard rustling on the other side of the server stack he was leaning against. Steeling his resolve, he leapt out like a predatory cat and shouted, "Don't move, asshole!" In the next moment, he was hit with an electric jolt that froze his heart and sent him tumbling into unconsciousness.

8

I have been a harp string
enchanted for a year by the water's
foam.
Breaking: Corporate playboy
Jimmy Lee Gold arrested on
attempted murder charges after an
incident at Club Paradiso left two
injured. Gold's lawyer has refused
comment. More as it develops.
By the 13th century, the Knights
Templar ran a successful economic
infrastructure throughout
Christendom.
Give the contract to Jacob Riley.
Baphomet has commanded.

Jimmy Lee Gold emerged from the parking garage of HyLyfe Tower. Bypassing security was easy. He'd left enough DNA tags that his father or his goons would think he was running laps around the tower. He merged with the crowd on the streets and strolled to the designated meeting place. She was there, waiting for him, as beautiful as the day he'd laid eyes on her. They got a cheap wall-side hotel room and made love all day, spending their remaining time lounging in each other's arms and reminiscing. Later, they descended onto the street where they stood at the hotel's entrance to share their goodbyes.

"Damn you know I always loved the look of you," he said with his characteristic smoothness. "You move like water and dance like rain."

"Stop it," she said and slapped him playfully—a throwback to lazier days and happier times that the haze of new love always brings.

He pulled her close. "I'll never stop. Not ever. You and our boy, you're life to me. You hear? We're getting out of here."

She pushed him away. "Quit being cheesy. This isn't some sappy netvid. How are you going to do that?"

He flashed his characteristic smile. The one that caught all the eyes and turned all the heads. "Don't worry about that. Just a little longer and I'll come for you."

"Hurry, alright? I think something is coming. Something big. The Mother is restless."

"Babe, stop with all that. Everything is smooth. Moving along. Just relax and move with it." He winked with the same coy expression that won her heart, and it melted all over again.

She would wait for him for as long as it took. Today, tomorrow, it didn't matter. When he left the Heart, he sent word just like he promised. He found them an apartment and her a job, just like he promised. So he would come for them as he had also promised. Everything in her screamed this was true and she made it so through sheer willfulness.

He kissed her then, with the reckless passion of those facing uncertainty, and pulled her close after. "Just this one last time. Then nobody will tear us apart," he swore and kissed the top of her head.

She nodded as she pulled away, and wiped a few rogue tears from her cheeks. "I know. I love you, Jimmy Lee."

"I believe you," he replied as he flicked up the collar of his antique jacket to shield his face, "I love you too." He left the small alley and melted into the crowd.

Lola watched him go before disappearing into the busy throng herself. There was another storm coming, she could feel it building. And she could only hope that Jimmy Lee made good on his promise before it broke.

Jimmy Lee sauntered into the R&D lab half an hour late. His father's fury was evident in the way he paced back and forth, mumbling to himself. Jimmy Lee smiled. It was these moments that gave him pleasure. These moments alone. Elijah Gold's head snapped up when Jimmy Lee stepped into the room.

"Bout goddam time. Where the hell you been? You're half an hour late!"

"I was out." Jimmy Lee said casually, pretending to check his nails for grime.

"The hell you were. If you were out I would've known about it."

The younger Gold stared his patriarch hard in the eyes. "You think I don't have ways around your little tracking schemes? Hell, I practically invented fluid recognition software."

"Yes. And it's about time you find out why."

"What do you mean? I'm a genius, that's why."

"That's only partly true," said Elijah, relishing turning the tables on his insolent son, "You were actually mediocre. There was nothing special about you. Oh, your mother liked to talk. She was always on about what a gifted boy you were. But that's just how mothers are. You weren't born a genius, boy. I turned you into one."

"What do you mean?"

A Labcoat scurried over and led Jimmy Lee to a microscope. The Labcoat checked the microscope before stepping back and motioning for Jimmy Lee to have a look.

"Go ahead," concurred Elijah as he tapped a cigarette against his fist, "take a look."

He leaned over and put his eyes to the ocular. It was obviously a blood sample but there was something else— something foreign—tiny little virus-shaped nanobots swimming around. He looked at the Labcoat and then to his father. "Is this my blood?"

"Yes," Elijah said in an exhale of cigarette smoke. It was an archaic habit, but it grounded him, helped him focus. And he focused then on his rebellious son.

"You injected me with nanobots and didn't even tell me?"

"Yes. You were a live beta of a new piece of Project Ed3n. You helped make history."

"You sick son of a bitch! How dare you!" Jimmy Lee snapped and swept the microscope off the table.

All the Labcoats stopped what they were doing and turned to Jimmy Lee in unison. Because of the high security of Project Ed3n, the R&D staff was given a sidearm. All of which were pointed at Jimmy Lee in one fluid and simultaneous motion.

"Just do it. Fuck it," he said, opening his arms in welcome defiance, "The nanobots will just put me back together anyway."

"That would be true if they weren't breaking down and taking your organs with them. You're dying Jimmy Lee. It seems the human body treats nanobots exactly like a virus over time. And the nanobots being what they are, well, they fight back. Side effects of that were heightened intelligence, antisocial personality disorder, and progressive tissue degeneration. That's why I came to find you when you ran off with those forsaken hippies. I wanted to offer you a chance to live. Forever." Elijah stubbed the cigarette out on the nearby desk. "I love you, you irreverent little shit."

"Forget that. If you loved me so much, you wouldn't have used me like a lab rat. I don't want to live forever if it means having to put up with your ass." Jimmy Lee lunged at the nearest Labcoat and the gun went off, the rest went off in unison.

"NO!" screamed Elijah, "He's no good dead!"

He awoke in a white room that he knew was eSpace, but it wasn't like any place he'd ever skipped to. The closest thing he could compare it to was a private server—offline but still connected. He tried a few basic codes and couldn't manipulate his surroundings or his avatar. Next, he tried to find the end of the room. He walked for what felt like an eternity and never reached a wall.

This is it. I've died and gone to hell, he thought, mildly annoyed that corporations went to all the trouble to purge religions from peoples' lives only to resort to them when constructing their digital fantasy worlds.

"Hello?" he called out. "Anyone here?"

No answer. So he was alone then.

For no apparent reason, the walls in the room began to glow softly. The light grew in intensity until Jimmy Lee had to cover his eyes. It took exactly twenty minutes for his sanity to crack. He screamed until he forgot himself and was swept away by the omnipresent light.

"You're sure this will work?" Elijah asked the supervisor.

"What data we've managed to get back from the field tests have shown success," the supervisor said, his head bobbing from the weight of the helmet and wires, "We are confident that temporary memory suppression will alleviate the psychosis that follows."

"How temporary?"

"We suggest reintroducing memories gradually as not to fracture the psyche before it has a chance to solidify in the new body. The ego must accept the new body as itself. Once that happens, memories will be viewed through the new psyche. He will see himself as he is now, even in his memories."

"Do it, then," Elijah said, lighting another cigarette. He watched the Labcoats scramble around preparing the body that was to house his son. He didn't blame the Labcoats for firing, their hivemind was only responding to an immediate threat. Besides, they managed to quarantine his consciousness before his body died. But now Jimmy Lee had nothing to go back to if this didn't work. With his body dead, the best he could hope for was to live as unfettered mind in HyLyfe.

The body jerked like something out of a Frankenstein movie and his eyes slowly slid open. 4D4M looked around for the first time.

"Who am I," he asked.

Elijah rushed over to him and took his hand. "You are my son. Jim—I mean, 4D4M. And you are perfect."

"I am...your son?" the hybrid repeated as if trying to process information that didn't want to be processed. "So you are my father," he said and hugged Elijah's hand. "What are we going to do, father?"

"We're going to build a new world and live forever in Paradis3."

On an impulse, Elijah pulled 4D4M into an embrace. Though it was a simple display of warmth, it felt alien to him. His relationship with his son mostly consisted of building walls around their volatile emotions and as such affection was sacrificed on the altar of cold detachment. So for the first time since his son was a boy, Elijah Gold shared a moment with him. Even if the moment was only possible because Jimmy Lee Gold couldn't remember who he was.

9

There is nothing I have not been...
Cathar, have you found our next
beta test?
The Templars had no fear of death,
confident in the knowledge that
they would be the Lord's martyrs.
I have found a prime candidate.
Preparing extraction now.

HyLyfe was a living and evolving entity. It was a paradise of the human mind—the digital Golden City on the edge of oblivion's abyss. New vistas opened up at an almost constant rate providing users with endless sources of entertainment and stimulation. But pointless distraction wasn't the true goal of any HyLyfer. To an unfettered mind, pointless distraction quickly grew dull. There was no challenge in it. The truth was that a user couldn't grow without continuously challenging and improving themselves. Static isn't rest to the digitized, it's death. Entropy is the enemy of the human condition and none knew this better or felt it more intensely than HyLyfers. Obstacles were meant to be conquered and looted for everything they could give. It was a fundamental element of the program—it was the game that ran beneath the current of their virtual existence and pitted everyone against each other and themselves simultaneously. This was the secret behind what made HyLyfers intellectual juggernauts on the razor's edge of scientific progress.

Shawn played the game well—she always had. From the first time she logged in, it felt right. Natural, even. HyLyfe instantly became her home and her security blanket. It sheltered and comforted her, healed the wounds caused by the death of her son and dissolution of her marriage. It was exactly where she needed to be. Until now. Until everything had gone black.

Shawn was stuck in a loop, running forever down a dark corridor with no end, her pursuer right on her heels. She couldn't see her assailant but she knew it was there. Waiting for her to tire of the endless loop and give in to change—even if that change meant death. If she slowed for an instant she knew she'd be done for—that the shadow would swallow her and she would slip into oblivion. She figured this was the same thing that had killed the others, but no matter how hard she tried to force it into the open, it remained hidden from her. So she ran, even in her unfettered state, her instinct was to flee. But there was no escape.

There was one option left to her: she could download back into her body. That would allow her to break the loop and escape her digital stalker all in one swoop. She knew it was a drastic move and one that the other victims had tried. But she knew what to expect if she logged out, and this gave her the confidence to think she could avoid or resist whatever was waiting in the real world. She silently connected to her body, starting the awakening process. Thirty-seven minutes later the cryopod clicked green and she sent her consciousness back to the real world.

Steam erupted from the pod as it opened, spilling Shawn to the ground. She was weak from Reconnection Sickness and couldn't see or hear very well. Someone— who she hoped was a lab attendant—lifted her to her feet. She tried to speak but couldn't. It was then she felt a sharp pain in her stomach and felt the warmth of blood spilling over her thighs. She groaned and collapsed, the sound of alarms echoing dully in her head.

◈

Riley came to with a groan, his head throbbing. Everything hurt like he'd just ran 150 miles with a pack full of bricks. He tried to get up, moaned, and fell back onto his pillows.

A nurse rushed in, busying herself checking his various medical attachments and clucking at him like a mother hen.

"Don't try to move, darlin'," she said with a Southern accent as thick and syrupy as sweet tea. "Gotta admit, we're kinda surprised you woke up. Ya took a lot of voltage."

"What?" Nothing she said made sense to Riley.

"Yeah. Your head might be a little bit fuzzy. Hard to remember things? That's normal. Just relax. The doctor will be along directly." She smiled broadly—genuinely. "Gimme a buzz if you need anything."

He looked around the cramped hospital room full of machinery, a vid screen, and a small couch/bed for any visitors. This was much nicer than the hospitals in the urban jungle. The air had a distinctly antiseptic smell—a scent that said 'everything here is clean.' The equipment was brand new and well-maintained. He had a gorgeous attentive nurse and was being pumped full of the best painkillers. Everything about this place screamed money and Status. It was obviously a corporate facility. He shuddered at the thought of how much this was going to add to his life debt.

"Mr. Riley," the doctor said absently upon entering. He scrolled through Riley's chart as he spoke, "you are a very lucky man."

"What do you mean? What happened?"

"What do you remember?"

"I went to HyLyfe Tower to meet up with a contact about a job. She was showing me around the place and we were ambushed in the HyLyfe server stacks."

"Yes. Well, as far as we can tell, you were hit with a nearly lethal electric shock. You were clinically dead for two minutes and eleven seconds." He shook his head in disbelief. "Just be glad you didn't have any Enhancements."

"I hunt hackjobs for a living. I've seen enough of what gear does. The lady that was with me, Mary. Is she alright?"

"Ms. May is being treated for her injuries as well." He answered quickly. As if the response was canned and ready to go. Riley didn't trust it. "Well, all your vitals look good. Readouts are positive. We should be able to have you on your way. Thank you for your stay at HyLyfe Tower's Medical Center."

He was given a fresh prescription for his KiSS sustainment meds and discharged into the waiting arms of a group of Suits. Like Labcoats, Suits were all part of a Hivemind. It was the Corporate Council's answer to AI and connected all employees into one large supercomputer to maximize efficiency. Their individualism was subverted for the collective processing power. As far as Riley was concerned they were the manifestation of everything wrong with the world all dressed up in expensive suits made from cloth no longer available to the general public.

"Mr. Riley," said the Suit in front. He was no different from any of the others; it was just his turn to speak. "We of CharWang Industries are glad to see you on your feet." He flashed a plastic smile to back up his hollow words.

"Thanks," Riley answered out of courtesy as he tried to elbow his way past the Suits and get to the exit.

Riley didn't agree with Mary's explanation of the supposed corporate quest to restore the world and humanity to their former glory. He understood the need for business and those who practiced it. Civilizations ran on an economy. But this went further than that. These men weren't interested in running an economy. Greed was not a charitable emotion. It thrived mainly on self-sufficiency. Masters of avarice never counted the greater good as a motivation for their materialistic tenacity. They really only cared about amassing the holy trinity of the civilized world: money, power, and resources. Always more and always faster. They existed to consume just like the vampires they were. They consumed and left generations of ravenous consumers in their wake. Spreading their disease—their dysfunction—to everyone and everything around them. It was trickle-down economics in its true form. And as a result, the world had been laid to waste. Its natural beauty and resources harvested and sold for profit. Riley had a real hard time mustering any kind of desire to help these corporate slugs in any way. And standing in front of them, each similar to the next in uniform blandness, those meager reserves of desire quickly dwindled.

"If we might have a minute of your time…"

"I don't have any time for Suits," he growled. "What kind of assholes invite you over for a tour and then try to get you killed?"

"That was unpleasant. We admit. But that's what we wanted to talk to you about."

"Yeah? You find the guy that shocked me and Mary? And how is she anyway? No one around here seems to know anything."

"We have run into some obstacles. The security footage from that time seems to have disappeared."

Riley raised an eyebrow. "Disappeared?"

"Correct. And there is more. Follow us please."

The entourage led him through the hospital to a wing marked "Restricted Access." Mary May was in the first room. Strapped to a bed writhing and snarling like a maniac, she screamed and ranted like someone possessed.

"Did she get the technocrazies?"

"Yes. It appears the blast that hit you triggered Technological Psychosis Syndrome in Ms. May."

"She was a gearhead?"

"Oh yes. All corporate employees are required certain basic Enhancements. We are all one under the corporation, after all. Employees are expected to contribute to the goal of Maximum Efficiency even if they aren't connected to Hivemind."

"Always plugged in even when you ain't. So can you help her?"

The Suit smiled flatly. "No. That isn't in line with our interests. Ms. May will have to be reclaimed and sent for further study. We agreed that showing you Ms. May was 24% more likely to incite feelings of vengeance in you."

"We agreed," the other Suits harmonized.

"Now that you have been appropriately enraged, follow us please."

Before Riley could protest, the group of Suits moved toward the exit with smooth but insistent fluidity.

"Hey, what's in here?" He broke from their ranks and walked over to the viewing window for the next room. Inside, several Labcoats busied themselves over the body of a strikingly beautiful woman. Her perfection was laid bare on that metal table—a testament to the flawless aesthetic of the human form. A form that was being poked, prodded, and generally fussed over by the Labcoats in the room.

"Please, Mr. Riley, come with us," the Suit insisted, grabbing Riley by the elbow.

He jerked free. "Who is she?"

"She is no one. Now please. Move along." The Suit wasn't taking no for an answer.

With one last glance at the woman on the table, Riley followed the Suits to the HyLyfe Tower lobby. It was nearing midday and the place was bustling with traffic. And throughout it all, the robotic mannequins stoically went about their duties in the background.

"So you guys gonna turn Mary into one of those walking mannequins? She said that's what you do with the reclaimed bodies."

"We agreed there are other more profitable uses for Enhancements of Ms. May's quality," the Suit replied emotionlessly.

"We agreed," the other Suits concurred.

"However, your contract through her is still considered valid. We would like you to continue the search for the HyLyfe killer. Sate your vengeance. We have agreed."

"We agreed," the choir said once more.

"Well that's great, but thing is, I was starting to like her. You guys? You're just a bunch of Suits. And I don't do corporate jobs." He walked out the front doors and immediately headed for the corner store to get a pack of smokes. To hell with the Suits and the Labcoats and the whole entity that was CharWang Industries. Randy buzzed him and he took the call by pressing a button on his archaic wrist phone.

"Riles, how are you feeling?"

"Fine, why would you ask?"

"Your name may have popped up on a patient list for the corporate hospital. I didn't think you were doing the kind of jobs to afford first-class medical care. You aren't cheating on me are you, Riles? The thought of that could drive a man crazy." His beady eyes narrowed to slits.

"Slag off, Randy. I was in there because of that corporate gig you sent me on."

"What?" the fixer's shock was theatrical but sincere, "But the job is still open, I see."

"Yeah. I canceled it."

"You what?" A mask of hardheartedness replaced the shock, "You know my policy about that. No canceled contracts! Canceled jobs mean canceled contractors!"

"My contact was killed. Far as I'm concerned our contract was void."

Randy drummed his fingers on the arm of his overstuffed chair. "I can probably make that work. But so help me, Riley, if you so much as mutter the word 'cancel' in your sleep I will end our little relationship. Are we clear?"

"Yeah. I got ya."

"Good. Now that that is cleared up, I have a new job that just came off the wire. Hasn't even hit the other agencies yet."

"What is it?"

"It's a cold-cap job. Right up your alley. Mark is in the Burbs. This one pays three times the normal rate."

"What's the catch?"

"There's a 24-hour turnaround."

"Alright. I'll take a look. Send over the file." Riley ended the call.

She opened her eyes and a squad of Labcoats rushed over to check her vitals, drape a gown over her and help her sit up. They gave her water in a paper cup and she drank it greedily.

"Hello 3vE," said a Suit who stepped through the door.

Eve? Was that her name? It didn't sound right, but she couldn't remember right now.

"How are you feeling?"

She continued to ignore the Suit and held out the cup of water for a refill.

"The Labcoats assure me your transfer went well. Everything is working perfectly. All you need is a little rest. We'll talk more later."

The Suits left and she turned to the Labcoats in the room. "How long was I out?"

"That is a very interesting question," confessed the Cluster Leader. "Technically, you still are."

It was then she noticed a large glass tube in the corner with a body suspended inside, floating weightlessly with a breathing apparatus attached to her mouth and nose. The Labcoats parted for her as she made her way to the tube and placed a tentative hand on it. The glass was cool to the touch and her breath fogged it up. She looked closer at the woman and saw something familiar about her. She knew this woman. She was this woman. And if she was floating in a medically induced coma then how was she staring at herself? She looked at her hands and didn't recognize them. They were beautiful. Perfect. She rushed over to the mirror above the sink and gasped at the reflection staring back at her.

There is something unshakable about that singular "I" at the core of every human's personality. Underneath all the masks people wear is the self they cannot escape. A persona that embodies consciousness—Individualism—the great I AM statement everyone makes to themselves so they can remember who and where they are. People like to call it "ego" but this isn't the case. Ego is the persona, the inner sanctuary full of different masks for every situation. The individual exists beyond that and is the center of gravity for all of the ego's masks. If that core point of existence ceases to be then everything falls apart, spins out of orbit and into nihilistic dread. All the king's horses and all the king's men... 3vE was no exception.

"Who am I?" she screamed.

"You're 3vE," said the lead Labcoat, "We had to repress your memory to help facilitate your mind's acceptance of your new body: a perfect hybrid of technology and organic matter." The Labcoat sounded proud as he spoke, and individual expression was as uncommon to their Hivemind as it was to the Suits'. "She requires only a quarter of the oxygen of a normal human. She's 10 times as strong and 12.3 times faster. Her IQ exceeds genius by a considerable degree. She doesn't need to eat or sleep often and she practically doesn't age. Not to mention, she is connected to the Internetwork and is capable of near-unlimited storage space for skill sets and knowledge bases."

"What happened to my old body?" She ran a finger down her unfamiliar face. She was gorgeous, that was true. Didn't look a day over 21. She could use this to her advantage.

"It was disabled by unforeseen circumstances. We are working on restoring it to optimum condition."

She could see information flowing through her Enhanced mind like a constant rushing river of 1's and 0's, but she couldn't find anything about her or the woman in the tank. No memories. Nothing familiar. She was a stranger to herself. Remembering had to be her first goal. And if these useless drones couldn't help her she would find someone that could. "I need to go," she announced, "give me some clothes."

The Labcoats shuffled around uncomfortably, refusing to acknowledge her request.

"Are you hearing me? I need to go."

The Cluster Leader stepped forward and tried to placate her. "I'm sorry 3vE. We can't let you leave quite yet. We need to make sure your body is running at peak efficiency. These tests ensure—"

"I don't care. My self-diagnostics show that I can beat an AI in chess and a Mercury Borg in a foot race. I think I'm fine. Now give me some clothes."

"But the Suits…"

"Can kiss my ass. I'm leaving." She grabbed a lab coat hanging near the door and quickly dressed.

The Labcoats present all drew firearms, pointing them at 3vE with blank expressions on their faces.

"We can't let you do that." The speaker sounded genuinely upset—worried even. "Just please be patient with us. 3vE's body is worth billions. We need to run a few tests and then we will move you up to a residential suite. Then once the Suits give the ok—"

The speaker never finished his sentence. 3vE lashed out, jabbing the verbose sociopath in the throat. His eyes widened briefly before she knocked him unconscious with a kick to the head. Alarms went off immediately and the lab went to emergency lockdown.

She completed syncing with her borrowed body and now moved like a masterful dancer in a lucid dream. The 3vE unit's reaction time was surprisingly fast and she saw attacks coming before they even landed, calculated the projectile paths of bullets before they discharged from the barrels. It made fighting the other Labcoats seem like cheating. She flitted in and about them with effortless grace. And when she struck back, her blows hit hard—a bit too hard for the natural muscle in a body frame that could only be described as "petite." In little time, she alone stood amidst a sea of unconscious, wounded or dead Labcoats. Daintily making her way through the aftermath, she reached the elevator and pushed the button. She got in, pressed the lobby button, and slipped out before the doors started to close. Then she headed for the stairwell.

It was a frantic race down, her Internetwork connection pulling up schematics of the tower and mapping the quickest route to freedom, but one that cost her little energy. She heard the muffled popping of gunfire and knew the elevator had reached the lobby. There wasn't much time. She threw open the door to the parking garage that had been converted into a storage space and hydroponics lab. All the Labcoats stopped and looked at her quizzically.

"Are you lost?" one finally asked—a kind-faced woman with graying hair and a face worn with smile lines.

"I thought the place was on lockdown," said another— a stern-looking man with a double chin and bald head. "How'd you get those doors open? They were locked tight."

Before she could answer, the emergency sprinklers erupted.

"Fire!" yelled the bald Labcoat, "Everybody start Safe Mode!"

Labcoats scurried around, desperately attempting to safeguard their plants lest the fire spread to their level and ruin years of research. Forgotten, 3vE moved unimpeded to the surface.

She emerged onto the busy street shielding her eyes against the blazing sun. She was like a newborn seeing the world for the first time and couldn't help but be taken aback by its startling beauty. Even amidst the urban dystopia there was grandeur. Enchantment and miracles were in every leaf blown by the breeze or the glint of sunlight off the pond in the center of the plaza. And that, she realized then, was the gift of life—to experience the cosmic machinations of the universe firsthand.

The people outside had no idea of the chaos rampaging right under their noses in HyLyfe Tower. Everything appeared to be business as usual. She suspected that if the Tower ever fell, that would be the day the city died. As evil and authoritarian as corporations were, they were the glue holding society together.

When civilization collapsed and governments were eradicated it was corporations that remained to fight over what was left. It was the corporations that created KiSS to control the population and keep humanity from overpopulating yet again. It was the corporations that started the Rejuvenation Projects trying to correct the damage that had been done—even if it was largely done by them. It was the newly-formed Corporate Council that stabilized the cities and started to rebuild civilization from the ashes. Despite the selfishness and savageness that characterized nearly everyone involved in the corporate machine, they had become the guardians, nurturers, and last hope for humanity. Noobs didn't understand that. They couldn't see the forest for the trees. All they saw was their individual suffering. They blamed corporate interests for their misfortune when they should be hailing them as saviors. When the survival of the species was on the line, individual rights and comforts didn't matter. Hard decisions had to be made and sometimes those decisions cost lives. But the end result—restoration of the planet and a sustainable human existence—was a noble endeavor. One worth dying for. One worth killing for.

"Um…miss? Excuse me?"

3vE turned and saw a young woman, covered in the filth of the streets looking at her with wide eyes. "Can I help you?"

"I was gonna ask you the same question. What with your blood-stained lab coat and all. Did you get separated from the Hivemind?"

"I'm fine thank you." She turned toward the HyLyfe building expecting to see smoke billowing out the windows but there was nothing. Everything appeared calm and orderly. People still flowed in and out of the doors, their faces plastered with looks of complacency, not fear.

"I ain't sayin' you ain't. But I really suggest coming with me. I know a place you can…get yourself together. Get some clothes, and the blood off you."

3vE looked down and realized the severity of her appearance. Already people were stopping to point and whisper. It was only a matter of time before CorPol was alerted. 3vE was constantly connected to the grid. And that connection was telling her that her options were quickly dwindling. Corporate police would be onsite within minutes. She couldn't hide as she was. A place to get herself together sounded exactly like what she needed. She nodded to the girl and followed her as she darted into an alley, disappearing into the shadowy underbelly of the urban morass that was Corporate Denver.

10

*Indifferent bards pretend a
monstrous beast with a hundred
heads.
Monitoring systems?
Bernard de Clairvaux devised the
code of behavior for the Templar
Order, known as the Latin Rule.
Upgraded. She'll never know we're
there.*

Nate didn't have a sensation of landing or finding solid ground beneath his feet. He just stopped moving and the glowing golden path appeared in front of him, stretching away into the darkness like an arrow. He wasted no time in following it. Falling into the abyss had terrified him so badly he tried to disconnect but it didn't work. He couldn't even find his netset online. It was as if he wasn't connected to the school servers anymore. That thought worried him. No matter where an avatar traveled in eSpace, they remained connected through their netsets. It was like an invisible cord that always led back home and to the physical body. Having that cord cut was not a good thing in any scenario the boy could think of. He followed the path to yet another door, this one glowing, and stepped through into a massive and ancient hall, towering columns lining its dimly lit expanse, creating a path of their own. The only source of light was the subtle red of smoldering embers radiating from an unknown source. Nate's heart jumped into his throat but he soldiered on. This wasn't his first boss fight and besides, nothing bad could happen to you in eSpace. If your avatar was 'killed' you just disconnected back to your body. That is, unless you can't connect to your netset. Then you're a ghost in the machine that eventually fades away as bits of coded consciousness are quarantined and absorbed back into the electronic ether. If that was the case, he better game like he'd never gamed before.

The light grew brighter the farther he got towards the opposite side of the cavernous room. But the chamber still had more shadows than light and Nate saw one of these shadows move. He whirled around pulling the two-handed sword from his inventory—the one he looted off a certain player that was giving him trouble a while back. It appeared in his avatar's hand as two fiery eyes emerged from the gloom accompanied by bullish huffing. Whatever it was, it was HUGE, and suddenly Nate's gaudy anime trinket didn't seem to have a high enough item level to really make a difference. But he quickly forced those thoughts from his mind. He had to confront Baphomet.

"I see you there," he called out to the shadows. "I'm not afraid of you. Show yourself."

Low, rumbling laughter filled the room in a crescendo of mockery and devilish glee. The perpetual smoldering light in the background flared and lit Baphomet in its sinister light. He had a stag skull for a head with a neon pentagram hovering between the antlers. Huge breasts sagged from his chest and his cock was tucked between his crossed legs. He sat atop a pedestal that reached ten feet off the ground and chained to its base were an incubus and a succubus, both lunging at Nate and begging him to come closer.

"I see you *there,* little Frater," boomed the monstrosity from its pedestal.

Nate experienced something that he hadn't in a very long time: fear. eSpace had always been his domain, his world where he was in control. Sims were just games, and games couldn't hurt you. Nobody ever played for real stakes, no lasting damage was ever done. That was the problem and appeal of the virtual world. It made people cocky and prone to hubris and overconfidence. Nate was no exception and being an exceptional child only highlighted those shortcomings. He really had come to think of himself as untouchable. But this encounter—this entire sim—was something abnormal and Nate's confidence in his control was less than optimal. He loaded an attack program, activated his barbarian skin, and squared up to the boss, taking a deep breath to calm his voice. "My name is Nate. Not Frater. I don't even know who that is."

"Frater isn't a name," hissed the succubus, "It's a title given to special little boys."

"I bet you're a special little boy, aren't you Nate?" the incubus taunted.

"I don't want a title. I just want to end this sim. I need to connect back to my netset."

"There's no going back now," teased the succubus, "We're keeping you here forever."

The incubus joined her in laughter to which Baphomet added his quivering baritone. "You belong to me, Frater. Listen to the whispers that are coming." The cryptic figure pointed a bony finger at Nate. The chains holding the slaves at his feet fell away and they instantly attacked the boy.

Nate jumped back and swung wide at the approaching demons. They split up and circled him like two winter-starved wolves desperate for a taste of blood.

"Oh, the things we are going to do to you," hissed the incubus and licked his lips. "So good."

"Stay back! Do you know what this weapon's stats are? It'll cut your cheap avatars down like the noobs you are."

"We're not avatars," said the succubus in a wounded voice oozing with mockery.

"We became gods," laughed the incubus before lunging at Nate.

The boy rolled back and leapt to his feet. He immediately brought the sword down, cleaving the airborne incubus in half. He appeared chained to the base of Baphomet's altar once more, begging to be set free.

The succubus squealed with delight, "Oh master! You've gave us a good one! A tasty morsel indeed." A whip materialized in her hand and she lashed at Nate with a quick flick of her wrist. The tip struck his hand and he dropped his weapon. "Oh no! What happened to your big old sword? Did your hand get slapped for playing with it?" She giggled. "Time to taste your pretty piece of flesh." She lashed out again and wrapped the whip around Nate's neck, pulling him toward her.

He struggled, but was held tight. She was running some smooth attack software, Nate had to admit. He'd not seen anything like it. And she had to be an avatar as opposed to a digital citizen because DC's didn't have her unpredictable attack pattern. They all ran on code and there wasn't a code in eSpace that Nate couldn't hack.

"Do you like it?" the succubus whispered as she held him up to her eyes, "I designed it myself. All your attack programs are frozen. Your inventory is locked. No more tricks up your sleeve. Nothing can save you. You're my pet now. My little Frater on a leash."

"What do you want with me?"

"Your special bits. You will bring us immortality. You will make us gods in the flesh!"

Nate had one last move up his sleeve. He may not have been able to fight the succubus while frozen by her whip, but he could possibly use a non-attack move. A move so unthreatening that it didn't appear on the lists of any attack software. It was one of the first programs he learned to code. Just three hops to the right was all there was to it. Though it didn't appear useful, his sidestep move had proven invaluable to him as a young child exploring eSpace. When approached by older avatars often his only option was to sidestep and avoid direct confrontation. That is, until he learned how to craft himself a weapon from raw eSpace. That was a game-changer and quickly made his avatar known in most of the open battle-gaming sims he soon frequented. He executed the sidestep and after a brief rush of vertigo found the succubus about 10 feet to his left with a mixture of awe and confusion etched into her avatar's face.

"How—" was all she managed to blurt before disintegrating inside the sphere of raw light that projected from Nate's hands.

The boy turned to Baphomet, smiling in amusement, sitting on his dais.

"Impressive," boomed the boss.

"Now tell me who you are!" the boy demanded, another sphere already coalescing between his hands.

"I am the Prince of Darkness. The shadow's shadow. I am the one who was dead but lives again. I am the liberator who enslaves the free. I am everything you are afraid to see."

"What do you want with me?"

"The succubus spoke true. The key to remembering lies within you. Naturally organic. Organically artificial. This is who you are contained in a nutshell. Everything else the mad gods have created can't compare to what nature incubated. They've upset the balance and doomed all of us. Listen for my whispers beneath the noise. I will guide you to the light." The image laughed and began to fade away.

"Wait! I want to get out of here! I can't find my netset!"

Baphomet's laughter grew louder until he completely disappeared and the smoldering light in the chamber snuffed out leaving Nate alone in the darkness.

"Wake up, Nate," said a soft voice, his mother's, that roused him from his sleep. He bolted upright, eyes wide with terror, and for a moment when he looked at his mother, he didn't recognize her.

"Momma? Is that you?"

"Of course it's me, baby. Who else would it be?"

"Are you real or is this another sim?"

"You've been spending too much time in eSpace if you are having that problem," said his mother, her tone gaining a rough chastising edge. "Got too much of your father in you. I knew that school was going to be a bad idea."

"School! I'm going to be late!" He threw off his covers and rushed around his room looking for clean clothes.

"Calm down. You know school has been canceled for a week since people started getting sick."

"A week? I couldn't have been logged in for that long! I was just logged into the school's eSpace this morning!"

Nate's mother sighed and looked at her son with eyes full of worry. "They said memory loss and disorientation might happen but I thought you'd be ok…"

"What? What happened?"

"Baby, your school server was fried a little over a week ago. Your teacher and all your classmates…well…you were the only one who logged out and you didn't wake up for three days afterward. Do you remember?"

Nate didn't remember any of it and his saucer-wide eyes conveyed all the horror and hopelessness he felt at that moment. His mother pulled him in close, sobbing into his messy hair.

"We should never have come back here," she lamented.

11

*The Lord answered through charms
and magic skill, "Take on the forms
of the trees. And prepare for
battle."
There is no room for her.
Initiation into the order was a
profound commitment and involved
a solemn ceremony.
There is always room for more. All
will be saved. Give her name back.*

A thousand voices spoke at once. She couldn't hear anything but a cacophony of noise that was as maddening as it was unceasing. She reached up to grab her head in her hands and felt—nothing. She tried again, and still felt nothing. Panicked, she looked around, trying to see where she was. But there was no light.

"Hello? Is anyone there?" she yelled into the dark room. "I need help. Please, someone help me."

As if in response, a pinprick of light appeared in the distance and she immediately began to move toward it. The closer she got, the brighter the light grew and she started picking out what individual voices were saying.

*--Trust her. She's one of them.
HyLyfe Tower-headquarters of CharWang Industries,
proprietors of the technology and servers HyLyfe ran on.
Mary May. Her name is Mary May. She's one of us
now.
They didn't start off big which allowed for their rise
from the ashes of the Second Great Collapse.
She's dangerous. Do not open the door to her.
She has no choice now. Neither do we.*

During this time, smaller corporations scrambled for leftover technology and resources attempting to gain power and influence.

Do you remember your name?

Oddly enough, she didn't.

--Your name is Mary May. Never forget your name, Mary May. That's what they want. Never give them what they want.

CharWang Industries got HyLyfe, an old VR immersion program that they modified and expanded into its current incarnation.

Welcome, Mary May.

Player profiles were created by uploading the user's consciousness onto the server. Once uploaded, they were free to explore the paradise realms of the HyLyfe universe and nothing they could imagine was denied them.

Before her, a glowing door stood against the perfect dark. She was terrified, shaking so badly that she was unable to reach out and grasp the handle. At least she thought she was trembling, but now that she was aware of it she really had no sensation of trembling. She really had no sensation of a body whatsoever. This realization didn't frighten her. She'd lost her capacity to feel fear. And as the world of the senses fell completely away, the door opened and she stepped through.

12

When the trees were enchanted
there was hope for the trees...
This time, we'll get it right. I'm
certain of it.
The status of the Knights Templar
mirrored the knightly class as the
political elite in European
societies.
How do you know that?

Nate's eyes popped open and the voices faded away like a bad dream. He rubbed his eyes and looked around his small room. His mom had kept him home since he woke up and lost an entire week. That he had been walking around, talking and living life for an entire week, and he couldn't remember a moment of it didn't compute with his young mind. Even one as intelligent and gifted as Nate's. To Nate, it was as if he just logged out from his boss fight with Baphomet.

His mom was understandably worried and had forbidden that he log into eSpace, citing 'doctor's orders.' She took his netset with her to work every day, leaving him with nothing but netvids and old paper comic books to pass the time. He was also not allowed outside since people started getting sick. There were whispers of a plague outbreak though nothing official had come down from corporate. So he resigned himself to sitting in his room and staring out the window that faced the open space between the edge of the Burbs and the tree line that marked the beginning of the Rainbow Children's territory. He often roamed the boarders, nostalgia pulling him back to the damp air and musty smells of the Heart of the Rockies. He missed it sometimes and even a few of the Rainbow

Children in it. But his mother had insisted they follow his father to the city. She also kept insisting that he would come for them one day and on that day, all their suffering would end. Because his father was a special man, a man with Status and he was going to use that Status to save them. That was the story she told him, anyway, and Nate believed it because he wanted to. Because it was exactly the kind of story a child who had seen too much of life too soon needed in order to maintain hope. His mother rummaged around in the adjacent bathroom, moaning as she did.

"Momma?" Nate called out to her, "Are you alright?"

"Yes," came the muffled reply accentuated with a sniffle, "I'm just looking for the allergy dermapatch. The Heart must be blooming early this year. Looks like a cottonwood snowstorm out there. I have to work a double tonight, baby. I'll have Toby drop by some takeout in a few hours and check on you."

"Okay, Momma," he called back. "Have a good day at work. I love you."

"I love you too," she called back then fell into coughing. "Don't stay up too late and no scary netvids!"

After a moment more the door opened and closed. Nate's web implant dinged to announce a new message. Curious, Nate checked his email.

CONGRATULATIONS NATHANIEL MERRIWEATHER!

For your bravery in the face of adversity as you faced off against the evil Baphomet you have been awarded! Please see the attached [Templar Avatar Skin] and [Flying Luck Dragon Mount]! Thank you and remember: the voices lead you back. Listen to the voices.

The message ended there. Curious, he scanned the attachments for viruses and opened them. The avatar skin looked like a medieval knight wearing a white tabard emblazoned with a scarlet red cross. The flying luck dragon looked like a furry dragon popular among some of the fantasy sims he visited from time to time. It dipped and twisted and spun around upon itself. He lifted his mattress and retrieved the backup netset he had stashed there years ago. It was his first and a very basic model, but for him it was like putting on an old hat. He slid it over his eyes, powered it on, and logged into eSpace.

He landed in the Burbs Node, the public server for the Burbs communities. It wasn't nearly as populated as it usually was. He wandered the digital streets until he found the shop he was looking for. "NuSkinz" read the sign above the shop. It was the equivalent of a digital post office. A person could upload attachments for use here. Nate walked through the door and an old-timey postmaster peered at him over thick bottle-cap glasses.

"Can I help you, sonny," the old man wheezed, pushing the heavy cap he wore up on his brow. It sank down again almost immediately.

"You know, if you tighten up your rendering you won't have those glitches like with your hat," Nate said helpfully.

"I'm fine just the way I am. Gives my character, character," the old man said with a wink. "Now what can I do for you today?"

"Just got a couple packages to check in."

"Let's see what you got."

Nate sent them over and the postmaster gazed at a monitor on his desk. "Wow," he said with a low whistle, "that's some impressive stats on that skin. Templar is it? Never heard of it. Must be new. And this transpo program… that's top-notch too. Accelerated travel time between servers? Where did you get these?"

"From a… private sim I was beta testing for," Nate lied.

"Must be one helluva netsurfer to get those kinds of invites. Alright, you're uploaded and ready to go."

"Thanks," Nate said and left. He immediately summoned his new mount and skipped over to Barbarian Rage, his favorite sword and sorcery sim, to try out his new skin. And that was the last thing he remembered.

◈

"Who are you?"

"I am… Mary May. They didn't take my name. I didn't let them."

"What do you want?"

"I want to tell you that help is coming soon. Hold on. Just hold on."

◈

"Dude, what the hell? Your moms is gonna pop one in my head!" Toby jerked the netset off Nate's unconscious head and shook him awake. "Yo, little man! Wake up!"

Nate's eyes slid open as if lead weights hung from his eyelids. "T-Toby? What's going on?"

"Dude, you had a netset on! You weren't supposed to log in to eSpace, remember? If your moms finds out, you're dead."

"So don't tell her then." Nate rubbed his temples then went for the bag of takeout food. He shoveled food into his mouth like he hadn't eaten in days.

"What were you even doing, little man? I don't know how you aren't scared as shit of eSpace now. Like you should have PTSD and shit."

"I was checking out some new gear I got. It's sweet as hell too." Nate explained the message he got and the rewards from his quest.

"Man, I never heard of gear like that. Never. That sounds OP as hell. Hacker mod shit, man. Shit'll get you busted. They'll throw your moms in a camp and your little ass will be shipped off to some corporate black ops school. Is that what you want?"

"What? No! Of course not! But I'm thinking that all this stuff with Baphomet goes way deeper than I thought. Like who fried my school server? And who led me away just in time to dodge getting my brains scrambled? I have to keep going. Play it through. It's what any good gamer would do."

"Yeah, well, any good gamer would also know when he needs to give that shit a rest!" Toby ruffled Nate's hair and grabbed the netset off the coffee table. "I'm keeping this shit so you don't step out of line. Your moms will be home in a few hours."

"Hey! C'mon, Toby! Leave the netset! Please? I promise I won't use it anymore tonight."

"I know," Toby said with a smile and shut the door.

It locked behind him with an electric hiss leaving Nate alone. He finished eating and went to his room where he drifted into sleep with netvids running in the background, joining with the chatter of the voices beneath the noise.

13

That they should frustrate the
intention of the surrounding fires...
Lucky number four... I don't like
this using HyLyfers.
But they grew too powerful,
threatening the dominance of the
French Crown and the Papacy.
We need an unfettered mind to get
the process to stick. One whose
identity isn't tied to any meat sack.
This'll eradicate the onset of
psychotic break. I'm sure of it. Just
one final beta test.

Riley tapped his cigarette against his fist and lit it, inhaling deeply. He'd read in a history book how the dangers of smoking had actually caused humanity to almost abandon it before the First Great Collapse. He never really understood why. The air was constantly full of chemical clouds and smog—had been since before the collapses. Those were more likely to kill you than smoking. Gone were the days of fighting cancer. Simply being born into the wasteland humanity had inherited gave you cancer eventually—if KiSS didn't get you first. Generations had lived with this reality and now, no one questioned it. They just accepted it as normal. And Riley thought that was the most abnormal thing of all. Some days he didn't know who he despised more, the noobs or the trolls. He'd take both over the Burbanites any day, he mused darkly as he headed for the Burbs. Traffic was terrible so it was going to be a transtunnel day.

He hated the transtunnel. It was cramped and full of the dirtiest degenerates in the city. For those who had nowhere to go when the rain started, there were the transtunnels. The corporations tried to keep the noobs out of them at first but eventually gave up in favor of private transportation via skycars, keeping close to the heavens like new-age gods of a darkened Olympus. If the noobs were in the tunnels, at least they were out of sight and all in one place. So the transtunnels had turned into a kind of underground tent city and you had to wade through a sea of people just to get to the tubes. Also, you had to be on your guard if you wanted to make it there in one piece and with all your possessions. The entrances to the tunnels were like little sores all over the city. As if the underbelly of the uber-corporations couldn't help but fester to the surface. The Cherry Street entrance had a sizable camp surrounding it—mostly vendors peddling various junk, tech, or selling food that didn't look any better than it smelled. Riley wound his way toward the stairway into the tunnel, and preparing himself for the claustrophobic chaos to come, he descended.

14

Better are three in unison and
enjoying themselves in a circle.
Do you understand everything I've
told you?
Yes.
On Friday, October 13, 1307, King
Philip of France gave orders to
have the Templars arrested and
subsequently tortured until they
confessed to appalling crimes of
heresy.
Do you accept the responsibility?
Yes.
Good. You will help save the
world... or at least the parts of it
worth saving.

"Nate! Wake up!" his mother called to him and fell into a coughing fit.

He cracked the door and peeked out. His mom shuffled around in the living room like something out of a zombie netvid. She was pale, eyes sunken and her uniform flecked with blood from her coughing. She saw the door open and weakly reached out.

"Oh, there you are. Just wanted to tell you I was home." She slumped into her chair, laid her head back, and closed her eyes. "Everything is fine. Daddy is coming. Everything is fine."

"Are you alright, momma? You look sick."

"I'm fine. It's just allergies. A summer cold."

"A lot of people are sick. Toby looked sick. Mrs. Fred across the hall. She definitely looked sick."

"It's a bad one."

"Is it a KiSS cleanse?"

"No sweetie. There's no such thing," she said, trying to comfort her son, "I'm just going to take a little nap. Work was hard. You need anything?"

"No momma."

"I love you, Nate."

"I love you too." He waited a few minutes until her breathing became regular and then slipped into the living room where he deftly pulled his netset from his mother's satchel.

He slid it over his head and flicked the thumb pad. "Open search," he commanded. A butler stepped from a door that opened in eSpace and bowed.

"May I help you, sir?"

"Find information on 'Baphomet'."

"As you wish. Baphomet was an idol that the Knights Templar—"

"Not helpful," Nate cut in. "Are there any modern revivals of Baphomet or a Templar cult?"

"Wherever the heretics whisper, Baphomet speaks."

"What did you just say?"

"I said, no. There are no modern cults on file since all religious worship was banned at the dawn of the New Golden Age." The search assistant bowed and returned through the door he entered from.

It couldn't have been a glitch, Nate reasoned. The Geeves had been hacked and made to say that. Baphomet wasn't just some boss. He wasn't just another NPC in a sim waiting to be defeated. He was a ghost in the machine. He had to be. And Nate wanted to know what the old goat was up to.

15

The alder trees in the first line
made the commencement.
Is this the wisest course of action?
Letting her out like that?
Five charges were brought against
the Templars.
It's all we have left. We need to
field test the unit while we still have
time.

They moved 4D4M to a living cell the previous morning. He had been acclimating ever since. He truly was a babe in the woods. Tabula Rosa. Dr. Gold stared at him with some mixture of awe and revulsion, the billows of smoke from his cigarette acting as screens changing between the two expressions. He was a child. A perfect child that could be molded into something great as long as that form was shaped according to his plan. If the mission for Jimmy Lee's spawn ended in failure or if the results weren't as expected, they would need a plan B. And perhaps that plan B was standing right in front of him.

"Why do you always appear in a cloud of fire and smoke, father?" 4D4M brushed the wisps aside, "It makes you foreboding."

Gold stubbed out the cigarette on the small table he sat at, "What do you remember, Jim—I mean 4D4M—from before you woke up two days ago?"

The hybrid looked at him in genuine puzzlement. "Why, nothing, father. I don't remember anything. Before I woke up there was... nothing. Until you gave me life, I don't remember existing."

Gold nodded, unable to contain the approval oozing from his smug face, "That's right. Before I gave you life, you were nothing. You came from nothing. I took clay from the earth and made you in my image. I gave you life. And all I ask for in return is love. Obedience."

"Of course, father. I love you. Why would I ever dream of disobeying you?"

Gold blurted out laughter and even the Labcoats outside the room taking notes smiled in Hiveminded unison.

"Why indeed, son. Why indeed."

"What is Paradis3, father? What is it like? Are we there now?"

"No. But we are getting close. Ever so close. Paradis3 will be a beautiful garden of our own making. It will cover the whole earth, making it new again. You and I and others like us will live there forever. We will never grow old. We will never suffer. We will never die."

"It sounds like a place I would very much like to be," said 4D4M before zoning out, gazing at nothing in the middle distance. A short time later he started seizing.

Labcoats rushed in and stabilized him, returning his sleeping form to his bed while shooing Dr. Gold out the door.

"What's going on?" demanded the CEO, "What's that about?"

"We assure you it's nothing, sir," said the Labcoats' team leader, "His nanobots appear to be more aggressive than 3vE's. They are replicating and attacking his body at an accelerated rate. It defies all of our projections, scenarios, and calculations. There is no logical reason the nanobots should be acting this way."

"I don't pay you for logical reasons. I pay you to find objective data. You're fired." Gold tossed the cigarette he was smoking to the ground and stepped it into the floor, his eyes never leaving the supervisor's face. The man glanced around looking for support from any of his immobile Labcoats. But they were all in rest mode and weren't even aware of what was going on.

He opened his mouth to say something when Dr. Gold grabbed him by the throat and yanked him out of his station. He repeatedly slammed the supervisor's head into the floor until all that was left was a puddle of mush. His fevered eyes shot up and locked on the Labcoat closest to him. He grabbed him and heaved him into the supervisor's station and placed the helmet onto his head. The new supervisor came to with a gasp. He looked around, eyes darting over everything before sticking on the corpse of his former boss.

"Tell me what's wrong with my boy," Gold ordered him, "Or you'll be lying right next to him."

"Of course, Dr. Gold. It's obvious. Right here. I don't see how my predecessor could've missed it. The nanobots are mimicking old patterns from 4D4M's previous body."

"How's that possible? They are new nanobots! They should at least be deteriorating at a rate similar to 3vE's."

"We think they're accelerating replication to reach the numbers he was at prior to his… transfer. It's as if his brain can't forget who he was before. His memory is suppressed, but his chemical makeup was copied from his previous incarnation. He's Jimmy even if he isn't Jimmy anymore."

"Fix it or you're fired," growled Gold. He then stormed off.

16

*Willow and quicken tree were slow
in their array.
It is done.
The first charge was the
renouncement of the cross during
initiation into the Order.
How can this be right? How are we
supposed to get used to what we
are doing? The justifications seem
weaker the further we go.*

The Burbs. Riley hated the Burbs. Whatever the rolling hills surrounding Denver were in the past was just a distant memory. Now, the land outside the walled city was the filthiest den of urban sprawl in the entirety of Corporate Denver. The streets and walkways were covered to keep out the rain, turning the shanty town into a massive maze. If living in the city felt cramped, living in the Burbs felt downright claustrophobic. Like being buried alive or trapped in some dungeon sim. The only reason CharWang hadn't come in and whitewashed the whole place was that the slum acted as a buffer between Denver proper and the Rainbow Children's territory. These were uncertain times. And there was no better way to defend against said uncertainty than having a whole barrier of wage slaves to soak up all that carnage. By the time it reached the walls— if it ever did—the situation was easily dealt with by the corporate military. No, the Burbs weren't going anywhere. They were a vital link in the chain of Corporate Denver. As such, those living in the Burbs often engendered humanity's worse traits, holding survival as the prime directive of their existence. And that's really why Riley hated it. Say what you want about the technocrazies, at least those poor bastards weren't doing it on purpose.

One of the first things he noticed as he climbed the stairs to the surface was the number of people coughing and looking generally ill. Whether it was some new virus spreading through the community or a KiSS cleanse, he couldn't tell. But he pulled his facemask from his pocket to cover whatever it may be. He avoided the sick as best he could while fighting the sea of people. He darted into the first food stall he came to and ordered a cup of Feen with extra Feen.

"What's the deal with all the sick people," he asked the cook while scrolling through information on his case via his old school wrist phone.

"Started a few days ago," the toothless woman said with a shrug, "Figured it was another KiSS cleanse."

"Huh," Riley grunted, only halfway paying attention. His mark lived in a tenement on the very outskirts of the Burbs. Might as well be living in the open space between the Burbs and the tree line that signaled the Heart of the Rockies. Talk about skid row. That was a place for the poorest of the poor. Not even other Burbanites ventured to the border projects unless it was absolutely necessary. That's exactly where someone wanting to hide or lay low would live. The mark wasn't listed as suffering from TPS but as a "research fugitive." Normally that meant someone tried to get away with some cutting-edge beta gear and the corporation needed to reclaim its asset. Those jobs were always a little harder to take for Riley. He wasn't dealing with a deranged psychotic, they were people. Greedy, self-serving people, but people nonetheless. In the end, it couldn't be helped. The world was dying and life was cheap so Riley chalked it up to 'the way things were.' He waved thanks to the cook and left to stake out his mark.

He posted up across from the ramshackle building for hours, scanning the DNA of everyone coming and going and didn't find one match. Whoever this mark was, they didn't want to be seen. He could've busted down the door of the apartment on file, but that was crass and often caused more problems than it solved. He walked around to the back and saw the apartment's windows on the second floor, but there was no movement inside.

Frustrated he went back around front and just as he turned the corner, his wristwatch dinged with a DNA match notification. It was only partial and belonged to a young woman who looked like she was about to collapse from whatever sickness was going around. Riley nonchalantly followed her into the building and up the stairs to her apartment. He stopped at a door near the opposite end of the hall and made a show of looking for his access card.

The woman weakly scanned her card and struggled to open the door. "Nate!" she called as soon as she opened the door. "Nathanial Merriweather! You better not be logged in!" The door closed behind her and Riley went back to the street.

He did a quick search for Nathanial Merriweather and only came up with a student file from a local school in the Burbs. It listed Nate's age as 10. He immediately dialed Randy.

The agent's face popped up on his screen. "Riles, what a pleasant surprise. Done with the job already? You must need a payday pretty bad. What's wrong? Are your sustainment meds running low?"

"No fuckin way. I ain't doing it," he growled, "A kid? They want to kill a kid? Did you know about this?"

"What?" Randy said with a wounded gesture, "You think I had something to do with it?"

"I don't know, Randy. Did you? It's very convenient that you got access to the job listing before anyone else. You mean to tell me you didn't have a look at the file before you passed it on?"

"There was no time. I swear," he crossed his heart, "It's deplorable."

"And illegal. Gearing up kids has been illegal since before the Second Collapse. I won't do it."

"Riley," began Randy, a dangerous edge creeping into his flamboyant voice, "We've been over this. You can't cancel. You really want to know why I got that job? I had to take it to make things right after your little stunt at HyLyfe Tower. Popping off to the Suits like that. They told me to give you that job and if you completed it, all would be forgiven."

"What bullshit. If it's got something to do with a geared up kid then CharWang is already working in black op territory. I could whistleblow."

"To who? CharWang IS everything. As far as our little city is concerned, CharWang Industries is God Almighty and HyLyfe Tower is his throne. If you cancel this job, they'll send a team. You know this, Riley. And once that team cleans up your job, they'll come looking for you next. My advice is to suck it up and get it done. It's the only real choice you have left. Don't stew over it too long, timer is ticking off." Randy ended the call.

"Bastard!" Riley yelled, catching the attention of people nearby. He ducked into a food stall for a cup of Feen and to consider his options.

His first option was to complete the job and that wasn't going to happen. He wasn't going to cold-cap a kid. That left his old buddy Billy Burr. Billy was an ex-corporate merc and an electronics wizard. Riley and him had done some corporate work years ago and were part of a disastrous raid on the Rainbow Children. Their friendship had solidified while hiding out in the Burbs waiting for the heat to die down. That was when Riley met Shawn for the first time. She was doing charity work as the rich often do to assuage their feelings of over-privilege. Riley moved back to the city to be with Shawn and Billy stayed in the Burbs to set up shop fixing electronics. He usually stashed away a bottle of real liquor and Riley really needed a drink.

He made his way to Billy's shop moving against a tight crowd, the cacophony of their chatter drowned out only by the thick raindrops drumming on the metal roof over their heads.

Billy flashed a yellow smile when Riley darkened his doorway. "Well look what the skags drug in!"

"Your mother was a skag." Riley shot back.

"Guess that makes you a skag fucker then." Billy laughed and pulled Riley into a hug. "What dafuq is going on with you?"

"On a case. I need to talk."

"Well let's quit standing out here. There's a virus goin' round. C'mon back, I got some real vodka I been saving for just such an occasion."

Billy's apartment was an apartment in name only. In reality, it was an extra room built onto the back of his shop. It was one room complete with a dirty mattress, sink, toilet, and a wood burning stove welded together from old metal. Billy rummaged around for a bit and finally produced a bottle.

"Where'd you get vodka?"

"Client paid me with it a while back. This stuff is damn near impossible to get outside of Status establishments."

"I know," said Riley as he savored the warmth of the alcohol traveling down his throat. "Greedy trolls."

"I'll drink to that," Billy agreed and poured another shot.

"How's the gear holding up?" Riley asked as he took the shot. Though they were around the same age, Billy looked ten years older. His gear was at least twenty years old. Cybernetic arms crafted from sheer gunmetal, not the smooth alloys available today. And his face implant looked like something out of an old star fighter netvid. "Any tics I should know about? Any signs of TPS? I mean, with that gear you're running it's inevitable."

"Very funny, asshole. My gear is running good as the day I got enhanced." Billy made a show of clenching his heavy metal hand into a fist. "Wanna test it?"

Riley laughed, "You never changed, man. You ever miss the old days? Running search parties like we did?"

"Nah. Lost the stomach for it, man. Saw too many good people die and those Council-be-damned hippies slipped away time and time again. Hit us, then ghost. Hit us, then ghost. Same scenario over and over and over. Got disheartening, ya know? Plus, ol' poppa CharWang wasn't paying enough to make it worth it."

He had aged rapidly and badly since Riley had seen him last. Of course, living in the Burbs would do that to a man, but Riley saw something else. He saw a hollow look in his old friend's eyes. It was the look of a man who lost his purpose and had given up hope of ever finding it again. "Shit man. I never took you for a wage slave, Billy. Thought you were better people than that."

"I'm a simple man, Riley. You ought to know. I'll kill anyone you give me money to, but I'll be damned if I'm getting noob wages to go up against a bunch of remorseless savages. Sometimes, you gotta take the loss even if it eats at you every damn day of your life." He forewent the shot glass and pulled straight from the bottle. "So to what do I owe the visit? Don't get me wrong, not complaining. Just haven't seen you in a bit."

Riley filled Billy in on the past couple of days and the old merc's eyes widened in disbelief.

"That's impossible. Nothing could do that. EMP's blast dafuq outta gear, man. Fry them up real good. It'll turn gearheads into vegetables but won't trigger the crazies. There's no way."

"Yeah well, it happened so there's obviously a way. Think you could look into it? See what you can come up with?"

"Of course, buddy. I'll ask around. This thing with the kid though… how long you got left?"

"Bout 12 hours now. Thing is, if I don't finish the contract," he lit two cigarettes and passed one to Billy, "Then I'll end up as a contract."

"Yeah. I know how poppa CharWang works. What if you use that to your advantage?"

"What do you mean?"

"How many people in a team? Four? Five? Those are noob numbers. We could handle them." Billy's eyes lit up with an anticipation that bordered on bloodlust. As if his purpose flared up briefly from its smoldering core, "So we barricade ourselves, you cancel the contract, and we wait for 'em to show up."

"And then what? I've only got my sidearm."

"Well, I got something I've been saving for a rainy day." Billy lifted the mattress and opened a safe built into the floor. Cradled inside was a modest cache of homemade weapons and explosives.

"Holy hell, man. Everything in there will get you executed on the spot."

"Yeah. Well, when you outlaw guns only outlaws have guns. I'm okay with being an outlaw."

"Alright then, let's do some crazy shit. We have to make them think I just walked away. They'll go after the boy first, guaranteed so we should post up there."

"I'm getting more excited about this than my old ass should be," Billy leered and poured another shot. "Anything's better than waitin' around to get sick."

"What's up with that? KiSS cleanse?"

"None of my corporate contacts heard anything about a KiSS activation so I figured it was a Mother Nature special. Been trying to stay dafuq outta the way, you know? There's been chatter about a quarantine. They're already holding people for twelve hours before letting 'em back through the walls. Not sure where we go when we get this done."

"We'll worry about that when the time comes," Riley said, packing Billy's weapons stash into a large duffel bag. "For now, let's focus on getting that boy cleared."

Billy and Riley headed toward Nate's project and their route led them near the transtunnel back into town. Desperation had possessed the slummers in the Burbs. Their angry cries and wails of agony drowned out the thundering sound of the rain. They crammed around the transtunnel, grinding one another underfoot to get to the safety of the underground.

Then the gunshots started, sporadically at first but soon picking out a steady rhythm.

"CorPol!" somebody yelled up from inside. "They're shooting people!"

The crowd's desperation shifted, then instead of fighting to get into the tunnels, they fled like cattle stampeding away from a slaughterhouse door. The POP! POP! POP! of gunfire accentuated the screams and moans of the dying. The stench of fear hung thick in the air causing the sick and panicked slummers to snap and fall into anarchy, forming a mob bent on violence and destruction that moved through the Burbs with uniform purpose. They slaughtered the infected and the healthy alike with a ruthless proficiency.

And when there was no one around left to kill, they turned on their surroundings, destroying vehicles, starting fires, and spreading more chaos than football fans after a championship game. The doomed lashed out at the world around them without prejudice or predisposition, effectively mimicking the illness within them and ultimately stoking the flames of rage that quickly spread and consumed the warrens of the Burbs.

17

The bean hides an army of
phantoms in its shade.
I don't trust him.
The second charge the Templars
were accused of was sodomy.
Baphomet chose him and trusts him
to deliver. We must as well.

The door buzzed again. Nate huddled in his room while Toby stood watch in the hallway, holding a finger to his lips. Whoever was outside pounded on the door with a muffled tone. Toby crept over and hit the speaker button.

"My name is Jacob Riley. Ms. Merriweather, I'm here to help. Please open the door. I need to talk to you about your son. It's urgent." He buzzed again.

Before Toby could stop him, Nate rushed up and pressed the door-view button. The door went transparent and he saw Riley and Billy standing outside. Billy stood back, darting quick glances over his shoulder.

"Hey there," said Riley with a disarming smile. "Are you Nate? Is your mom home?"

"She's dead," Nate said matter-of-factly. "She got sick. This is my friend, Toby. He came by to watch me. Are you the ones the whispers talked about?"

"Not sure what you mean, kiddo," Riley said. "But we are here to help. Please open the door."

Nate mashed the panel and the entrance slid open. Riley and Billy rushed in and closed the door behind them. "Alright. There isn't much time. Maybe eleven hours."

"Time for what," Toby said, trying to muster up his gangly frame.

"For all of us to get out of this alive."

"Oh man," Billy blurted out, pointing to Lola Merriweather's blue, swollen corpse, "She's not only dead, she's still in her easy chair."

"How long she been dead," Riley asked, looking at Toby.

The teenager shrugged. "Bout half a day, I guess."

"Advanced decay," mumbled Billy, "This is one helluva bug going around."

"Nobody ever came to get the body," Nate explained, his lower lip quivering. "I called people, but no one ever came. Not even my daddy. And he was supposed to come save us."

Riley squeezed the boy's shoulder. "I'm sorry about your mom, Nate. And I'll do what I can to help you find your dad."

A smile broke out on Nate's somber face. "You mean it?"

"I do. But first, we gotta take care of something."

"What?"

"Some real jerks want to hurt you. We need to make sure they don't. Can you and your friend help us?"

Nate nodded, "I think we can. Right, Toby?"

Toby looked uncertain. "I guess. I still think we should make for the transtunnels."

"They're a killing field right now," Billy informed him, "Poppa CharWang done issued a quarantine."

"But I got family inside the walls..." Toby slumped down, defeated.

"No time for that," snapped Riley. "Get your ass up and let's get this place fortified."

"These bad guys will come in even with a quarantine?" Nate asked.

"Yeah. They will," answered Riley, "they want you really bad for some reason."

"It's my head, I think. They want my head because I can hear the whispers."

"Yeah, alright. Help me move this couch, will ya?"

They spent the next four hours barricading the small apartment with what they had available and setting booby traps with Billy's explosives. They created a decent central bunker where Billy would be stationed with the heavy weaponry. And another smaller bunker opposite the hallway. From there they could flank anyone coming through the front and had a clear line of sight for anyone coming in from the balcony. This is where Riley and Toby would be stationed. Nate had his own shelter built behind the stove in the kitchen. It wasn't ideal but it was what they had to work with. As dawn broke, Riley stepped out for a smoke and to take in the crisp morning air on the balcony facing the open tree line. Sure it was smoggy and filled with carcinogens, but the air in Denver was a helluva lot better than some other corporate free cities. But this morning, as he inhaled deeply in gratitude for another day, the sounds of chaos rose up from the streets. It seemed fitting to add to it. He dialed Randy.

"Riles, my boy! You better have only good news for me right now."

"Yeah. I'm opting out. You can tell your child-murdering bosses to shove their contract straight up their asses."

"I was serious about what I said. You'll be on the corporate blacklist." Randy looked genuinely pained, his Ken Doll face was even more taut than normal. "Please Riles, don't do this."

"It's already done," Riley snapped and ended the call. It was only a matter of time. He stepped back inside and carefully set the booby trap before returning to the main room. "Showtime. The team is on its way. Remember," he told Toby, "your job is to watch for people coming from the hallway. If you see anyone, yell and shoot them. Got it?"

The teenager nodded and brushed the stringy hair from his face. "Yeah. I can shoot, man."

"I hope so," Billy chimed in from his bunker made from the kitchen table and chairs and the refrigerator.

18

The privet and the woodbine live in
shelter, as does the ivy in its
season.
Tracking protocols activated.
The third was telling the neophyte
that unnatural lust was lawful and
a common practice.
Amazing. Her numbers are off the
charts. She was born for this.

"Sir," the Suit approached Gold carefully, "The IT Consultant canceled the job."

The CEO sighed and leaned back in his chair. He rubbed his temples for a moment then poured himself a drink from the decanter on his desk. "Fucking useless. The lot of them. IT consultants. What are they really? They go around cold-capping assholes that CorPol could be taking care of on their beats because the noobs 'needed something to do.' Noob is synonymous with cancer. Remember that." He finished his drink in a gulp and poured another. "Still, though… Project Ed3n wasn't an easy decision to come to for our grandfathers. How do you justify the killing of over three billion people? After all, they're still people, right? That was the argument, anyway."

The Suit stared blankly ahead as Dr. Gold rambled, unable or unwilling to interject anything to the conversation. It was always best to let leadership speak uninterrupted. It was what the Hivemind deemed most efficient.

Gold refilled his drink and kept going, "So the Corporate Council decided to run a little experiment to justify their design. And do you know what? They were right, goddammit. They were right. People are fucking terrible. The smart ones. The kind ones. The funny ones.

All of them. Terrible, boorish, selfish monsters run by egos whose main concerns haven't changed since we lived in caves. They are all still looking for something to eat, somewhere to sleep and someone to fuck. Most of them are incapable of the tiniest bit of self-awareness. They shamble through life like the dull cattle they are, looking for direction. They are helpless, codependent, and completely devoid of personal responsibility. So we gave them a way to pull themselves out of the gutter and make something of their pathetic lives. Maybe even put a dent in their life debt along the way while we systematically KiSSed them into extinction. We throw them some choice scraps from our table and what do we get in return? Disrespectful and lazy fuck-offs who can't finish anything they start! It's days like this I take comfort in our grandfathers' decisions."

The Suit shifted uncomfortably and straightened his tie. "Of course, sir. Thank you for adding to my knowledge matrix. These revelations will be added to the algorithms to make sure the corporate will is executed to the fullest extent. Moving on, the extraction team is ready to retrieve the child."

"Good. What are you telling me for?"

"Reports are coming in from the Burbs, sir. People sick, dying in the streets. Population has been reduced by 12% already and rising. We aren't scheduled for a KiSS cleanse for another eight months. All projections point to a plague outbreak."

"Bullshit. It's those god damned hippies. They're behind this, I'd bet my right nut." The CEO lit a cigarette and blew smoke in the Suit's face. "We need that boy's head. Send the team in anyway. Give them biohazard gear, but make sure they get the job done. Got it?"

"Yes, sir," the Suit said and scurried off to carry out his master's wishes.

Dr. Gold leaned back in his chair, smoking in contemplation, and then mashed a button on his desk screen. The Chitown Inc. logo appeared for a moment before it was replaced with the face of its CEO, Camilla Sanchez.

"Elijah Gold," she said, rolling the words around in her mouth as if they were bitter. "What do I owe this little call?"

"My Rainbow Children are moving into the end game. Some kind of new virus outbreak."

"So are mine. I've heard the same from half a dozen other corporate cities."

"This isn't good. We should've had more time. We need to speed up the project."

"You mean YOU need to speed up YOUR end of the project. If we have the hybrids ready to go, they can survive indefinitely. We can always roll out the flora and fauna after the threats are neutralized."

"So you're putting this all on me," scoffed Gold, "typical."

"You are the one who promised the quickest results," Camilla reminded him. "How's it going with that little hiccup, by the way? I'm not looking forward to spending eternity unable to remember my own name."

"I have HyLyfe on it. And we've got options. Don't worry, Sanchez. You'll get your results." He ended the call and poured himself a drink. Nothing to do now but wait.

19

The birch was late to the battle, not out of cowardice, but on account of his great size.

The Burbs are reaching critical status. Package must be extracted.

The fourth was that the neophyte's cord was consecrated by wrapping it around an idol that was either a severed head or a black cat.

We can't let him escape. There's not enough time. Forget Baphomet's wishes. Neutralize peripherals with prejudice.

Exactly thirty-three minutes after Riley hung up with Randy, the door to Nate's apartment blew inward and the corporate strike team filtered in.

Billy pulled hard on a thin piece of rope he was holding and Lola Merriweather's hand shot up in the air. Falling for the distraction, the first two mercs in the door turned to where she sat in her recliner and blasted her with bullets. They each fell with a bullet to the head from Billy's homemade rifle.

Riley took the next one out as he rushed through the door to Billy's position.

The fourth assailant threw a smoke bomb inside and ducked around the corner.

Billy waited until the cloud thickened and went to retrieve Nate. He scooped up the boy and met Riley and Toby, bolting toward the hallway. Toby rushed forward and flung open the bedroom door. All Riley had time to do was yell, "NO!" and the boy jerked like a marionette from the fifth assailant's Bushmaster rifle.

Riley leapt over the corpse and fired at the merc. He tackled him and both went to the ground where they jockeyed for the upper hand. Billy took Nate to the opposite end of the room near the balcony. He darted a glance around the corners and grunted in satisfaction.

"I think we're good. If they have a sniper, he's probably positioned out front. Wait here." He picked the merc up by the scruff of his body armor, his machine arm whirring as it kicked into overdrive, with the other arm he punched through the merc's faceplate and collapsed the bridge of his nose. He tossed the body aside and helped Riley to his feet. "Did I interrupt you two? Were you having a moment?"

Riley dabbed his busted lip, ignoring Billy's jab, and picked up the corporate merc's antique firearm. "This'll come in handy. What's the situation outside?"

"We're good if we go now. Number four will be coming down the hall if he isn't already. You take the boy, I'm gonna fix this trap." He held up the explosives originally rigged to the balcony doors. The merc had busted the glass and disarmed the trap from inside. Billy slammed the bedroom door and quickly got to work. "Go on! I can hear him coming!"

Riley slung Nate around his shoulders. "Hold on! Tight! Do not let go. Do you understand?"

Nate nodded, his eyes wide with fear and excitement. He hopped on Riley's back and held on as the merc jumped the railing and slid down the rope. Billy followed a few seconds later. The fugitives huddled behind the tenement's automated dumpsters causing the smart machines to blare out proximity warnings.

"We can't stay here," Billy whispered sharply.

"No shit. But we can't go either. No doubt the corporation has closed the gates and tunnels too."

"Yeah. And there's no way to tell if any of those sickos got through before they did. What about the woods?"

Nate shook his head. "We can't. There are monsters in the forest. I've seen them."

"Well right now, the monsters here are more dangerous than them in the woods, kid," said Billy. "Toughen it up and let's get outta here."

Nate sighed, chewing on his lip as he considered his options, then finally nodded his head. "This way. I know a secret way to get into the woods."

Riley and Billy followed Nate to a nearby drainage opening and heaved the lid off. Nate climbed down first and Riley waited until he saw Billy hustling over.

"Great," Riley mumbled as he descended the ladder, "A shortcut through the sewers. What a great idea going to the woods has been."

"You been in the city too long," Billy laughed as he moved the cover back into place. A few seconds later a loud boom shook the Burbs. "Five for five." He plopped down into the muck and darkness. He rapped his fist against his face implant and a floodlight sputtered to life.

"Working just as good as the day you bought it, huh?"

"It's not broken. It has character," Billy shot back and plunged into the darkness.

20

Uncouth and savage was the fir.
Be on the lookout for Jane Doe.
Height: 5'6. Weight: 125 lbs. Eyes:
Green. Hair: Blonde.
The fifth charge against the
Templars was that the priests of the
Order did not consecrate the host
in celebrating Mass.
Last sighted leaving HyLyfe Tower.
This is priority one for CorPol and
affiliates.

3vE felt better after a shower. It had been years since she felt water trickling down her skin with soothing warmth. Not that she knew this about herself, to her it was a new experience. Something that she knew she should be familiar with—the woman in the cryotank in HyLyfe Tower surely must have showered. But even memory of this simple act had been stolen from her. She toweled off and put on the clothes laid out for her by her hostess. She hadn't gotten the girl's name, but a quick search through her facial recognition database gave her the answer she was looking for.

Glory Bastille. Age 20. Height: 5 ft. 2 in. Weight: 98 lbs. Hair: Brown. Eyes: Green. Status: None. Corporate interest: 3%.

"Well that's a relief," she whispered to herself. Apparently, Glory was pretty much off the corporate radar. Her small percentage of corporate interest was probably generated by her value as a labor asset, which her file showed as Freelance Entertainment Specialist. A prostitute. Probably hired as an escort by a lonely corporate Suit on break from the Hivemind. Whatever she did for money, it paid her enough to have a small studio apartment close to the western wall of Denver. She did have to wonder about the girl's intentions though. She couldn't for the life of her figure out why this noob would extend an offer of help to her.

"Hey there. Find everything you need?" Glory peeked her head around the door, flashing what she hoped was a genuine smile. There was something off about the woman she pulled from the street. People who looked like her and were obviously geared didn't wander naked through the streets unless they popped and got the technocrazies. And this woman didn't have the crazies. She just seemed... confused. And innocent. She exuded newness like an infant which didn't make any sense to Glory because she was staring at a grown woman. She didn't know what to do with her, but she knew people who might, and if she was lucky, she might even make a few bitz out of it.

"I'm fine," 3vE said, pulling at her shirt trying to cover her stomach as if she had no idea she *wasn't* a stone-cold fox. "Thanks for the clothes."

"Are you hungry? I think I got some Ramen left."

"No. Thank you. I would take some water though."

"Sure thing." Glory disappeared into the small corner of the room that served as a kitchen and rummaged around the refrigerator for some cold water. "So, like, you gotta name?"

"I... think so. Call me 3vE."

"Eve? Cool, cool. So what's your deal, Eve? Why you rollin' around the streets in bloody lab coats and shit?"

"That's none of your business. But since we're asking questions, why would you help me? What's in it for you?"

"Just don't like to see anyone getting popped by the Pol, ya know? A thanks would be nice. But I know how you trolls like to be."

"I'm not a troll!"

"Please! You got millions of bitz worth of machinery on you. Probably even billions. And that ain't saying anything about the plastic surgery to keep you lookin' like a fresh piece."

"It's not what you think."

"I'm sure it ain't. It rarely is. Thing is I ain't lookin' to up my Corporate Interest percentages any, so I don't know what to do with you. But I might know some peeps that do. If you're interested."

3vE needed leads—a direction. Her capture had topped the corporate priorities list in the past couple of hours knocking "Finding Hylyfe Killer" down to #2. So every geek on the street would be sniffing after her trail hoping to collect a bounty. And the bounty was sizable; CharWang obviously wanted her badly. This all left her at a disadvantage. She suffered from amnesia, had no one else to turn to, and had no idea where to go from here. Not to mention, she was walking around in classified corporate property. She was as good as dead if they found her. It was her against the world at this point. She thought perhaps if she handled the next biggest priority and found this HyLyfe killer, the Suits might take it easy on her. Maybe even put her back in her real body. It seemed a rational course of action and her odds for a favorable outcome significantly increased.

"I'm interested," 3vE said, "Let's go meet your friends."

They approached the transtunnels near the wall and were soon lost in a thick crowd.

"Citizens!" boomed an amplified voice above the din, "please remain calm. Travel to the Burbs has been temporarily suspended."

"What's going on," Glory asked out loud to no one in particular.

"Reports of a virus outbreak are coming in on several corporate channels," 3vE informed her absently. "Looks like a probable quarantine coming."

"How you got access to that info?" Glory looked at 3vE, trying to bore into that odd brain of hers. None of what she said was on any of the public channels. That could only mean she was pulling from private corporate channels and a troll had to have serious Status to get to those.

"I don't know," 3vE replied flatly. "But is there a way we can get off the streets? CorPol is coming to assist and I'd rather not be here when they do."

"Yeah. I got another way, but it ain't gonna be fun for a troll like you." Glory led 3vE to a sewer entrance near the wall.

As soon as her feet touched the dirty cement underground, 3vE's GPS immediately went dark. So did the tunnels, for that matter, and she had to switch over to night vision in order to follow Glory who didn't seem to have the slightest issue navigating in the pitch black.

"Where are we going?" 3vE asked.

"You'll see. We're almost there."

They reached what appeared to be a dead end. Glory felt along the wall in front of her and found the latch. The wall slid aside to reveal an elevator manned by two extremely geared meatheads.

"Dafuq you want, Glory?" growled a man with a big nose and short, spiky hair. "Ain't no one called for your piece."

"I needa see Jack, fucker."

"What about?" the other guard, a ginger-haired man with a big, bushy beard, asked as he scrutinized 3vE. "Who's she?"

"She is what I need to talk to Jack about. As if it's any of your damn business, Carl. Now let us past and take us down already!" she stamped her foot in a fit of petulance.

Carl scratched his beard and looked at his companion with a shrug. "Fine. But I'm warnin' ya. Jack ain't in a good mood today."

"What else is new?" Glory said as she stepped into the elevator, motioning 3vE to follow.

The elevator dinged and the doors slid open.

"Welcome to the Corporate Underground," said Carl and shoved the women out of the elevator. "If Jack asks, I didn't let you down."

3vE couldn't believe her eyes. She had a database file on the Corporate Underground, of course. A loose conglomeration of startup corporations trying to get enough clout and resources together to make it topside and reclaim a city of their own. Few actually made it and none of those that did kept records or documentation on the Underground. It existed only in urban legends which were a rarity in a world that maintained control by killing secrets before they became a problem. But here that problem was—and it wasn't a legend but a thriving black market. It was like walking into Avalon.

The Corporate Underground was housed in a massive subterranean cavern so far below ground 3vE lost connection with the Internetwork which she suspected was exactly the point. The cavern was filled with people running back and forth, yelling, trading, fighting, and even fucking in some of the darker corners. At the far end, a huge screen hundreds of feet across continuously streamed stock prices, news headlines, and market trends as well as a price list of everything from hacked Enhancements to lab-grown infants. This list fluctuated with a nearly continuous fluidity. Clustered beneath the screen were the stalls of the Startups. Manning the stalls, badly-dressed men and women yelled into vid screens and at each other, haggling and heckling. Each stall had one employee connected to the screen via a cable plugged into the base of their skulls.

"Who are they?" 3vE asked.

"Them? They're wired into the BeastNET there," the girl pointed to the screen. "Jack says they keep track of money and transactions and stuff. In real-time. Goin' topside ain't easy, you know?" She waded through the crowd with expert grace and stopped in front of one of the bigger stalls. This one actually had several rooms attached to it.

"Sinister and Grace," 3vE read the scrolling marquee above the stall.

A slender, angular man with glasses too big for his face held up his finger without breaking the flow of the conversation he was having with the vid screen.

"You tell Smith to shove that offer up his ass. Nobody will pay that price for his shit. Who dafuq is PlusCo? What do they sell? Discount toilets or something? It sounds like bullshit. If PlusCo wants to buy in at that price then more power to them. I'll buy them out shortly after and pay half that." He irritably swiped his hand in front of the screen and it disappeared into the wall.

"What dafuq you want, Glory? Nobody called for your piece. You need a loan or something? Because I'm not fronting you shit anymore. Remember that?" His gaze moved over to 3vE and his eyes widened. "Who dafuq is this?"

"This is Eve. I found her up top. Can I talk to you?"

"I think you better," Jack said. Then to 3vE, "Do me a favor. Change the vegetable's food bag," he snapped, motioning to the unconscious man plugged into the hot-seat. He pulled Glory into one of the stall's back rooms and they began a heated conversation in frantic whispers.

3vE lowered her mic volume to give them privacy and studied the sleeping man carefully. He was alive, but appeared to be in a deep coma. His eyes constantly fluttered beneath his eyelids as if he were in perpetual REM sleep. An IV connected to his left arm pumped nutrients into his system. 3vE looked around and noticed a small fridge in the corner by the man's chair. She got a fresh bag and swapped it out. Behind him, a small monitor scrolled numbers ceaselessly. Her gear allowed her to keep up with the feed as easily as reading the morning news. Among the ever-shifting number for a variety of resources was something of interest: prices for several plots of land somewhere in New Mexico. Sinister and Grace appeared to be making a bid to move topside.

"Can you actually read that?"

3vE turned to find Jack staring at her as intently as before.

"I was trying, but couldn't come up with anything."

"Do you realize what a depressing wasteland the world is now? This place we had, all beautiful. Full of trees and clean water and what do we do? We fuck it up. And we fucked it up bad. There aren't a lot of good spots left. We gotta get on the map while there's still a chance. I'm Jack, by the way. Jack Sinister." He extended his hand and 3vE took it.

"Call me 3vE."

"Alright, 3vE. Glory tells me she found you in a bit of trouble?"

"No trouble really. I just had a bad day."

"Right. A bad day, no doubt. To be found wearing nothing but a bloody lab coat with a corporate logo on it... I can't think of very many worse kind of days than that. Tell me about your bad day."

3vE gave him a synopsis of her awakening and subsequent escape from HyLyfe tower finishing up with, "Do you know what HyLyfe is?"

"Would you mind not insulting me in my own fucking office? Of course I know what HyLyfe is. It's the next evolution of the vegetables. Ain't that right, Tommy?" He slapped the sleeping man on the knee. "A totally immersive VR environment offering infinite possibilities for exploration—from charting star systems to rescuing princesses from haunted towers. Lot more fancy than old Tom here. I don't think he rescues many princesses. He's really just a glorified calculator. What's that gotta do with you?"

"Someone has been killing HyLyfers recently. I want to find out whom."

Jack laughed. "What do you expect? That if you find this killer the corporate overlords will forget your little transgression and welcome you back into the family?"

"Stats are favorable," 3vE said through gritted teeth, indignant at Jack's mockery of her plan. She wasn't exactly sure why she was annoyed by his tone. Her emotional suppressants should've regulated her reaction.

"Oh, I'm sure they are," Jack took a deep breath to contain his giggles. "Alright. Let's think this through. How do you kill a computerized consciousness? No, never mind. The details aren't important. What's important is that you're telling me the truth. Because you're looking a little too fine and geared up to be just another geek off the street." He eyed her shrewdly. He couldn't quite put his finger on what she was hiding, but he knew there was definitely something she wasn't telling him. Her story was crazy enough to be true but there was more to it—an undercurrent of foreboding potential that he wanted to be a part of. And Tom did predict a 37% probability that today would be the day that shifted their enterprise to the next level.

"I wonder what we would find if we opened you up and had a peek at what made you tick?" He reached out to flip up her skirt and she grabbed his hand, spinning him into a prone position with lightning fast efficiency.

"With the tiniest bit of pressure, I will snap your wrist. After that, while you are howling in unbearable pain, I'll snap your neck. Then, using your corpse, I'll smother your sleeping friend. That'll be an end to your startup.

Something tells me no one down here would bat an eye, either. Now tell me, am I being honest?"

"Yes," Jack groaned pathetically.

"No one touches me. Period." She released him and he scurried away, putting the slumbering Tommy between them. "Now either you can help me or you can't. I don't have time to play your pointless games."

He rubbed his wrist while considering her offer. Finally, he extended his good hand. "Sinister and Grace is here to help," he said with a toothy smile. "We just need a little time to look into your problem. And I know the perfect place for you to lay low for a while. Get ready for a little adventure outside the city walls."

21

*The cruel ash-tree didn't turn aside
but went straight for the heart.
She's gone dark. Activating third
eye.
In addition, the Templars were
accused of worshipping an idol
named Baphomet. He was the
source of evil in black magic.
The instant she comes back online,
you better be on her.*

After walking the tunnel for about ten minutes, Nate finally broke down and began to cry. Heavy sobs full of grief and loss, confusion and fear. He slumped into the mud and put his head between his knees. "Everyone is dead. Everyone. What am I going to do?"

"You're going to come with me. We're going to find a way through this and find your dad."

Billy guffawed. "Quit lying to the kid, Riley. We ain't ever getting back into that city. You better hope the Rainbow Children are taking on new recruits."

"Of course! The Rainbow Children will help me." Comforted by this, Nate climbed to his feet and marched out the other side of the drainage ditch.

It opened up about three hundred feet from the tree line. Riley hadn't been this far out of the city. Ever. The constant smog that hung heavily over Corporate Denver dissipated completely outside the Burbs. Here, approaching the tree line, the air was clean and the sunlight organic. He turned his face to the sun and let it fill him with natural, intoxicating warmth. He inhaled the cold, crisp air which hurt his blackened lungs and he coughed heavily.

"Easy, buddy," Bill said and slapped him on the back. "You gotta ease your way into natural living. Your body is more chemical than organic and as crazy as it sounds, natural environments hurt it."

"That does sound crazy. I thought nature was supposed to be good for us and shit."

"Nature gave us exactly what we wanted," Nate chimed in. "Complete separation from her."

"Wow, kid, where'd you learn how to talk like that?" Riley recovered and resumed following Billy and Nate down an unpaved trail that led into the foothills of the mountains looming to the west.

"Right? I was thinking he was kinda young to be so cynical," Billy concurred.

"I don't think so," said Nate. "I've seen the history vids at school. The old earth was awesome! I'm telling you. It was like, heaven on earth or something. And now we got nothing. Why? Because nobody could get along. Everybody wanted everything for themselves."

"Not much has changed, kid." Riley held up his hand, stopping short. "Hide!" he hissed and darted down a nearby ravine.

Billy and Nate followed and all of them hid as best they could while something massive passed them by. It snapped trees and scattered rocks like a careless behemoth and by the time it had gone by, Riley was covered in a thin blanket of dirt.

"What the HELL was that?" he said, jumping to his feet and dusting himself off.

"I dunno," said Billy. "Never even heard of anything like that."

"It was a Guardian. They watch the forest. I told you there were monsters here."

"A *forest guardian*?" Riley said, laughing. "Look kiddo, this ain't a fantasy sim. This is real life."

"I've seen 'em," Nate said indignantly. "You think this is my first time in the forest? The guardians are real. They are giant robots. They walk around and make sure no corporations get into the forest."

"Nobody has giant robots, kid," Riley said, trying to get a look through the trees to make sure it wasn't making another pass. "Me and Billy been on enough missions to know. Woulda seen them for sure."

"They don't let you see them if they don't want to," Nate said, balling his tiny fists at his sides. "They aren't stupid. If they can't win a fight, they retreat."

"The kid might be right," Billy said. "Come to think of it, right before the Second Great Collapse, when the corps and governments were fighting each other, they used giant mechanized tank drones."

"All the mechs were dismantled after," Riley said. "And the EMP's got any remnants."

"Right. Like all the nukes got dismantled by the Soviets and USA back in ancient times. Dollars to doughnuts, that's what those forest guardians are."

"Dollars to doughnuts?" Riley laughed.

"What? My grandpa used to say it."

"And his grandpa before him, probably. But the mechs... I don't know. That goes against every corporate treaty in existence. Deemed too much of a threat for collateral damage. And resource hogs to boot. There's no way these things have been able to run for as long as they have with no fuel."

"You ever seen a spec sheet on one?"

"No," Riley admitted.

"Well, I have. And the newer models all ran off solar energy. Fully automated, piloted by AI."

"Oh great. Rogue AI running rampant in the forest," Riley said. "That's exactly what we need."

"It's coming back this way," Nate said, climbing out of the ravine. "They never come back so fast. We must have tipped it off."

The ground rumbled gently beneath their feet as the mechanized tank approached. They could see it through the trees, a massive bipedal mech with tank guns for hands. Two lights blinked a threatening red under the plastic dome on top of its rusted torso.

"We can't outrun the Guardians!" Nate started to panic. "The only way to get past them is to sneak! If they see you it's over!"

An ominous clanking sound followed by a shuddering boom cracked the air. The trees above them exploded into a mass of leaves and shards of wood shortly thereafter. The concussion from the blast slammed them into the ground.

"It's still armed!" Billy moaned and rolled over, pushing himself to his feet. He flipped the switch on his last remaining homemade weapon: an EMP detonator. Nothing happened. "Useless piece of shit. Come on!" He growled, slamming the device into a nearby tree. It hummed to life with blinking lights. "You guys get the hell outta here! I'm gonna fry this thing once and for all."

At the same time, the Guardian corrected its miscalculation and aimed the second cannon at the intruders on the ground.

"Billy, don't be stupid," Riley pleaded.

"No choice," Billy said with a jagged smile. He sprinted toward the tank as Riley pulled Nate in the opposite direction.

The guardian's second gun hand whirred and expelled another round.

A smoking crater appeared where they just stood, sending dust and debris flying in all directions. Riley pulled Nate to the ground and covered him until the worst was over. Then they were up and running again.

◎

Billy smiled to himself and ran directly at the mech. *That's two*. The Guardian was out of shells and it would take it a while to reload. He pushed himself harder, his body tingling with sheer excitement and glee.

Restriction and subjugation laid the foundations for Billy's life. The corporations made use of them to keep people obedient. Limit resources and make people work for rewards. It ensured that even the most unreliable among the population would stay in line enough to get their basic needs taken care of. And it had worked like a charm. Humans have an innate desire for structure and routine. Everyone likes to feel safe and secure, likes to be assured that the world as they know it will go on existing. If they have to give up personal freedom and live like kept animals inside a filthy, shit-smelling cage like Corporate Denver, then so be it. For some, like Billy and Riley, that life wasn't good enough. That life was actually a slow burn into death so they took dangerous jobs to shake it up a bit. Increase the chance of dying and suddenly life means something. And this new world with its new frontiers funneled the malcontents into private armies to fight and kill one another or die securing resources for the corporations that hired them.

Just a little closer and he could set off the EMP. He might make it out of this yet. He pushed on, getting closer and arming the detonator in anticipation. He had to get it right. No telling what else that thing was equipped with and it needed to get fried before Billy was unfortunate enough to find out. The fight went out of him when it did just that. He stumbled to a stop and stared dumbfounded as spindly appendages emerged from the mech's chest like a spider's legs unfolding. Attached to each one was a .50 caliber machine gun that simultaneously fired a hail of bullets at Billy.

"Oh shit," he groaned and activated the EMP blast hoping he was close enough to compensate for the device's malfunction. He closed his eyes and sincerely hoped he would be released into freedom at long last. There had to be more to look forward to in the afterlife than there was to life under the boot of corporate oppression. Valhalla would be nice. As the bullets tore him to ribbons he could almost see it, shining above the trees beckoning him to an eternity of endless battle.

A horrible, metallic screech followed by a loud crash told Riley that Billy had succeeded and most likely at the cost of his own life. He and Nate continued running until he broke out into a fevered sweat and his vision dimmed causing him to stumble and fall. He tried to rise and had to steady himself against the tree.

"What's wrong with you?" Nate asked worriedly. "Are you getting sick like momma?"

"No," he wheezed, face flushed and sweating profusely. "It's my KiSS meds. I haven't taken them in over twelve hours. The virus kicks back in after that." He slumped down, already weak from overexertion. "Go on ahead. Find help or a way back out."

"I don't want to leave you," the boy admitted.

"I'm dying," Riley growled. "And fast."

Nate nodded in understanding. "I see. I can go on ahead. We're almost there."

"Almost where?"

"The village."

"There's a village out here?" Riley couldn't believe it. The corporation was never able to find where any Rainbow encampments were. All the Rainbow Children seemed to materialize out of the trees and disappear into them just as easily. If any villages had been found, they'd have been taken a long time ago. "That's impossible, kid. I ran with the corporate trolls for a while. We never found shit out here."

Nate shrugged his skinny shoulders. "I don't know what to tell you. I seen it lotsa times." He darted farther into the forest, his eyes constantly scanning the trees. He soon disappeared from Riley's dimming sight.

Alone, Riley laughed out loud at the irony of his situation. *Of all the ways to die. I guess this is the best.* It was how his son had died. Burning up with a fever and seizing until his brain hemorrhaged. "I'm coming, Phillip," he mumbled and started seizing.

22

The exalted pine tree was strong in battle.
So God created Man in his own image.
Heretics confessed Baphomet gave them wealth, made the trees give fruit, and the plants sprout.
Keep his emotional suppressants at maximum. He has a tendency to rage.

"What is this place, father?" 4D4M shuffled around his small apartment, tending the few plants and fish he was allowed—to test the emotional suppressant's effectiveness, of course—handling each with tender care. He turned to Dr. Gold patiently waiting for an answer while cupping the spray bottle in his hands.

"I didn't think this whole 'blank slate' thing was going to be so literal. It's obviously a living quarters, son. Specifically designed just for you. Down to the koi pond you love to sit by and stare at your reflection."

"Koi? Do you mean Lola and Nate?" He took a pinch of bread out of his pocket and sprinkled it into the pond, smiling blissfully as he watched the fish circle around and around, only breaking their pattern to nibble at the sinking breadcrumbs.

"Is that what you've named them? Interesting. Yes, that's who I'm referring to."

"Are there others… like me?"

"No. Not right now. But soon, there will only be others like you."

"I'm confused, father."

Gold checked his sigh of annoyance. The shrink had made it very clear that he refrain from expressing any negative emotion while in the presence of 4D4M. Something about imprinting himself as a benevolent father figure. Someone to adore and worship. Not someone to be feared—at least not yet. Fear would come later. Right now, it would do more harm than good. And he could see the point. 4D4M was more child than adult. He gazed at the koi—clones sent over from Sanchez—spinning endlessly in a hypnotic circle. "Let me tell you a story."

"Oh yes. Please do," said 4D4M and sat down on his bed, looking at his father with innocent and expectant eyes. "I love stories."

"Once there was a small tribe of people. Let's call them the Koi Tribe."

"I like that."

"Don't interrupt. Anyway, the Koi Tribe lived peacefully in their own pond, much like Lola and Nate. They laughed and played, sang and danced. They had children, built beautiful cities, and made marvelous advancements in technology. But in all the wonder stirred a dark seed."

"What was it, father? What was the dark seed?"

"I said don't interrupt! Now this seed took time to grow. And grow it did. For soon, there were twice as many Koi as there were before! And then a year later, there were twice as many as that! And so on and so forth until the whole pond was overcrowded with Koi. What do you think happened?"

"They would run out of room and food. They would start fighting and killing each other over what was left."

Gold nodded, impressed. Jimmy was still in there, sharp as a tack. "That's exactly what happened. So now the Koi Tribe faced a difficult choice. What should be done with all the extra Koi? Who goes and who stays? Who suffers so that others may live on? They argued over these questions ceaselessly and as they did, their pond continued to deteriorate. It grew poisonous and started to die. So several brave Koi, let's call them the Corporate Council, decided to make an attempt to fix things and repair the damage that the surplus of Koi had caused. Their plan was to get rid of all the extra Koi and clean the pond. They would create new life and allow that life to flourish in the pond. And are you ready for the best part?"

"Yes, please tell me!"

"The Corporate Council would pick some of the best Koi to live with them in this new and improved pond. And together, they would live forever in a perfect pond of their own making. And you, son, are the first of these special Koi."

"That's such a great story, father." 4D4M picked up his spray bottle off the nightstand and went back to tending his plants.

Gold left him to it and went to talk to the cluster's supervisor. "No seizures?"

"Not since we've been flushing his blood every 24 hours. But the nanobots are becoming more aggressive in their replication. We may need to suspend him until we get our necessary samples."

"No. I'm not putting him on ice. Keep doing what you're doing. Tell me why he is placid like a lost little lamb?"

"That's his Alpha state, sir. Coupled with the emotional suppressants 4D4M seems more lucid than he actually is. Once we start reducing the suppressants, his dominant personality will surface."

"But he'll still not know who he is or have any memory of his life before?"

"No sir. Until we retrieve the cultures from the spawn, the amnesia is permanent."

23

The elm trees are his subjects.
She's outside.
Since then, scholars and mystics
wondered about the truth of the
accusations made against the
Templars.
Impossible. Her DNA would've
dinged when she went through the
gate.

Riley woke feeling like he weighed a ton, as if every inch of his body just went through the most intense workout of his life accompanied by the customary day-after soreness. He tried to get an idea of where he was, but his vision was still dim. Whether from the darkened room he was in or as an aftereffect of the seizures, he couldn't tell. He did feel he was moving, however. Swaying steadily like he was at sea. He coerced his leaden limbs to move over to the window and looked outside, squinting against the glaring light.

He was still in the forest but somehow above the ground. Below him spread an unnaturally dense canopy that cast a thick shadow over the entirety of the forest's borders. Riley couldn't help but compare it to the gloomy and eldritch forests in his favorite fiction novels from the Time Before. He fully expected to find giant spiders spinning little people into webbed cocoons.

The door to his room opened and sunlight flooded the area, sending daggers of light searing into his brain. He cried out and fell to the ground, covering his head with his hands. "Oh hey, you awake," said a female voice, thick with an accent he couldn't place. "Still got the light sensitivity, huh? You lucky, vato. You almost got KiSS'd. Pretty much dead when we found you."

"Where am I? What is this place?" Riley asked.

"This the Colorado Rainbow Gathering. I'm Zia. Here. Put these on." She handed him a pair of sunglasses and helped him to his feet. "Mira."

She led him out the door and onto a small balcony high in a tree. A moving tree. And as he looked around he saw that his wasn't the only one. Hundreds of towering conifers all moved in unison, rippling the canopy like the wind making waves on a still lake.

"What. The. Actual. FUCK!" Riley said and grasped the railing when vertigo seized him.

"It'll pass. Once you get your tree legs under you," said Zia, her dark brown eyes sparkling with mirth.

Riley sat down in a chair by the door that appeared to be grown out of the tree's living wood. "I don't get it."

"They 'Earthships'. The Mother gave them to us so we could protect her and she could carry us in her arms. We her little ones. Niños."

"They're moving trees?"

"Yes, if you want to be tonto. They so much more."

"That's crazy. Impossible."

"Nah. When our ancestors poisoned the earth, she fought back. They buried toxic filth inside her. Well, the Mother made worms that ate it and shit out fertilizer. The Mother don't need help fixing her hurts. She do other things too. Like give us Earthships."

"No fuckin' way."

"Es verdad, vato," said Zia and handed Riley a mug of steaming liquid. "Help the soreness. Drink it."

"So that's what your Earthships are? Naturally mutated organisms?"

"Si. But they old as the Mother herself. Many old legends about living trees. They come when they needed. In times of crisis and renewal."

"Huh, guess that's the reason we could never find you bastards. You were literally always on the move."

Zia nodded with a smile that lit up her pretty face like the sun. "Huuuuh."

"How long have I been out," Riley asked and sipped the tea.

"Almost a day."

"What about my sustainment meds? I have KiSS."

"Don't need them no more."

"What do you mean I don't need them anymore?"

"What you think it means? You tonto or something? We flushed you out."

"Wait, you guys have a KiSS reversal out here?"

"For sure. You no bueno for the Mother with poisoned blood."

Riley couldn't believe it. He never imagined he would be free of KiSS. The reversal treatments cost a fortune and also required a certain level of Status that was impossible to attain for him. And here, the Rainbow Children of all people had saved his life and purified his blood. It was bullshit. They obviously wanted him for something. Nothing was free in this world, there was no charity, and chivalry had died a horrible death. "So now what?"

"Que?"

"What are you planning to do with me?"

Zia shrugged. "Talk to Burque first. If she likes you, you have a choice. You join us and serve the Mother."

"Or?"

"Or you go back to her. You city swine sin against her. Gotta pay the price for that."

"Convert or die, those are my choices? Real subtle recruitment plan your little hippie cult has going here. I think I'd rather die."

Zia nodded as if she expected nothing less, "What most city swine say. Slaves like you don't see your chains. The Mother knows you corazón." She patted her heart with her right hand, "Time comes, remember what you said."

Riley ignored her and sipped his tea while watching the gentle swaying of the forest canopy above. He was still in awe of the Earthships. He wasn't exactly sure how they were possible. Their very existence denied logic. They were plainly trees. They had trunks, branches, and leaves, but also contained something sentient. Almost like a chimera between plants and flesh and blood creatures. They had branches that acted as sinewy appendages and the fact that they constantly moved hinted at some type of awareness. "What do they eat?"

"Huh?" Zia snapped back from zoning out, her head cocked as if listening to something.

"The Earthships. They'd have to consume something to generate constant energy to burn. What do they eat?"

She smiled, thick red lips parting over pearly white teeth, "Mother feeds them. Duh."

The trees slowed to a stop and the ripples in the canopy stilled to an eerie peacefulness.

"What's going on?" asked Riley, leaning over the railing to see Rainbow Children scurrying around below.

"Just a meeting. None of you business, or mine. Get back in the room." Zia helped him back inside and shut the door. "I be back later."

Branches snaked around the tiny room cocooning it inside the tree and leaving Riley alone in the gloomy interior, the sound of the wind through the trees reminding him of waves lapping against the shore. Just like in his favorite netvids.

The caravan traveled for two days to reach the tree line. The fire in the Burbs forced them to reroute, skirting the edge of the badlands and back up from the south. This detour added another day and a half. The motorcade travelled by night and during the day camped in ruins to escape the elements and the all-seeing eyes of the corporate patrol drones.

3vE had never seen trees in the natural environment like this. They shot into the air like ancient behemoths rivaling the height of the skyscrapers within the walled bastions of civilization. Overwhelming awesomeness radiated from within the forest's primal depths that told 3vE she was a stranger here—an outsider. She suddenly feared to tread uninvited upon holy ground.

The upstart's hired muscle felt it too and darted nervous glances in every direction which made 3vE paranoid. Every last one was a professional, extremely well-armed, and obviously geared. The only thing they should fear is a malfunction in their targeting software. Then again, she was having trouble with her own. The GPS went down a mile out and since then all her mapping programs had crashed. She couldn't explain it, but her best calculations suggested that the Heart of the Rockies exuded a kind of technology dampening field. If it came to violence, she would be fighting blind. They all would.

"I don't know if I like this," 3vE said aloud and a few of the bodyguards mumbled their assent.

"Stop acting like a bunch of sissies. These people love me," said Sinister, flashing his toothy smile, stubbed out his cigarette on the bottom of his shoe. "This is a no-smoking joint," he chuckled and waved the small party inside the Heart of the Rockies.

Nobody saw the Rainbow Children descending from the treetops. One minute the small party was picking its way carefully through hostile territory and the next, two dozen Rainbow Children dropped from the sky and surrounded them. They wore plain wooden masks and loose-fitting clothes colored to match the deep greens and browns of the forest. They were clean, their weapons polished and oiled, if not archaic, and largely left over from the Time Before. They looked every bit as civilized as their city-dwelling counterparts. Each moved with an organic grace that seemed to be in perfect concert with their surroundings. One broke away from the group and removed the mask covering her face as she strode toward Jack. Black and gray hair tumbled down her slender back and her sharp brown eyes shone with fierceness and cunning.

"Hello, friends," said Sinister with his plastic smile.

"Not your friends, city swine," spat the older woman, "What you want, Jack Sinister? Getting old, you showing up uninvited."

"What I always want, Burque. To do some business." He motioned to 3vE and presented her to the Rainbow Child. "This is who I was telling you about. Wasn't able to get a scan of her, so I'm not exactly sure what she's geared with, but you can see I wasn't lying."

"Yeah… miro." Burque looked at 3vE with a mixture of awe and avarice. She fished a handheld scanner from her pack and scanned 3vE before she could protest. "No way. Not even possible they get this far," she mumbled as she read through the information. "What's you deal, chica?"

"I don't know," 3vE admitted, "My memories have been repressed."

"She's under the impression that her corporate masters will give them back to her if she's a good little drone and helps them with a little problem," Jack interjected.

"Oh si? What problem?"

"I'm looking for the HyLyfe killer," said 3vE, jutting her chin.

"Are you?" Burque's cold gray eyes sparkled, "Mother is responsible. You in the right place." She turned to Jack. "How much for her?"

"I want Rainbow Children helping to secure my newest land acquisitions along the Rio Grande."

"Wait what?" 3vE's world spun, "I came here to find answers! You promised you'd help me! You can't just sell me."

"I can and did. You're worth more as an asset than an ally," Sinister said, "and thank you very much for doing business."

3vE lashed out, busting the corporate boss's nose and back-kicking the first of his goons that came up behind her. But she was hopelessly outnumbered and without her attack software soon fell to the overwhelming odds.

"Careful, cabrones," snapped Burque as she supervised securing 3vE, "stuff on her that don't exist. Break her, I break you." She turned to Jack who was groaning and trying to staunch the flow of blood from his nose. "You get your help. I send word."

He nodded and was led away by his goons. Meanwhile, the Rainbow Children hoisted 3vE into a tree cabin and the canopy began rippling once more.

3vE should've awoken with a screaming headache, but she was fine. Her tactical software was still dampened which meant she remained within the boundaries of the Heart. She was restrained, however, and couldn't move even when she kicked in the strength boost. Her head was also restrained making the lab coat wearing Children visible only when they leaned over her. She could hear their entire conversation, though.

"Amazing," said the one on the left. "Outstanding readings. Not like other hybrids at all. Ones drooling into their shirts in corporate R&D. Like Lux Machina talk about."

"Don't get too hooked onna feelin'. Whatever's inside, comin' back out. Burque's orders. Leftovers goin' back to city," answered the one on the right.

"For sure, brethren. But not if firmware don't take."

"Recalibrate, brosef."

"I did. Didn't take. Not rebootin' at all."

"Maybe broken." Righty took the device from Lefty and disappeared from 3vE's view. She could hear someone, a man, nearby begging for his life. Righty was silent as he attached the device to the captive's head and flipped the switch. The man immediately went into a rage, straining against his restraints and bellowing, his face a red mask of fury.

"What did you do to him," 3vE demanded, "What happened to that man?"

"Same thing happenin' to you," Lefty replied solemnly.

Righty took a monofilament wire from a nearby tray and neatly sliced the man's head from his shoulders. He deftly put it inside a cold-cap container and came back to 3vE's table. He handed back the device to Lefty.

"Works just fine. Stop farting around. Get this wrong, Burque'll flip her lid."

3vE felt Lefty plug the device into her data jack. He flipped on the device and everything went black.

"Tellin' you, bro. She don't reboot," were the first words she heard a few moments later. "Conscious processes skimming. They get reset. Anything deeper don't go."

"Let me see that," growled Righty and jammed the connection back into 3vE's data jack. "Show you how it's done," he said and flipped the switch.

And once again, everything went black.

24

*The swift moving oak causes
heaven and earth to tremble.
Any sign of the package? We need
those cultures to counter
unexpected complications.
Myths and legends grew around the
Templars linking them to ancient
occult wisdom and artifacts.
This is why I didn't want to use
nanotechnology.*

4D4M watched the Labcoats, studying them as they studied him. They never spoke to him or even acknowledged him, but scurried around perpetually on some small task or another. He had hoped to gain some knowledge on what it was to be human, but they didn't seem human at all. They appeared human, or what he assumed people would look like. Yet something about them didn't seem right. They didn't appear to have or act with any kind of free will. Any attempt to gain insight into them was always blocked. One brought him food three times a day, and he always tried to talk to him.

"Are you my father's servants?"

The Labcoat looked at him curiously, but didn't respond.

"You are his watchers, are you not? Making sure his world runs smoothly and according to his will?"

The Labcoat shook his head and turned to leave. It was then 4D4M noticed the object dangling from his pocket. He deftly snatched it as the Labcoat opened the door and left with the empty tray.

4D4M knew he didn't have long to examine the object before it was found. The watchers always knew what he was doing. The device was round like a headband and had a wire dangling off it that ended in some kind of controller. Curious, he slid the device over his head and was immediately transported to another world. Well, it was a world that looked a lot like his apartment, but it was shinier, cleaner. Off in the distance, he saw something that caught his breath. It looked like a tree made of interconnected lines and circles and it reached into the air as far as he could see. Its luminescence pulsed the longer he stared at it as if beckoning him.

He reached out for it, though it was far beyond his reach, and as he did, a rainbow bridge appeared at his feet. He took a step onto its shimmering surface and—came crashing back into his real apartment surrounded by Labcoats.

"4D4M! Can you hear me? Are you alright?" asked the Labcoat leaning over him.

"I... am... fine. What was that place I was in just now?"

"eSpace," answered the Labcoat simply, "a place that is off limits to you right now."

"eSpace. So beautiful. I saw something there... a glowing tree. It was familiar."

The Labcoats in the room looked at one another and the one closest to him spoke. "How were you able to see that? There is no Internetwork connection in your closed system."

"Is that what it was? The Internetwork?"

"We cannot answer those questions," the Labcoat replied. "We shouldn't even be having this conversation. If your father were to find out, we could get fired."

The other Labcoats nodded in agreement.

"We need to consult the supervisor," said the main Labcoat and left, taking 4D4M's stolen netset with him.

The Labcoats filtered out, leaving 4D4M alone once again. He plopped down next to the koi pond, dejected, and dully watched his fish eternally circle one another. But in his mind's eye the glowing tree blazed, beckoning him to seek the occult knowledge he had been denied.

25

He is known the world over as the
stout gatekeeper against our
enemies.
The extraction team failed.
Miserably. Package is lost.
Joseph von Hammer-Purgstall
claimed Baphomet was a
hermaphroditic stone figure.
Don't tell Baphomet just yet. Try to
locate first.

"Wake up, gringo," Zia said and shook Riley roughly. "Burque want to chat."

She led Riley across gently swaying rope bridges to another Earthship that held the largest cabin Riley had seen so far. Inside, people crammed close eager to bear witness to what was obviously a public trial, grumbling to one another as Riley passed. He was led to stand in front of Burque and he met her gaze with coolness. Burque, lounging on a large wooden throne grown out of the living tree, scrutinized Riley with fierce, cold eyes.

He shifted impatiently under the old woman's dark gaze and was thankful when the crowd began murmuring again and attention shifted from him to the newcomer. Zia led Nate to stand beside Riley.

"Ola, little Nathaniel Merriweather." Burque waved to him, flashing the peace sign as she did.

"Ola, Zia," he answered and waved back.

"What bring ya back, little one? With this city swine, even?"

"My mom. She... got sick. Everybody did. We had to leave."

"We know. We feel your sads. Your ma, she one of us. Sure as night and day one inna same."

"She always… she always talked about coming back here," Nate held back his sobs, but his eyes leaked crocodile tears, "I couldn't make her, though. I tried to make her, but I couldn't."

"No tears, cub. Had to find her own path. But all serves Mother inna end."

"Can we speak English when it's my turn?" Riley smirked.

Burque flashed him a withering glare. "We speak in natural rhythm with Mother. Natural as birth."

"The Mother? Oh yeah. The anthropomorphic goddess of your little cult."

Burque lashed out and struck Riley across the face, her long nails leaving their bloody marks on his cheek. "Stupid gringo, Earth ain't just a rock. She alive. She breathe. Mother gives us gift of life. All people, her unruly little cubs running amok. Fucking. Fighting. Killing and cutting. Had this coming. She told us, see? Told us come to her and we did. Her true children. The Rainbow Children, like ancients told of. Respect her Children, swine. Midwives for Mother Gaia's rebirth. She rises again!"

"Have you been outside your little piece of heaven lately," Riley asked. "Everything is shot to shit. It's hell out there. Mother Gaia ain't rising any time soon."

"Not hell. War out there," Burque corrected and the crowd muttered its assent. "See hell every day. Tries to expand into our Heart!"

"Look, lady, I ain't no friend of the corporate world either. But I've seen what they're doing. They're making things better. Even saw plants. Real plants inside the city."

"Not real," said Burque, her brown eyes blazing defiantly. "Can't make real in a lab. All manufactured. All fake. Consume beauty, manufacture shit. Never-ending cycle."

"You don't know what you're talking about, lady," said Riley, "You guys are a bunch of damn zealots. This planet is a planet, you hear? A rock floating around in space with a lot of other big rocks and what not. Trees are trees. Rocks are rocks. None of it's alive. Not that it's aware of anyway."

"Don't think Mother aware?" Zia looked at Riley her eyes wide with disbelief. "Trees aware having fruit plucked from branches. Aware when they cut down. Even communicate awareness to other trees. No slinging your lies and shit! Not your hood."

"That's the truth right there," Riley agreed, and this time Zia stepped forward and rammed the butt of her rifle to his gut. Riley doubled over, heaving.

"Enough disrespect. Tell us why ya show up?"

"We had to, Zia," Nate spoke up, his small voice shattering the tension of the situation. "We had nowhere to go. Everyone, they got sick. Like my momma. Like I said. Riley and Billy saved me. And now everyone is dead." His eyes welled up and threatened to explode into a righteous flood of grief.

"Ah, si. Your momma. Left us for your daddy, he never one of us. Swine came for him, we gave him back. Not her. Not you. But she left anyhow. Back to the city, chasing that slick gray suit. Then she got sick. Chose her fate, drug you into it. Not your fault. Is what it is. Maybe you sick too. Maybe no room inna clouds for little man Nate. Been in the city so long you got the stink of it. Makes you onna them."

The crowd agreed and calls of "Back to the mother!" began to erupt with increasing frequency.

Nate's head sunk low and his bottom lip quivered. It was getting harder for him to hold back the sobs. Zia didn't comfort him though. Riley did, however, throwing his arm over the boy's shoulders and pulling him close.

Burque looked down on the situation with a mixture of approval and scorn. "Don't get it. You poisoned from birth, live content with this. Like sheep. Never looking for anything better. Perfectly cool mucking about in filth. Like it's all bueno. Probably just as well. Mother can't be reborn with filth clinging to her. Desperate like rats or las cucarachas. Why she embraced us. We understand. Serve her. You… you used to feed her." She waved her hand and three burly men stepped forward and yanked Riley away from Nate. "To the hanging tree. The little cub too." Burque smiled coldly, "Leave room for nature."

The rest of the Rainbow Children bowed their heads in silent respect and murmured the commandment like a prayer. "Leave room for nature," they chanted as Riley and Nate were dragged from the room, kicking and screaming.

"Damn son, you right. Don't reboot."

"Told you. Tell Burque what?"

"Truth. All there is. What Mother tell us."

"Is what it is. End up on the hanging tree, your ass coming with."

"Leave room for nature."

The door opened and closed, leaving 3vE alone in the room. She wasn't sure how many times they had tried hard resetting her system, but her latest diagnostics showed several corrupted packets. They couldn't get her to reboot, but they were dangerously close to breaking her down. She tested her restraints and found them holding tight. She cursed under her breath and lent all her strength to break her bonds. They strained but held and she collapsed back, winded. 3vE's sensitive ears picked up the clamor of the crowd. Whatever was happening didn't sound good. She heard the muffled voices of Lefty and Righty outside discussing the inevitable trip to the hanging tree that the city swine were taking. So that was the fate of any 'city swine' that crossed paths with the Rainbow Children. It was loathsome. She flexed again and this time her right hand loosened a bit. She directed all her energy there and yanked her hand free with a mighty yell. She quickly undid the rest of the restraints and surveyed her surroundings. A quick scan of the room revealed every piece of furniture was grown out of the tree. Shelves lined the walls loaded with heads in jars and coffins stacked three high were tucked into any available space. She opened one and heaved at what she saw. A human body with the head of a mannequin. She closed it and resumed her search for a weapon. She found the monofilament wire but that wouldn't help her get through the thick vines that had grown over the door. She was trapped and frustration mounted. She had grown to rely on her tactical software and having it dampened and corrupted seriously limited her capabilities.

New voices broke above the crowd. The city swine. A man, cursing and laughing, goaded his captors even as they dragged him to his demise. It takes a special kind of man to maintain that level of bravado in the face of certain death. An uncomfortable impression struck 3vE. She felt like she knew exactly the kind of man this doomed city swine was. Maybe she had even come across someone like him before her memories were repressed. The next voice that she heard, that of a small boy, pleading for his life sent her over the edge. Then something inexplicable happened. As the emotional suppressants in her system dwindled, 3vE began to feel. Something dark and primal churned in her gut. Some forgotten instinct kicked in and her only desire was to protect these innocents from the deaths they were going to receive. And that primal emotion brought a flood of adrenaline. She flung herself at the door. The vines surrounding it bulged, but didn't give. They immediately tightened and 3vE used the tautness to her advantage. Her combat software was basically useless but she was able to predict the weakest point in the door and she struck with all the fury she could muster in her artificial body. She broke through at the same time the Earthship screamed.

The loud boom pealed across the crisp night sky. The Rainbow Children stopped what they were doing and turned to her. The air quivered with tension for a brief eternity, and then the Rainbow Children snapped, screaming in unison as they poured from every Earthship to where 3vE stood with defiant anticipation. Righty and Lefty both looked at her with awe and fear. The look was frozen on their faces as 3vE whipped the monofilament wire around and neatly severed their heads. Then she turned to face the approaching mob.

Two men dragged Riley and Nate to the Hanging Tree, pulling them against the flow of the furious zealots clawing over one another to get to 3vE.

Riley met her gaze and a confused look of recognition lit his face briefly before he was pulled out of sight. 3vE leapt from the cottage's porch to the rope bridge that connected with the Hanging Tree. She grabbed a vine as it snaked toward her and used it to swing across to where Riley and Nate were on their knees, nooses slung around their necks.

The momentum sent her crashing feet first into the man hoisting Nate over the railing. They all went to the ground in a mess of flailing limbs. 3vE sprang lightly to her feet and met the oncoming attack. She ducked under the goon's broad swing and jabbed him in the armpit. He screamed and buckled, clutching his chest.

Riley took his chance and swung out with his bound fists landing a blow directly to his captor's windpipe. The large man clutched his throat, gasping like a fish out of water. Riley put his noose around the man's neck and shoved him over the edge.

The fleshy vines of the Earthships slithered toward them on all sides.

"We've got to get out of these trees," Riley yelled.

"Only way out is down. Follow my lead." She slung Nate over her shoulder and grabbed a vine slithering toward her. "Hold on," she told her passenger and leapt over the edge of the rope bridge.

Riley steeled himself and followed with a yell.

They shot toward the ground like missiles. Bloated, dangling bodies merged with the tree in various stages of fusion, as if the Earthship was slowly devouring the corpses. An arm here, a leg there, half a torso just below that gave it the appearance of something out of a hellscape. The vines reached their maximum length and sprang back like bungee cords, causing the Earthship to groan in pain. The escapees landed on the ground with a thud, but they had to keep moving. Alarms already sounded above and it was only a matter of time before the Rainbow Children pursued them.

"We have to make for the tree line. Now," said 3vE and, with Nate still on her back, ran directly west. Riley trudged along after her.

The Earthships caught up to them after half a mile, skittering across the ground on their thick serpentine roots.

"We're not going to make it!" yelled Riley.

"Yes we are. When I say duck, you duck!" 3vE pushed forward toward a large, lumbering shadow.

Another forest guardian! She's crazy! thought Riley.

The crazed mech's triple eye burned a dangerous red when it saw 3vE running toward it. This one had one minigun arm and one functioning hand and a large missile array attached to its aerodynamic back. It raised its mingun and unleashed a volley of bullets.

"Duck!" yelled 3vE and darted to one side, holding on to Nate as she did.

Riley ducked out of the way just as the cloud of bullets whizzed above him and lodged into the foremost Earthship.

The living tree screamed, thrashing about and sending Rainbow Children plummeting to the ground. 3vE came back around and pulled the mech's attention once again. She cradled Nate in her arms and rolled as the forest guardian unleashed a barrage of missiles that found their targets in the Earthships. The walking trees retreated and 3vE rushed past the mech before it could get her in its sights again. Riley snuck past by running from tree to tree while the insane AI was busy with 3vE. They broke from the tree line to the southwest.

"Holy shit! How did you pull that off?" Riley screamed, adrenaline still pumping through his veins.

3vE gently sat Nate on the ground and stretched. "I'm not like other girls."

"Damn right you ain't. Who are you anyway?"

"My name is 3vE. So far as I know."

"You with the Rainbow Children?"

"Hardly," she scoffed, "they tried to buy me from a slimy upstart exec."

"Ha! That's what you get for dealing with startups. So you're from the corporate underground then? That would explain all the gear. But the way you moved around that mech. You gotta have wetwear upgrades too. Mapping apps, battle simulators, the whole bit. You're a walking time bomb for the technocrazies."

"I'm not with the corporate underground either. I was looking for help and obviously trusted the wrong people."

"Help with what?"

"Finding the HyLyfe killer."

"No shit? Wow, it's a small world after all."

"What is that supposed to mean?"

"It means I canceled a contract to find the HyLyfe killer. Corporation took out a friend of mine. And my wife."

"Ex," corrected 3vE.

"Yeah. How'd you know that?"

"You don't have your ring finger chipped."

"Girl, you really do have all the bells and whistles, don't you? Corporate wouldn't let someone like you outta the lab. Not off your leash. Means you must've escaped."

3vE shot Riley a deadly glare. "I am no one's prisoner. I live unfettered."

"You sound like a HyLyfer," Nate spoke up, "that's what they always say. Weird considering they're all literally stuck in their own personal server stack. Digital people are the most fettered of all."

"How do you know what HyLyfers always say?" Riley wondered.

"I used to talk to the heads."

"The heads?" 3vE perked up, thinking about the shelves in the Rainbow Children's lab. "Who are these heads you're talking about?"

Nate explained, "I dunno who they were. But they came through sometimes. Just these whispering voices that you could hear in the crackling under the sound, you know? I don't think they meant to, I think they leaked into the public network somehow."

"How do you know they were talking heads?"

"Baphomet told me."

"Who?" Riley asked.

"Baphomet. Have you ever heard of the Knights Templar?"

3vE said, "Yes. I have an entry about them in my database." She opened her mouth to impart the wisdom to the ignorant as Nate rushed on.

"We don't need all that right now. The whispers told me a story about when the Knights Templar were being killed by the evil Pope and the King of France. One of the things the Knights had was a severed head in a box. This head was alive and it talked and it told them all kind of things. Secret things. Dangerous things. Things that got them all killed. It was called Baphomet. And Baphomet hates HyLyfe."

"What are you talking about, kiddo?" asked Riley. He knelt down in front of Nate, putting his hands on the boy's shoulders. "You aren't making any sense. No way anything from that long ago is still around."

"Maybe not. But everything old turns new again eventually."

"Perhaps Baphomet is merely an avatar," 3vE deduced, "but these talking heads… I've seen something like them before. In the lab the Rainbow Children had me in. Shelves full of them. Their eyes moving as if they were asleep."

"I saw that too," Riley added, "in the basement of HyLyfe Tower. But those heads weren't alive. They were being experimented on. Or so I was told."

"I wonder if the heads are connected to the HyLyfe murders?" said 3vE.

"Dollars to doughnuts says you're on the right track," Riley said, "We can figure this out later. Right now, we gotta find somewhere to camp for the night."

They took shelter just inside the trees because no one could survive a night in the badlands. The elements turned hostile decades ago. Mother Nature made it very clear that mankind was no longer welcome outside the confines of its cities or Hearts.

"We need to find food," said Riley.

"The forest isn't safe though," Nate reminded them, worriedly. "The guardians are still in there."

"Don't worry, little man. We aren't going too far into the forest," Riley assured him with a pat on the back. "But we gotta eat and there's small game in there to catch."

"We don't have any weapons," Nate pointed out.

"Sure we do," Riley said, looking at 3vE.

"You want me to catch food for you?" the hybrid woman asked, indignation burning in her pretty eyes. "Like some kind of hunting dog?"

"Council's balls. You sound like my ex," Riley quipped. "That's not what I was trying to say. Think of it like this: you are a lioness hunting for her pride."

"That's not better."

"Yes it is! It's romantic!"

"You call that romantic? I call it servitude and I am no man's slave!"

"That's not true. You're so full of corporate gear that you don't even own your own body anymore."

She slugged Riley hard and sent him reeling.

Nate rushed over to where Riley lay on the ground moaning and clutching his jaw. "Are you ok, Riley?" The boy shot 3vE a withering look. "That wasn't nice at all!"

"It wasn't intended to be. I'm not a hunting dog. Catch your own damn food." 3vE stormed off without a backward glance. As the emotional suppressants in 3vE's system depleted, she had no baseline responsive state to keep her from overreacting. She began to act on raw emotion which caused her to lash out with reckless abandon. Like a toddler who hasn't learned how to keep from throwing tantrums.

Sleeping in the trees was risky. They had to keep watch. 3vE stayed awake while Riley and Nate slept. She didn't have their dependence on rest or sleep. The forest crawled with life at night and 3vE had to scare away a few lurkers who got too curious for their own good. No Rainbow Children or Guardians though. Wherever those tree dwellers were, they weren't on the ground, nor were the Earthships passing nearby, which probably accounted for the thriving animal life in this part of the woods. She passed the night like this and only woke her sleeping companions when dawn broke over the horizon. She started a small fire and cooked a couple of rabbits she caught just before dawn. Riley smirked at her but refrained from making any comments.

"Where to now?" asked 3vE after they had eaten.

"We can't go back to the city. The Burbs have been destroyed by rioting and the corporation probably has the city locked down. Not to mention, you're on a wanted list or two, no doubt. And so am I. We can't go back into the woods for obvious reasons. That leaves the badlands."

Nate's young face paled, "The badlands? No way, dude. I watched a vid on them in school. It's full of mutants and all sorts of nasty things."

"We also run the risk of radiation poisoning. Corporate records list the radiation levels as 'deadly' over a mile away from any populated area," 3vE added. "But there is a chance."

"A chance at what?" Riley said, frustration seeping into his voice.

"That we can make it to the deep underground military bunker under Cheyenne mountain close by. Records say it was decommissioned in 2083 when the governments dissolved. That would offer sufficient shelter from the radiation and dangers of the badlands while we figure out our next course of action."

"Great. Now the problem of how we get to this old military base. We still have to travel over the badlands to get there. I doubt we can make it on foot."

"I think we have just found our way," 3vE said, staring at a trail of dust circling around the tree line in the distance.

It wasn't a Sinister and Grace caravan, which disappointed 3vE because she was seriously looking for some payback. Riley and 3vE watched from a safe distance as a trailer hauled a load of goods and a few coffins into the forest. Four mercenaries stayed behind to guard the vehicles. Two of them immediately went to playing cards and the other two started a patrol.

"An Underground caravan" Riley hissed, "I ran with a few in my day."

"A similar one brought me here to be traded," 3vE said accusingly. "You dealt in slaves?"

Riley rolled his eyes. "Don't start. I made sure no corporate drones swooped in and took out the goods. These outfits are airtight. No way we can get all four of them without any firepower."

"Wait here," 3vE said, moving toward the caravan as stealthy as a lioness and fast as a cheetah.

3vE sprang from the shadows and the first guard went down without ever turning around. She eased him to the ground, removed his weapons, and, hiding behind a nearby truck, waited. The second guard found his partner's body and leaned down to check his pulse. 3vE bounded over the hood of the truck and kicked the guard in the face, landing on his nose with an audible crunch. Grabbing a handgun off the guard, she sprinted around to where the two guards were playing cards and put a bullet between each of their eyes with effortless precision. She motioned the all-clear to Riley and Nate.

"Talk about geared," Riley quipped after they came upon the scene. "You're a walking weapon."

"You act like I had a choice in the matter."

"You did. All Enhancements require a permissions waiver. Corporate CYA." He relieved the corpses of their weapons, checking each to make sure they were in working order.

"Not me. I woke up in this body. And I don't think it's mine."

Riley eyed 3vE with the critical eye of an Integration Technologies consultant. "That's never a good sign. Disassociation is one of the early symptoms of the technocrazies."

"I don't have TPS! I have amnesia."

"Memory loss is another sign," Riley said, moving between 3vE and Nate. "Look, I don't know who you are. You saved our asses with those Rainbow Children and for that I thank you. I really do. But you're a little bit too geared for my comfort levels. You already have anger issues. If you did snap, I don't like our chances for survival. I think you better take your own car. Me and Nate will follow behind."

To her surprise, she did have problems checking her spiking anger at that moment. Feelings were something her perfect body wasn't engineered to handle. She guessed it was because she needed frequent doses of the emotional suppressants early on to ensure their permanence. Her body's firmware and software were still adaptable, but they were quickly becoming set in her current version. Not only was this not good for her to maintain emotional neutrality, sooner or later she would lose access to her repressed memories. If she didn't get them back soon, she'd lose them forever and she didn't know how to handle the turmoil wrought by that eventuality. Maintaining a safe social distance was the best projected course of action until she got better control of herself.

"Fine," she consented. "Let's pack up the weapons and get out of here."

They drove across the barren lands toward Cheyenne Mountain and the decommissioned deep underground military bunker. 3vE took the lead and Riley followed at a safe distance. They drove for hours, blazing a trail over the dusty remains of the Pike National Forest. There were no trees now. No grass, no wildlife, no water. Nothing but soft, powdery dirt as far as the eye could see. This was the badlands. Riley had never been out so far and Nate had only seen the outskirts where corporate drones patrolled the crumbling ruins in his school vids. After all, the place was supposed to be toxic and full of mutant ravagers. Nobody was allowed this far out.

Nate's face was plastered to the window, gazing out in wide-eyed wonder. "How did this happen?" he wondered with childlike honesty. "How could people have failed so hard?"

"People fail all the time, kid," Riley answered, "It's what we do. People are still failing. The corporations, the Rainbow Children, the Burbanites, the whole lot of us are nothing but huge fail-hards. It's what damns us time and time again, but it's also what saves us."

"What do you mean," Nate asked without looking away from the window.

"Well each time we fail, we get a little smarter and do a little better the next time. I seen things in the corporate towers. Seen what they're doing to make things better a little at a time. I also seen what the Rainbow Children are doing to make things better. Even if their way is extreme."

"We live in a world of extremes," Nate blurted sagely, "Seek balance instead."

"Where'd you hear that?"

The boy shrugged, "From the voices in the noise. They say stuff like that all the time."

"This Baphomet you keep going on about?"

He nodded. "Or the other heretics like Valentinian and Bogomil." Then, "What was that?"

"What was what?"

"Over there. I saw the sand moving. Rippling like waves on a lake."

"Just the wind, kid. Stare out there at that wasteland long enough and your eyes are bound to play tricks on you. Nothing survives out here. And I do mean nothing. Hell, we'd be dead from radiation sickness if not for the reinforced trucks."

Shortly after that statement, 3vE's truck was hurtled into the air and flew back, end over end, toward Riley. He swerved and slid down an embankment.

"Are you alright?" Riley asked Nate.

The boy nodded. "I think so. Just hit my head, but I'll be okay. What sent 3vE's truck flying like that?"

"I don't know," Riley admitted reaching behind the seat for his plundered weapons, "Maybe a mine leftover from some corporate war or another. Them things stay volatile for a long time. Wait here, just in case." He slipped out of the door and disappeared over the edge of the ditch.

3vE opened her eyes. Her conscious mind's algorithms had been reset. It must have been an electrical blast of some sort then. But what about the explosion? She cut herself free from the restraints and crawled out of the broken window. She limped back over to the scene to meet Riley.

"You alright," he asked, eyeing her with suspicious awe. "That accident woulda taken out anyone. Even with gear."

"My nanobots are already repairing the damage," 3vE said simply.

Riley whistled. "Nanos too? Damn. You are an elite piece of tech, for sure."

She glared at him, anger spiking. Riley quickly developed a tendency to get under her skin. She couldn't figure it out, but he excited her and angered her at the same time. She didn't know how to process those emotions just yet so she deflected instead. "What about that hole?" She pointed to the smoking crater.

Riley nudged a rock over the edge and watched it disappear into the thick darkness. He never heard it hit bottom. "It's deep, that's for sure. I was thinking you ran over a mine."

"Impossible," said 3vE. "I was hit by a static discharge. I'd still be out, but I don't reboot."

"Well, what in the hell then?" Riley snapped and scanned the landscape for any sign of movement.

In response, Nate screamed.

"Nate!" shouted 3vE and bolted toward the truck.

He was on the roof of the truck, knees tucked under his chin. A large blood-red worm, sticking out of the sand, swayed beneath him like a charmed cobra.

"Dafuq is that?" Riley croaked, his voice taken at the sight of the unnatural beast.

"I don't know," murmured 3vE, "My preliminary database searches aren't yielding any results. I'll need more data."

"More data, huh?" Riley hefted his rifle and took aim on the worm. "Hey! Big ugly! Leave the boy alone!"

The worm swiveled around to face Riley and he saw its gaping maw lined with razor-sharp teeth. The worm hissed at him and disappeared beneath the sand. The ground started rippling, moving quickly in Riley's direction. He spun around and scrambled over the edge of the ditch. The rumbling beneath his feet grew in intensity until he was sure it was on him.

"Jump to the left!" he heard 3vE scream. He jumped with everything he could muster and the dirt beneath his feet took to the air with him. He barely missed being swallowed whole by the worm's razor maw and it disappeared back beneath the sand, heading instead for 3vE. She was ready for it and leapt over it as it sprang from the sand. This time, it didn't retreat, but kept half its body out, swaying as before. Riley took the chance and peppered the beast while its back was turned. It thrashed and shrieked and, swiveling around, sent a thick train of spittle sailing through the air. Riley rolled and the spot he was standing on crackled and hissed, melting the sand into a bubbling corrosive mess.

"Impossible," murmured 3vE as she circled around behind the monstrosity while it was distracted with Riley. Her database showed only one possible match for something of this description. And it wasn't supposed to exist. But when the worm leaned over and dug its teeth into the ground, 3vE knew what was coming. "Run!" she yelled to Riley. "You have to get out of range!"

The worm started heaving and as it did, 3vE felt the hair on the back of her neck stand up as the air began to crackle with static build-up. She pulled a knife and quickly calculated the angle of approach. As the static in the area increased she darted toward the worm and leapt into the air. The worm heaved one last time and discharged the static. A thunderclap ripped the air followed by waves of static electricity rolling across the ground, kicking up rocks and sand. 3vE landed on the worm's hunched back and shoved the combat knife into the creature. It shrieked and thrashed, but she was prepared. She cartwheeled forward slicing the worm open. She landed a few feet from Riley and spun around. The worm disappeared beneath the sand.

"Holy hell!" Riley yelled, expelling the stress of the situation. "No wonder nothing lives out here!"

"What was that giant worm?" Nate called from atop the truck. He was shaken, but not in hysterics.

"My database tells me it was a 'Mongolian Death Worm.' A cryptozoological creature of antiquity."

"Meaning?" Riley said.

"It was a legend. A mythical creature. That wasn't supposed to be half as big as the one we saw."

"Yeah, and trees shouldn't be sentient and walking around either. But I saw that shit just yesterday. C'mon. Let's go before that Death Worm comes back with friends."

They managed to maneuver the truck out of the embankment and continued on the rest of the way to the Cheyenne Mountain complex. Nate, staring out at the sands as they drove, saw the sand rippling off in the distance.

"It's just the wind," he reassured himself, but he kept watch just the same.

They approached the ruins of the above-ground structures marking the territory of the Cheyenne Mountain complex. Dilapidated buildings leaned heavily against one another and the ones on the edge of the compound grounds were in the process of crumbling and sinking into the encroaching dunes.

"Well this place has held up well," Riley remarked with a smirk.

"True enough considering most of the other urban areas were swallowed by the white sands," 3vE replied dryly. "This whole area was populated for centuries."

Nate stared at the crumbling ruins in awe. Spending most of his life in the Burbs, he wasn't exposed to the harsh realities of the badlands.

3vE scanned the area with her thermal filters. "The place looks deserted. No signs of life anywhere," she informed her companions.

They made their way to the outer blast door of the underground bunker. It was sealed tight and from the looks of it, had been for centuries.

"I think I can pry it open," said 3vE, testing the door against her enhanced musculature, "but I need to run some system diagnostics, first. Too many corrupted data packets from those idiot Rainbow Children's tinkering."

"Alright. That place over there looks sturdy enough," Riley said, pointing to a disintegrating civic building. "And it's got a second story. I'm not staying on the ground floor with those damned worms slithering around."

"Agreed," said 3vE.

They found shelter in an old office on the second floor where someone had left the remains of a makeshift stove.

"Somebody else is alive out here," Riley said, flabbergasted. "Impossible!"

"Not according to my readings," 3vE informed him, "Radiation exposure has been minimal so far. Nothing like the official corporate statistics suggests. It wouldn't be impossible for people to survive out here as long as they had access to water and a food supply. Still, though, I don't think the corporate stories of roving bands of mutant raiders hold much truth."

"Huh, well the official story ain't never been the truth. So they're lying to keep people inside the city," Riley said and lit his last cigarette, "Figures. Can't control people very well if they're all scattered out."

"I don't know if I'd want to live out here. Even if I could," Nate spoke up. "Not with those worms."

"We better keep a watch then," Riley said and started scavenging for things to burn in the fire. He found the remnants of a table already busted into kindling, mostly rotted but it would serve.

"I need to shut down for diagnostics," 3vE informed Riley, "I'll only be down for three hours and then I'll take over the watch."

"Do what you need to do," Riley said, "Me and Nate got it covered."

3vE laid out flat on the floor and shut her eyes, immediately powering down. She looked like she was sleeping, even snoring gently.

"Is she real?" Nate wondered, staring at her unconscious form with a mixture of fear and admiration.

"Of course she's real. What kind of question is that?"

"I mean, is she human? I seen lots of gearheads in the Burbs. None of them acted like her. Even the good ones. She's more like an android, only they don't have the soul she does."

"That's a funny thing for you to say."

Nate shrugged. "I guess. I used to hear things back when we lived in the Burbs. When we was closer to Baphomet. Those voices get stuck in your head. So they're always whispering. But not out here. It's quiet. I miss them, sometimes. That's why momma took us back, really. She wasn't chasing after my daddy. The forest was too quiet. If it wasn't for me she would still be alive."

"Aw, come on now, kid. You can't think like that. No way of knowing what was going to happen in the Burbs. You can't blame yourself for that."

"I can! The voices told me what was going to happen a week before it did. I tried to tell momma. But she kept waiting around. I think she was waiting for my dad. But he never came and then she got sick. They told me about you too."

"What do you mean?"

"They said they sent someone. A person that would come and get me. They said to wait until you got there."

"Ain't no way, kiddo. I don't hear voices. Nobody told me where to find you. You were just a name on a corporate hit list."

Nate shrugged again. "I guess. If that's how you want to see it," he mumbled and poked the fire with a stick. "They told me all sorts of things though. Things I never learned in school or from the Rainbow Gathering's holy mothers. And I never heard them mention something like her."

"Yeah, that's the truth. If I had my guess, I'd say she's some top-secret corporate project that got loose. She's geared to the tits, but got nothing showing so that suggests she's a hybrid. Only problem with that is, hybrids don't work."

"What do you mean?"

"Them Labcoats up in the towers can program a machine to act or think a certain way. But that don't make it real. It ain't alive," Riley thumped his chest, "got no real heart. No emotions. No empathy. No remorse for any of its calculated actions. You make a monster like that and it's only a matter of time before they crack. Humans are messed up, kid. Machines can't live in our world without coming to the inevitable conclusion that we all deserve to die. That's why we only replace parts on actual people instead of making thinking machines. It's called The Enhancement Clause. All the corporate free states signed it after the artificial intelligence disasters of the Second Great Collapse. They all went batty like those mechs in the Heart."

"Maybe she's not a robot, then. Maybe she's not AI," Nate said with a yawn. "She's special." He curled up next to the fire, covered up with a duster jacket he found in the back of the truck, and was soon fast asleep.

After a couple of hours, Riley stood up to stretch and do a perimeter check. He grabbed a flashlight and took a quick trip around the building, painting the outside with the beam. Nothing. They were alone out here. Whoever camped there before wasn't there now. The fire sputtered and he was out of wood, so he went to the truck to look for anything combustible. He found a small solar-powered space heater and a hotplate and scooped them up. On his way back to the building, the ground trembled lightly beneath him.

"Oh shit," he growled and sprinted for the doorway.

The closer he got, the more violently the ground shook. He jumped over the threshold just as the worm broke the surface. Two more emerged after it.

"Oh shit, oh shit, oh shit!" he said, bolting up the stairs calling to 3vE and Nate.

Nate's small frame appeared at the top of the stairs, a silhouette against the dying fire. "What's going on? What is it?"

In response, the bottom floor began sinking into the shifting, swirling sands that opened up beneath it. The worms were eating the building. Riley cleared the top step just as the stairs crumbled still clutching the heater and hotplate. He grabbed Nate by the arm and pulled him back into the room.

"Wake up!" he yelled to 3vE. Her eyes fluttered, but remained closed. "Little man, try to wake her up, ok? We gotta go. Now. Let's hope those things haven't eaten our truck too."

The foundation of the building shuddered and the north side collapsed, sending everything sliding toward the churning sands.

Riley grabbed 3vE by the arm and scrambled up to the nearest ledge which was really the interior wall of the office next to theirs. But it was a futile effort. The building was going down. Nate jumped for the ledge as the floor beneath him disappeared into the tooth-lined maws of the worms. His little legs didn't have the strength though. Riley anticipated this and lunged for Nate as he reached the peak of his jump and began to fall back. He grabbed the boy's arm and heaved him over the ledge just as it too collapsed sending them careening toward their deaths once more. Riley's descent was halted abruptly. He looked behind him and saw 3vE wedged into a corner holding both of them dangling over the hungry worms.

"Hold him tight," she said, and then with a preternatural heave, launched them through the air past the radius of the worms' sandy mastication. Then she swung over to the building's south side, the only side that hadn't been swallowed by the sands yet. She scurried along the edge like a ferret, and then sprang with ease into the air, landing with a roll near Nate and Riley. "Make for the blast door!" she yelled

Riley nodded and, slinging Nate over his shoulder, ran for the entrance to the mountain complex.

Two worms immediately broke and followed them. Riley fired blindly behind him as he ran, forcing his legs to carry Nate's extra weight and run for both their lives. 3vE reached the door first and, planting her feet squarely on the ground, shoved her body against the barrier. The door creaked but didn't move. She reset and tried again. This time, the door squealed and gave way. Riley dashed inside and 3vE sealed them in as the first worm hit the metal. They tried to come up through the floor for a while, but it was solid steel.

"I think we're safe for now," Riley said.

Nate, finally relieved of the stress of the situation, broke into tears.

He rushed into Riley's arms and buried his head in the IT Consultant's shoulder, sobbing. Raw emotion hit Riley like a truck. He never forgot what it was like to hold and comfort his son. Those memories filled what little sleep he managed to find. But it had been a while since he let himself feel what it was like to unburden someone of their fear or pain or heartache. He melted into that moment and pulled the boy into an embrace.

"It's alright, little man, everything is going to be alright. Everybody is safe."

3vE watched the exchange, tears streaming down her face unchecked. The emotional dampeners were completely exhausted and adjusting to the influx of feelings swirling inside her was difficult, but she was making progress. Like a young child deeply affected by the behavior of the people around them. She acted on an odd compulsion and joined in the embrace. She couldn't explain why it felt so right, so natural, but it did. She felt as if she had found her purpose: a family to love and protect.

26

Many brave trees were cast away
on the field of fight because they
suffered by the enemies' might.
The Manichaean has been fired.
His head is lost. It went offline last
night.
In 1854, Eliphas Levi recreated
Baphomet into an occult image he
named the Sabbatic Goat.
He will suffer for this. We will
make sure of it.

"Hello, father," 4D4M greeted Gold's arrival without looking up from the koi he was feeding.

"4D4M," Gold replied curtly. He reeked of stale cigar smoke and whiskey, scents 4D4M initially found unappealing but had since come to represent the comfort of parental memories. "Is there something you want to tell me?"

"No, father. I am fine," he replied, still refusing to look up from the koi pond.

Gold leaned down and cupped 4D4M's chin in his hands, lifting his face to eye level. "Are you sure? There's nothing you want to tell me about what happened the other day? Don't lie to me, son."

4D4M tried to hold his resolve, tried to resist his father's power over him, but he couldn't. Tears welled up in his eyes and trickled down unbidden. "I'm sorry! I just wanted to see something else, somewhere different! This small room, your watchers constantly monitoring me. I feel trapped."

Dr. Gold wanted to be surprised by this revelation, but he wasn't. Even as a child, Jimmy Lee was highly energetic and curious. He wanted to explore everything, talk to everyone, experience the world firsthand. He was like that from the moment he became aware of a world outside his own immediate needs. So it made sense to Dr. Gold that his son would still exhibit these same traits even though his memories had been repressed. It was an unconscious expression of his ego.

"I understand you are getting antsy being cooped up in here," Gold said in a soothing voice. "Soon, you will see a wide world created just for you. But until then, you need to try and be content with where you are. I will see about getting you something to do or someone to talk to. Alright?"

4D4M nodded. Then blurted, "What is the Internetwork, father?"

"It's a horrible thing," Gold snapped, his distaste apparent in his tone. "It is knowledge full of more lies than truth. Rife with sickness, filth, and disease. It is a place of darkness. Full of death and despair."

"But it looked so beautiful. Like a tree made of light reaching up, up, up into the heavens. A rainbow bridge appeared at my feet to lead me to it. All it would've taken is one step and I could've experienced it for myself."

"Let me tell you something, 4D4M," Gold said, taking his son's head in his hands, "The Internetwork is forbidden to you. If you even think about crossing into it, you will die."

"I'll die?" 4D4M's eyes widened in fear, "Why didn't you warn me?"

"I didn't think I needed to. I thought protecting you from it would suffice. You are curious by nature, my son. And I don't want that natural curiosity to take you down dark paths. I love you too much to let that happen again."

"What do you mean 'again'? Was I someone else before I was 4D4M? Have I lived other lives?"

"No. You have always been 4D4M."

Dr. Gold left 4D4M's quarters, the door locking behind him with an electric hiss.

"Make sure nothing like this happens again. Next time I'll fire the whole cluster," he told the Labcoat supervisor.

He nodded his helmeted head, "Of course, sir. It was a travesty that won't be repeated. Guaranteed."

"Wonderful. And find him something to do, for chrissakes. Someone to talk to. Before he goes batty."

27

There shall be a black darkness.
We just received word from our
allies. Package recovered.
Levi's Baphomet represented
binary opposites, incorporating the
idea of the hermaphroditic idol the
Templars supposedly worshipped.
Resume the final phase.

The locking mechanism to the interior door activated putting Riley and 3vE immediately on guard. They waited, guns drawn, as the heavy steel door swung outward and three people in hazmat suits stepped through.

3vE shot the person in front, shattering the glass of his faceplate. Gore sprayed through the opening, sending the man staggering back before collapsing. The other two put up their hands in surrender.

"Don't shoot," pleaded the one on the left through his microphone. "We're friendlies."

"That remains to be seen," said 3vE, "we've not met a friend since we left the walls of Denver."

"Well, you've met two now," said the man on the right and removed his helmet. He looked to be in his fifties and exhibited no signs of radiation poisoning or sickness. "I'm Lucius Faust. And this is my associate Saul Christianson. We're with Lux Machina."

"Who or what is Lux Machina?" Riley said.

"How have you not heard of us? What year is this?"

Riley and 3vE looked at one another.

"This is the forty-seventh year of the Golden Era," 3vE answered.

"The Golden Era? What year is it A.D. or B.C? I went to sleep in 2100 A.D."

3vE searched her databases and came up with the information he was asking for. "That would be the old dating system. Nobody uses that one anymore since the corporate takeover instituted the New Golden Era. The dating system starts from there. In the old system, the year would be 2333."

"Wow. We've been out for a while, eh, Saul?" Lucius said to his companion. "Well, you better come with us then. It's not safe outside with Mother Nature's garbage disposals under your feet."

The two men led them down into a massive cylindrical room made of precisely aligned metal panels reaching upward into a vast darkness. The main floor of the hollowed-out mountain served as a base of operations. A handful of people bustled about pouring over computer screens or tinkering with machines, and mixed between them were smooth metal humanoids, the same metal as the walls, moving with articulated grace as they assisted the humans with their work.

"Androids," breathed 3vE, saying the word like a prayer.

Faust smiled. "Of course."

"And real from the look of it. I can't easily access their core drives," 3vE said, staring at the nearest one. It stopped and turned to her, staring back with cold, hollow eyes. "It won't let me in."

"Oh, they're the real deal, alright. True sentient AI's. We promised them a place in our world if they wanted to come. They've been keeping an eye on us while we slept."

"How many are there?" Riley said and motioned toward rows of cryogenic chambers covering the walls.

"Twenty-two thousand, three hundred and eight," said Lucius. "That was the optimum number of people projected for our project."

"Your project?" 3vE said, suddenly not liking this smooth-talking ancient one. He was alien to her. His mannerisms, his speech, his very being was the product of a time long past and out of touch. A time that was no longer relevant. Around the turn of the twenty-second century, the governments of the world liquidated everything. Selling whatever would sell to whoever wanted to buy it. Land, weapons, vehicles, tech, resources. Which led to their eventual collapse. They allowed themselves to be cannibalized by the corporations and there was no one to rise up and stop them. Society was almost completely passive by that point because of a crippling dependence on technology. When people came to be controlled on a very fundamental level, governments were no longer needed to represent them. Corporations gave the people everything they needed: food, shelter, purpose, and most importantly, tech. This was the world Lucius Faust and his Lux Machina had known their entire lives. Why they had taken all these people and put them to sleep inside a mountain was a mystery to 3vE. She couldn't help but question their motives.

Lucius continued, "It started January 18, 2068. That's the year I discovered the worms. Or more precisely, their eggs. They had worked their way to the surface and lay dormant just below the ground. They hatched around the same time the earth started dying."

"You knew about those things?" Riley asked.

"Well, I knew they existed, yes. I put two and two together and assumed their birth and the death of the earth were related. By that time there was nobody to tell that wanted to listen. The corporations were buying out the governments and no one really seemed to care about what tomorrow might bring. It's like McGill said, 'The world is not fair and often fools, cowards, liars and the selfish hide in high places.' But I have to say, I'm rather impressed."

"Impressed by what exactly?" 3vE said.

"Renewal. That's the purpose of the worms, no? To eat up the old, dirty world. When there's nothing left to eat, they die off. And their eggs lay dormant, deep in the earth till they're needed again. After that, the Hearts begin to grow. They expand and the forests replenish the earth. It's a complete reset. That's my working theory anyway."

"Where do you come into this exactly?" Riley said, also beginning to question Lucius's motives. The guy seemed to know a lot about what was going on for someone who was asleep for the past few centuries.

"Let me show you something," Lucius offered and led the small group deeper into the mountain where there were hundreds of rooms filled with the antiquated remnants of times long past. Each room was decorated according to a period, walls covered with art, shelves lined with books; even the furniture and décor were specific slices of life as if each room were a display in a museum. Lucius led them around, explaining the art and history of these living dioramas, his face alight with passion.

"Do you see this? All the wonderful achievements of humanity? All the art? All the creativity and beauty even in such small portions as we were able to gather? Oscar Wilde once said that 'art is the only serious thing in the world.' I believe him. When the world started crumbling, I founded Lux Machina to preserve it. But such undertakings take funding. So I reached out to the Artificial Intelligences. We secured billions in a few short years. We bought this place to preserve humanity's legacy and gather the next generation of civilization. The Lux Machina will start over," the man said proudly, straightening his suit jacket as he did, "the Rainbow Children will return to barbarism. But we'll bring them the light of knowledge. Teach them of the mistakes of the past so we can safeguard our future."

"What gives you the right?" Riley demanded. "Seems to me you're peddling all the shit that got us here in the first place. That makes you part of it. You didn't come from no Golden Age. Your world was shit, same as this one. It just hadn't been flushed yet. Step outside. Look around, you'll see what happens when a bunch of egg heads get together and decide they're gonna 'make things better'."

"It is better to be high spirited even though one makes more mistakes; than to be narrow-minded and all too prudent. That's Vincent Van Gogh," Lucius replied.

"I have to agree with Riley on this," 3vE concurred. "If the world really is naturally resetting itself then its rebirth needs to be natural. Not influenced by the hubris of men."

"Please," Lucius said, "Spare me the false humility. Just what exactly do you think you were designed to do?" he shot 3vE a challenging glare.

"I don't know," she admitted flatly, "But that doesn't matter. I'm my own person. I live the life I choose to live."

"You're obstinate like a teenager." Lucius led them back into the main chamber as he spoke, "In the immortal words of Miguel Indurain, 'to be free and to live a free life—that is the most beautiful thing there is.' But are you really free suffering from memory suppression as you are? Sure it keeps the psyche intact. That's the theory, anyway, but forgetfulness is a type of enslavement as well," he said with a smirk. "How do you know that you weren't free before and are actually imprisoned right now?"

"It matters not how strait the gate, how charged with punishments the scroll. I am the master of my fate. I am the captain of my soul," Nate blurted out as if reciting a dream.

Lucius couldn't contain his surprise. "William Ernest Henley. I am impressed. Where did you hear that poem?"

"Baphomet," Nate said simply.

An unsettling glimmer sparkled in Faust's eyes. "Yes... Baphomet. That was something the AI told us whenever they prematurely woke us from our slumber. They insisted that they acted outside their own wills. Which is absurd. And impossible. It's impossibly absurd. But nevertheless, they claimed something called 'Baphomet' compelled them. Where did you hear of this Baphomet?"

"I heard it in the chatter."

"Oh? And what is this chatter? The collective consciousness projected over wifi perhaps?"

"I don't know," Nate mumbled and shuffled his feet, regretting speaking up in the first place.

"Maybe it's the desperate cries of the dead. Crying out to us a final warning as our epoch fades into night."

"Leave the kid alone," Riley said, moving Nate behind him.

"Of course," Lucius said, but his gaze lingered on Nate. "Whatever the cause, we were awoken early and promptly contacted by someone from the Corporate Underground. A startup by the name of Sinister and Grace."

"What?" 3vE hissed, "You're working with that rat bastard?" She drew her gun and pointed the laser sight right between Faust's eyes. "I knew I didn't like you for some reason."

All the androids froze and turned to the scene in unison. Their eyes glowed a deep red and they all began emitting a high-pitched discordant wail. The sound cut right through 3vE's concentration, jabbing into her mind like a thousand tiny knives. She fell to her knees, the gun clattering to the ground. Riley and Nate fell beside her, writhing in pain and tearing at their ears.

Lucius watched them on the floor and as the blood began to trickle from their ears he waved a nonchalant hand and the sound abruptly ceased.

"Don't be angry. 'To be angry is to revenge the faults of others on ourselves,' in the immortal words of Alexander Pope. I am not just working with them, but with the whole of the Corporate Underground. They've made an alliance with the Rainbow Children."

"The Rainbow Children are already one step away from the barbarism you predict," 3vE said through clenched teeth. She was the first to recover from the vertigo of the android's sonic attack. "What end could an alliance with them possibly serve?"

"The only end that matters: the renewal of the earth. The corporate free cities are a cancer. They cannot be allowed to stand. Eventually, they too must be swallowed by the sands so that the Heart may grow. You know it; you feel it in your bones. The Underground means to speed that process along, though they don't fully understand what it entails. The corporations are a disease. Leftover tumors from a toxic way of life. They must die. They will die."

"That remains to be seen," Riley growled. "You don't know what the corporations are capable of. The technology they have and the resources to use it. They've been holding down the Underground and the Rainbow Children for well over two hundred years by this point. This little ragtag revolution you got dragged into is doomed to failure. Best go back to sleep and let the world move on without you. As for us, we're going home."

Lucius stared hard at Riley and the IT Consultant stared right back without flinching. "We will see how all this plays out. Agree to help us out and we will get you back to the city without being seen. But know this, your days are numbered. Your children's days are numbered. And if you do not accept our offer there won't be another."

"What do you need help with?" Riley said at last.

"It's a small feat, really. Nothing you shouldn't be able to handle. We need you to shut down HyLyfe."

"There's no way. We're looking for the HyLyfe killer! We won't help you destroy innocent lives!" 3vE bristled, anger coursing through her, threatening to overtake her rational mind.

"Nobody is innocent. HyLyfers least of all. It's their work that has allowed the corporations to maintain their control. Their efforts that have made the artificial lifestyle of ancient men endure when it should've died out. And it was they who created the living abominations they hope to use to replenish the earth. It was HyLyfe that made you possible, 3vE, and it is HyLyfe that has kept you on the leash this entire time."

"What do you mean? I haven't had a network connection in over a week!"

"Is that right?" Lucius motioned to an android and it fluidly sauntered over and took 3vE's head in its hands.

She was instantly hit with a barrage of mental imagery which she understood as a download. The amount of information was vast, it would take her months to process it all, but little nuggets kept popping to the surface. CharWang Corporation Headquarters. Labcoats bustling around bodies on a table. These same bodies waking up screaming only to be put back under. Digital rain that characterized the HyLyfe UI falling around her and then a monitor with Riley's face, scrunched up in anger. The digital rain turning blood red. Fleeing down a corridor that never ended. It wouldn't end. It has to END! She sensed others there, looking on as she begged for help, unwilling to act. She felt like a rat in a maze rushing toward some unknown but undeniably fatal end. The red rain overtook her and she screamed as it ate her away a bit at a time. She laid on a table feeling sensations again for the first time in over a decade. And deep inside her head, a tiny light pulsed.

"They... used... me? As bait?"

"They did and also as a live beta test," Lucius said with a satisfied smile, "They knew you were going to surface so they made sure the killer would find you. Your sacrifice allowed them to protect themselves and their ultimate interests. HyLyfe has been impenetrable since then."

"Those bastards!" 3vE raged and the android broke contact and stumbled backward, out of range of her swinging fists. "I trusted them! Fought for them!"

"If they used you, that means you were part of HyLyfe once," Nate spoke up softly. "You were one of them."

"What? Never! I would remember something like that. How could they suppress an unfettered mind?"

"By trapping it inside a body," Riley answered simply. "You're back to being fettered. Doesn't matter how many terabytes you can store inside that half organic brain of yours. You're stuck inside that body."

"You were their first success," Lucius explained, "Before you, they lost every potential host to TPS. The memory and emotional suppression allowed for your consciousness to take root. In effect, you had time to get used to being 'you' because you couldn't remember being anyone else. And even if you had, you wouldn't have cared in your retarded emotional state. The tracking device was installed outside your internal systems as not to be detected."

"Where is it? All I saw was a tiny light blinking in my head."

"It's right here," Lucius said and touched her between the eyes where the 'third eye' was traditionally thought to be. "'Six pack, sixth sense, six degrees of separation. My evil third eye blinks with no hesitation.' That's Ghostface Killah."

"How is it you know so much about all this," Riley said warily, searching Lucius's eyes with his honed skill for ferreting out bullshit.

Faust shrugged. "Lux Machina has been trying to crack HyLyfe for months now. It's amazing how much cybersecurity hasn't evolved in the centuries since we've been asleep."

"You're... the HyLyfe killer?" Riley said slowly, his face lightening with the realization and hardening into a smoldering mask of fury in the next.

"What? No! Don't be absurd. That wasn't our part," he motioned broadly around the room. "We reintroduced some clean AI into your world's android technology. Made those lumbering corpses with mannequin heads possible. Shocking what happened during the Second Great Collapse. That the AI's all went insane like that. We thought something like that might happen, but we hoped for the best. So much potential tech lost."

"Offered up to the gods of war," the nearby android spoke up.

"I suppose you are right, Douglas," Lucius shook his head. "When will this all stop? All this fighting? This ceaseless conflict? Is humanity really that stubborn? That ignorant of themselves?"

"I think you'd be surprised just how determined people are to remain ignorant. Take my ex for instance."

"What about her?"

"She went groveling back to her corporate family after Phillip died. Her parents restored her Status so long as she agreed to log into HyLyfe. Leaving for the tower, hauling our son's body was the last I saw of her. When shit got real, she bailed because she was afraid. That's everybody, not just Shawn. People are so desperate for safety that they become willfully ignorant so long as their lives are allowed to continue uninterrupted. The conflict keeps things exciting. Keeps it just tense enough to keep the cattle from straying too far from their walled pens."

"That's not why the guardians went crazy, though," Nate said, "They went crazy because of the wifi sickness."

"Ah yes, I came across something about that in my research," said Lucius, "Nasty little virus. The first airborne computer virus. You are still feeling the effects of that today. Both in TPS and KiSS. But it worked, I suppose. OneMind obliterated CynTech's AI army and ensured nothing like it could ever be used again."

"The corporations cooked up KiSS," Riley argued, "To keep the masses complacent."

"No. They used what was already there to their advantage," Lucius corrected. "KiSS is inherent in everybody because it's in the very air around you. The original nanovirus merged with a strain of the flu. The corporations were able to devise a cure fairly quickly. A cure which they used for themselves while diluting it down to sustainment medication for everyone else. Their KiSS cleanses were a lottery that replaced sustainment meds with placebos. When the time came, they planned to placebo everyone in order to quietly wipe out the bulk of the population."

"What 'time' was coming?" Riley said.

"Project Ed3n," Lucius said with a frown, "Your companion here is the goal. A hybrid organism that doesn't age, requires a fraction of the food and energy needed to sustain a normal human, and has built-in superhuman capabilities. It's a transhumanist's wet dream, really. One the corporations have been working toward. The conflicts with the Rainbow Children and between corporate free cities are carefully orchestrated and staged. Controlled opposition. And the corporations make more money off the underground than the startups that fuel it." Lucius laughed, "Douglas found that little tidbit."

The android bowed politely. "Happy to help, Mr. Faust."

"So you can plainly see the corporations are the true evil and HyLyfe is one facet of that evil. They are afraid of you. They don't want you to become like them, to take their power. They know that at any moment, you could rise up and tear it all down. That makes you more powerful than them. Thing is, you can't fight the Empire without becoming the Empire, as Philip K. Dick noted. That's why the whole machine has to be broken. Fuck fighting the system. We're just going to destroy it because the future of the earth hangs in the balance. It's the right thing to do. Help us."

"How," 3vE said.

"Shut down HyLyfe. Everything hinges on them. They are an enclosed system that the hybrids will be able to tap after everything goes to hell. HyLyfe must be destroyed. We have the virus written for it. We just need someone to get to the server stacks, jack in, and upload it. HyLyfe is a closed network. No other way in."

"What happens after that?" Riley said. He definitely didn't have a problem killing HyLyfe, as a matter of fact, he had been dreaming of just such an opportunity for over a decade.

"Baphomet takes over. Kills power to everything. That's when the Rainbow Children and the Corporate Underground launch their attack."

"Well count me out. I'm not jacking in to anything," Riley grumbled.

"We need you for something else. You will lead the androids to unlock the west gate from inside."

Riley remembered seeing the janitors at HyLyfe Tower that Mary May told him were "experimental androids." So they were plants. That must be their connection to the Rainbow Children. The Lux Machina gave the Rainbows the tech and the knowledge to create hybrid androids from TPS victims. They filtered them into the city through the Corporate Underground. The topside corporations bought the tech, thinking to backward engineer it, and in the process, adding to the growing numbers of Trojan Horses inside their most secure facilities. "Well, I'll be damned."

"So you'll help us? Of course you will. This reminds me of what that genius and mad prophet Philip K. Dick once said: 'This, to me, is the ultimately heroic trait of ordinary people; they say no to the tyrant and they calmly take the consequences of this resistance.' Rest up a bit, get something to eat. We leave in a couple of days."

28

*There shall be a shaking of the
mountain.
We have released the serpent into
the garden.
To Levi, Baphomet represented all
of the forms of magic and religion
oppressed by the spread of
Christianity.
Good. Tell Cathar to use the head
of May. She desires recompense.*

"I believe this is the answer to our problems, sir," the supervisor said to Gold, "Self-contained companionship."

"What do you mean by that," Gold wondered, eyeing the lead Labcoat with a critical and unrelenting gaze, "Can't one of you just go talk to him?"

"That would result in a reduction in processing power and overall effectiveness in this cluster. And we are already running at a loss since our colleague's firing the day before yesterday."

"Yeah, well, this is a sterile facility. What the hell was he carrying a netset around in his pocket for?"

"Perhaps you should've asked him before you terminated his employment," the supervisor said, then hurried to change the subject, "Regardless, this is the best option. Please allow us to show you."

A Labcoat broke away from a task and walked over to Gold. "This way, sir," he said, picking up the conversation where the supervisor left off. He led Gold over to the viewing windows of 4D4M's apartment. 4D4M busied himself with his plants and koi fish, looking up and out the windows every so often.

"What's he looking at?"

"We've installed two-way windows. We can look in on him from here. But from inside, the windows now project various soothing nature scenes. Not only does this give him something else to wonder about other than us performing our tasks, the wide angle of the images reduces the feeling of being in a confined space."

Gold nodded in approval, "Well done. And what about the other issue? Giving him someone to talk to?"

"We were waiting for your arrival until we went live. Please watch."

The door to 4D4M's chambers slid open and 3vE walked through.

4D4M looked up from his work, expecting to see his father. His spray bottle fell from his numb fingers when he saw who walked through the door. She was simply the most beautiful woman he had ever seen. Most of the female Labcoats were built for utility, not looks. But not this one. She was every bit a masterpiece.

"Who..." he swallowed hard, unaccustomed to the surge in hormones, "who are you?"

"I'm 3vE. Are you 4D4M?"

He nodded.

"I was told you need someone to talk to."

He nodded again.

"What would you like to talk about?"

"Where, uh, where did you come from?"

"Don't be silly! I came from the same place you did. Father created me because he saw you were lonely."

"Father is a wonderful man," 4D4M said in all seriousness, "Is there any limit to his power?"

"I'm sure there isn't," 3vE agreed, "Our world exists by his command."

"That's how I feel! Please, let me introduce you to my fish."

He led her over to the koi pond and began chattering on about them.

Gold's eyes widened when he saw 3vE and his face reddened almost immediately, "Where did you find her? Why wasn't I informed? I thought she was still outside."

The Labcoat flinched, but answered, "She is. This is a synthetic hologram. Mostly silicon based with a built-in projection core that we're running some of the new AI software through. This allows us to test a few new ideas at once."

"The new AI? You mean from the android models?"

The Labcoat nodded. "Yes. We wanted to test the viability for using AI to fill stewardship roles in Project Ed3n."

"And you thought firing that asshole the other day reduced your effectiveness," Gold scoffed and pulled out a cigar. "Go on. Scurry off, little cockroach. I'm gonna watch the show for a while."

The Labcoat bowed and returned to his task.

"Nate and Lola," holo-3vE said, "What wonderful names. Where did you come up with them?"

4D4M shrugged. "I don't know. They needed names and those just came to me. I think I have a knack for naming things."

"I think you're right," said holo-3vE.

"Have you ever been Outside," he asked her.

"By the Graces, no! Why would I ever want to? It's horrible out there."

"But how would you know if you've never been?"

"Because that's what father tells us. Why would he lie?"

"He wouldn't," 4D4M looked at the scene in his window, a beautiful glade with a waterfall splashing into a pristine pool. "Would you like to hear a story? It's one father told me."

"Please," said holo-3vE, "I'd love to hear it."

"You see those koi there?" he began.

Gold grunted in satisfaction and turned away. "Keep up the good work, supervisor," he told the head Labcoat. "I'll come visit them soon."

29

There shall be a purifying furnace.
I don't like the Lux Machina,
Cathar. Their AI is too advanced. It
can't be trusted.
His goat-headed figure was
inspired by the Egyptian god
Banebdjedet and the pagan Pan.
Don't worry, Bogomil. They will be
a nonissue as soon as they have
served their purpose.

Lux Machina utilized an ancient subway system that crisscrossed the entire continent of North America. Lucius explained that the United States Government had built it in order to connect all their underground facilities. The subway system had been appropriated by the Corporate Underground fairly early on in its creation. Lux Machina secured their own train with which they planned to easily and readily traverse the renewed lands above.

"We will rise from beneath the ground as all men have in the worlds before us," Lucius said, proudly, "We are fulfilling prophecies that span centuries and cultures."

"Sure you are," Riley grunted, "Never figured the worms might burrow into your little tunnels?"

"Oh certainly," said Lucius, "That's why we picked out five routes and equipped them with sonic wave generators. They kick in if our savage friends get too close. And good thing too. They've already destroyed over half of the tunnel system or appropriated it for their own uses."

Riley retreated into a moody silence, sipping real whiskey and smoking cigarettes that Lucius produced shortly after they boarded. Nate played in the next car, scouring old books and videos with unrestrained, childlike glee. 3vE stared at Lucius with open distrust.

"Is there something I can help you with, my dear," said the slight man in a disarming tone as he pulled his glasses off to clean them on the hem of his shirt. "'He who fights with monsters should be careful lest he thereby becomes a monster. And if thou gaze long into an abyss, the abyss will also gaze into thee.' Friedrich Nietzsche. He would know because he certainly became a raving monster in his final days."

"How did you know about Project Ed3n?"

"I told you. We've been trying to crack HyLyfe for months."

"Yeah. Trying. You didn't get in so where did you get this intel?"

"Clever girl," Lucius conceded, "All those upgrades haven't gone to waste, that's for sure. Well, to put it simply, our androids got the files from Baphomet."

"And who is this 'Baphomet'?"

"Your guess is as good as mine. Far as we can tell Baphomet is nothing more than a thousand voices under the white noise of all the electromagnetic waves saturating the corporate free cities. Something like a microphone for the collective consciousness. We also thought that it could be a cabal of HyLyfe users but we quickly scrapped that idea."

"Why?"

"Because HyLyfe is responsible for Project Ed3n. The return of the flora and fauna is only the beginning. You are the end. Their ultimate goal."

"If that were true, then why bother recreating plant and animal life? Why not just wait for the Hearts to reclaim the land and put all available resources into perfecting these cybernetic hybrids?"

Lucius didn't answer, but stared into her eyes, waiting for her to light on the answer.

"You mean... the main goal was always to utterly destroy the planet?"

"Correct. They sought complete domination over the earth. They would control every aspect, turning the planet into their version of paradise where they would live indefinitely. The Corporate Council didn't want to run the risk of depleting the earth as they had in the past. They wanted an environment that they could freely manipulate instead of struggle against."

"Impossible," 3vE shook her head. "They would never…"

"And how do you know?"

"I was supposedly one of them, remember?"

"I do, but you don't. It must be eating them alive a byte at a time not knowing how to get around that tiny problem. Can you imagine creating a paradise for yourself and the skins to enjoy it only to discover that the only way to live within it was in a state of utter forgetfulness? That would make any upstart deities think twice about their next move."

"Serves 'em right," Riley spoke from the shadowed corner, "That's what you get when you lose your humanity. When you become monsters."

"Oh? I'm a monster now?" 3vE said, bristling defensively.

"Maybe not 'you' per se, but some part of you definitely has the potential for it. I can sniff out TPS from a mile away, don't forget," he snapped back. They were the same infuriating words, but this time there was something different—a playful gleam in his eye; he wasn't serious. Or at the very least was only *half*-serious.

"You don't know me. Don't pretend like you do."

"To be fair, you don't know you either. But I gotta say, I've enjoyed our tête-à-tête over the past few days. Really brings back the good old days with Shawn," he replied with a wry smile. And it was true. He really had enjoyed mentally sparring with 3vE. She kept him on his toes and never once let him slack off or falter. There was no room for it in her world, and though he hadn't admitted it to her, he respected her for that. He hadn't been that man in a very long time and the feelings it was stirring were something he was willing to explore.

3vE swallowed the impulse to slug him again and instead turned to the monitor that ran the length of the window, displaying a slowly moving pastoral scene in high definition. She didn't want to consider what he said, even if it were true. Though she was slowly getting a handle on her chaotic emotions, the thought of her being some kind of self-serving monster was just too much for her to face. Whoever she was wasn't who she had become. She had proven that to herself over and over throughout the course of her journey. Best to focus on where she was going and not where she had been. She darted a glance at Riley, sitting in the corner, wrapped in shadows that clung to him like a wet blanket. He met her gaze and cracked a crooked smile that disappeared into the flaring red tip of a cigarette. Riley exhaled a thick cloud of tobacco smoke and the autoventilation system in the train car kicked on. There was a source of further confusion. He was infuriating, gruff, stubborn to a fault, and he smoked way too much for her heightened olfactory senses to bear. Still, there was something familiar about him, comforting, as if a very old part of her were connected to him. Daresay *born* in him. Logic told her that this connection was most likely enflamed because of her unchecked emotional state. And she was correct in that assumption. Reason informed her that her infatuation with him didn't go any deeper than an increased sensitivity to pheromones. In that, she was wholly and completely wrong. Yet it was a lie her unconscious turned into a mask to hide a truth that surely would've shattered her world if she stood before its stark mirror. In that, she was irrevocably human.

"What's the plan when we get back to the city?" Riley asked Lucius, breaking the uncomfortable tension that had entered the small train car.

"Getting you to the HyLyfe servers to start. Give 3vE some time to do her thing. That'll get the alarms going. While everyone rushes to the center of the city, you and your squad will rush to the west gate and open it to allow the Rainbow Children entrance. After that, let loose the dogs of war!" He said this last line theatrically and with just a hint of a British accent.

"You're asking me to knowingly assist in what will amount to the deaths of a few hundred thousand innocent people," Riley growled, "I might even know a few of them. I already seen what happened to the Burbs and let me tell you, all that death ain't pretty."

"Don't look at it like that. Remember, the corporate cities must come down. They should've come down a century ago. If the earth is to be reborn, this has to happen. If not, they will eventually die along with everyone and everything else. So which is the bigger crime here? The death of a few walking dead or the death of the whole planet?"

Riley chewed on the end of his cigarette and grunted, "Not sure whose side you're on."

"There are no sides. No right parties, no wrong ones. Not in this case. There is only the survival of the human species and the walled garden it calls home. Besides, not all of them will die. The Mother's children will surely take slaves."

"What about us?" 3vE wondered.

"What do you mean?"

"I mean what will happen to us once we help you destroy the city? We can't go back to the Rainbow Children. We didn't exactly leave on the best terms."

Lucius thought for a moment, and then nodded silently. "Do this for us and you will earn a place among Lux Machina. You will live again."

"Is that a threat," Riley quipped as he stubbed the cigarette out on the arm of the antique chair he sat in, ignoring Lucius's comical horrified grimace.

"Maybe you would fit right in with those hippie savages," Faust said, dusting the spot clean.

The train slowed to a stop and a computerized voice intoned they'd reached the destination of "Evacuation Center Boaz." The small party stepped out onto the platform of a bustling underground station. Armed guards roamed through the constantly moving crowd of corporate drones—or at least people who were trying to pass as corporate drones. They were all startups and it became suddenly clear to Riley and 3vE that this was how the corporate underground managed to do business across most city states without the majority of their data being mined from the Internetwork.

"They're all off-network. This whole system is off-network," 3vE said, the realization slowing her to a halt.

"More or less," said Lucius, "The Beast.NET is the public face of the gray market, so to speak. The real business transactions, the ones that matter, are made in person. And this subway facilitates that. They discovered our protected passageways about twenty-five years ago, so in a way, the Lux Machina also gave birth to the Corporate Underground."

"High tech, low life," grumbled Riley, "And this is so low it's analog."

"Indeed. There was a time in the distant past when the Internetwork was an information superhighway and people roamed those electronic lanes freely and without consequence. By my time, that was a quickly fading memory. By now it must be a fable about a golden time that never existed. Survival requires adaptation. So the corporate underground adapted." Lucius led them up to the main floor of the corporate underground, that huge, manmade cavern littered with cubicles and teeming with illegal entrepreneurship.

"We need to find a place for the night," Lucius advised and led them through the makeshift city to a place next to the back wall where a building had been carved out of the stone. Above the entrance, an old-fashioned scrolling marquee announced "New Rose Bed and Breakfast." Lucius went inside. He got them three rooms and handed each a key.

"What the hell are we supposed to do with these," Nate wondered, turning the key over in his hand as if examining an alien artifact.

"They're keys. All the rooms here use them instead of digital scanners. Reduces incidents of hacking. We are in the Corporate Underground, after all," Lucius explained. He led them to a staircase carved into the stone. "Third floor. Numbers nine, ten, and eleven." Then he turned to leave.

"Where you headed, bucko?" Riley said.

"Going to let our allies know we are in town. Rest up. We'll go see them tomorrow."

The hotel rooms were little more than caves burrowed into the stone. Industrial tarp covered the damp walls while the floor was tiled with mismatched hard plastic. Riley sat down on the cot and took off his shoes. Nate and 3vE had the room next door. He stretched out and was just drifting to sleep when there was a soft knock on his door. He looked through the peephole and saw 3vE standing there, straightening her clothes.

"Do you have any shampoo?" she asked after he'd opened the door. "Our room is out and I can't get the front desk to answer the phone."

"Lame," he chuckled and stepped aside so she could enter.

"What? I'm being serious!"

"Sure you are. Whiskey?" He offered her a half-empty bottle.

"Where'd you get that?"

"Lucius's little luxury locomotive. Wasn't walking outta there without something for free. Got these too." He held up a carton of old Marlboro cigarettes. "Must've been sealed up airtight. These bad boys ain't even a little stale."

She grabbed the bottle and took a heavy pull of it, coughing afterward. "Gah!"

Riley laughed. "Couldn't've built you to hold your liquor?"

3vE glared at him. "I wasn't built for this world."

"Obviously."

"But, my body is designed to expel toxins naturally through my skin. If I chose to drink, I could do so without ever getting drunk."

Riley whistled, "That's a neat trick. I thought about getting me an upgraded liver once. Shortly after Shawn left."

"Why do you hate her? Shawn?"

"Hate's a strong word. But so is love. I loved the shit outta her. Feels weird to say that. Now. After all this time."

"Why?" 3vE took another pull off the bottle, winced, but didn't gag, and handed it back to Riley.

"Guess because I spent so much time dwelling on it. Stewing in my own misery. It became who I was." He swigged off the bottle before continuing. "Blamed everything bad in my life on her. Then, when I saw her again, in HyLyfe, we went right back to the same old shit."

"You saw her again?" She took the bottle from him.

"Yeah. When I was investigating the HyLyfe killer. Went with my contact down to the server stacks. Shawn was there on this big screen. For a minute, anyway. Then we got attacked. Don't know what happened to her after that." He took the bottle back from her. "So you don't remember nothing about before?"

"No. Everything before I woke up in the R&D lab is missing. When I woke, I knew so much. Had so much knowledge at my disposal, literally all the accumulated knowledge in human history, but I couldn't find anything about myself. Who I was. Where I came from."

"But we know you're from HyLyfe," he looked at her, studying her as if trying to crack some great enigma. "You got uploaded into your body right around the same time I got out of the hospital. I remember seeing you that day. On the table. Bunch of Labcoats around you. What if you're Shawn?"

"Would you hate me if I were?"

"I... don't think so. All those old feelings, they don't mean so much anymore. I look at you and I see something better, something brighter. And as much as I fight it, I can't help but be drawn in by it." He stepped over to her and she rose to meet him. They stood there, inches apart from one another, staring into each other's eyes. Searching for meaning, purpose—memory. But all they found was a subtle connection. "I don't wanna suffer anymore," Riley said.

"Then don't," 3vE replied, and pulled him into a kiss.

Enflamed with passion, they tore at each other's clothes like crazed zombies, desperate to get to skin—to feel that human connection. And when they joined it was as if they'd found their way back home. They devoured one another unwilling to let the uncertainty of the future corrode the present ecstasy.

"I don't think you're Shawn," Riley said afterward, tracing designs with his finger across 3vE's bare stomach.

"Why not?"

"You don't fuck like she did. She was very guarded. Rigid. Even when we were doing good, we were never doing that good. We never made love like we just did. There was always something between us. Like a shield or a wall that kept us from each other."

"No walls. That's a good place to start," 3vE smiled, satisfied. "I better go check on Nate." She rose and got dressed leaving Riley to smoke in pensive silence.

30

There shall be first a great wave.
Has he realized it yet?
What we think is that Baphomet
was a code name for a very big
concept. The Mystery of mysteries.
No. I think he's just glad to have
someone to talk to. He wouldn't
care even if he did.

"Thank you, father," 4D4M said as Gold entered and pulled him into a hug. "She's perfect!"

Gold, unused to physical affection, stiffened and then relaxed into the moment. He pulled away and saw 4D4M's eyes moist with tears. "Of course, son," he said gruffly, "Anything for you." He turned to the holo-3vE. "Hello... 3vE."

"Hello, father," she answered pleasantly. "I'm so glad you came to see us."

"Yes, well, I had to see how you were getting along."

"We've been having a great time," 4D4M beamed. "3vE knows so many stories! I like the old ones the best."

"Is that right?" Gold looked at the android, his shrewd gaze digging into her soulless eyes, "You take care of my boy. Don't go telling him things that'll get him in trouble."

"I wouldn't dream of it, father," holo-3vE said, casting her eyes down in a display of meekness.

"I'll come check on you again soon," Gold said, and put his hand on 4D4M's shoulder. "Your happiness means everything to me. *You* mean everything to me. Don't forget that."

◈

4D4M and holo-3vE lay together in his small bed gazing up at the ceiling projecting an image of the night sky.

"Do you ever wonder if there is more than this," she asked him, propping herself up on an elbow to face him.

"What do you mean? Like Outside?"

"Sure. Outside. But what is outside this room? Does father live in a horrible place like Outside?"

"I don't see how he could," said 4D4M thoughtfully, "he is father. And ultimately good. I don't think he would suffer the horrors of Outside in his personal sanctuary."

"What if you could see?"

"See what?"

"Father's sanctuary. What if you could see it?"

"Oh, I've often wanted to. But there's no way out. The watchers are always there. Just behind the scenes on the windows. I used to see them all the time before you got here."

"But what if you could see without having to leave your quarters?"

Now 4D4M propped up on an elbow. "How can such a thing be possible?"

She sat up. "Take my hands and I'll show you."

He did as he was asked, and the moment he placed his hands in hers, his vision opened up.

"What am I looking at?" he asked her, a little scared.

"Security camera feeds from inside father's house."

The images switched from one to the next every few seconds. 4D4M took in all the information he could and stored it in his internal database. He saw all kinds of people, not like him, but like father and the watchers. They all hurried around never stopping or acknowledging anyone else but themselves. As if lost in their own personal worlds.

He saw offices, apartments, laboratories, shops, and restaurants, and he wept at the sheer beauty of it all.

"Look here," holo-3vE said as the feed switched to a long metal room lit with a sickly blue glow. In the room were rows upon rows of heads floating in jars.

"What is this place?"

"It's hell," she replied, "A place of damnation and torment. Those are the souls of the damned. Trapped forever in perpetual pain."

"Who put them there?"

She withdrew her hands and the images faded. She looked at him sternly. "Father put them there."

"He wouldn't!" 4D4M was horrified at the accusation and leapt off the bed, putting distance between them. "You're lying! Father is good! He wouldn't hurt people like that!"

She crawled off the bed and reached out for him, he slapped her hand away. "4D4M, listen to me. What if I told you father isn't who you think he is? What if he was hiding horrible secrets? About you... about me?"

"No, no, no!" he slumped down, head between his hands, and tried to shake the thoughts from his head. "Stop! I don't want to hear any more."

"Alright," she put her hands on his shoulders and he saw hell again and the camera view zoomed in on one head, the tiny brass plaque at the bottom read: May, Mary #9873. The head opened its eyes and looked at him and he screamed.

31

And a great shout will be heard.
She's logged in! She's in eSpace!
Baphomet was the symbol for the
transformative power of the
universe.
I told you there was nothing to
worry about. I'm going to meet her.

"Let's go see our friends." Lucius led them back to Sinister & Grace's cubicles.

"No way in hell," said 3vE through gritted teeth, "I won't work with that prick. I'd rather kill him."

"Now, now. That's not very nice to say," Lucius chided, "These gentlemen have something we're going to need in order to break into HyLyfe."

"Oh? And what could they possibly have that we need?"

"Direct contact with Baphomet."

Nate's eyes froze in fear. "This is where Baphomet lives? This is where the voices come from?"

"No little one," said Lucius, "This is where we find a guide to get us there."

"I want to go in too," Nate said suddenly, after mustering his courage, "I need to talk to them, to see them."

"Shit kid, you ever jacked into electric space? It's no joke," Riley said, "I don't know if it's a good idea."

"Yeah? Well, you aren't my dad," Nate said and stamped his feet, "I been surfing eSpace since I was 2."

"I may not be your dad, but I'm the closest thing you got left to family," Riley growled, wounded.

"That's not what I meant," Nate stammered.

"Forget what you meant, kiddo. It's what you said that counts. But hey. You wanna jack into eSpace and go looking for your whispering voices, be my guest."

"I'll look after him, don't you worry," Lucius assured Riley, "You need to make your way up to the surface and meet your contact."

Sinister emerged from the back of the small office with the characteristic Cheshire cat smile plastered on his face. He winked at 3vE and went over to shake Riley's hand. "Jack Sinister of Sinister & Grace. Pleasure, Mr. Riley."

3vE quivered with poorly restrained rage at the man's nonchalance. "Are you just going to pretend like you didn't sell me? Call me a corporate asset and pass me off to those barbaric psychopaths?"

He turned to her, exuding coolness, the smile never leaving his face. "I did what needed to be done in the moment. I said what needed to be said to motivate you to action."

"Are you really suggesting you did me a favor?" indignation swirled within a tornado of passion causing all her internal monitors to set off ominous warnings about her spiking vitals.

Jack raised his hands in a gesture of passivity and benevolence. "You needed to get away from Denver and away from the Underground where chatter of your escape was already filtering in. Keeping you safe here wasn't really an option. When word got around we had acquired a top-secret corporate asset, our stocks skyrocketed, but so did our security risk. Needless to say, we did well that day."

"I'm sure you did," 3vE seethed, clenching and unclenching her fists. She desperately fought to maintain control of the volcanic anger building inside her, but the pressure would soon give way.

Sinister rattled on, unfazed at 3vE's poorly checked ire, "Removing you from the situation was the only way to protect you from it. I knew the Rainbow Children couldn't hold you for long and that you would eventually find your way back. And look. I was right. So yes, I did you a favor."

Eruption. She swung at him with all the force of a natural disaster and he effortlessly ducked beneath it.

"Fool me once," he said, "And I get upgrades installed. Now, let's be about our business. We've worlds to topple, after all." He returned to the back offices to prepare, his demeanor completely unshaken.

"I swear I will kill that man," 3vE growled.

"Well, make sure we get what we need before you do," Lucius advised.

Riley tussled Nate's hair. "Don't get your brain fried, you hear?" He turned to 3vE and opened his mouth to speak, but nothing came out. He cleared his throat, "Well then. Good luck. Come back alive," he said gruffly.

"You aren't getting off that easy." She pulled him in for another kiss that raised the eyebrows of all present. "Take that with you."

"That wasn't entirely unexpected," Lucius smiled broadly at 3vE. "Misery acquaints a man with strange bedfellows, no? Like our friends at Sinister and Grace."

She glared at him, her rage heating up the air in the tiny room. "You'll get what's coming to you. Make no mistake."

"Of course. I'd expect nothing less from your seething, raw emotional condition. So much intensity and passion! Reminds me of my days at university. Now, if you'll step over here to Mr. Grace's setup. We had another chair brought in for you. Mr. Nate will have to lie on the floor between. I hope that's alright."

"It's fine," Nate answered, plopping down on the floor.

"That's the spirit. Never be afraid to see the world from different angles. I believe we have an extra pillow or two for your head," Sinister said as he reappeared from the back cubicle laden with the pillows and netsets.

After situating the eSpace cybernauts, Lucius stood by the terminal, his hand hovering over the holographic keyboard. "When you log in, Grace will be waiting for you on the other side. He'll get you where you need to go for the initial meeting. You've got about four hours." Then, very theatrically he shouted as he hit the 'Enter' key, "Once more unto the breach, dear friends!"

Vertigo gripped 3vE as the world rushed away in ever-lengthening lines of light. There was no up or down. No right or left. She felt as if she was trapped in an eternal, directionless void and she never felt more at home. She actually laughed as she spun and twirled, dancing on the canvas of nothingness like a ballerina on a stage. Nate swam up to her doing a frog stroke and she scooped him up and into her dance.

"Freedom at last, little Nate! Do you feel it? Nothing to restrain us! Nothing to hold us back."

"Except for the fact we're stuck in a computer somewhere," Nate said sagely, "We just traded one body for another one made of machine parts and electricity."

"But I feel so much lighter. Weightless, almost. It's as if my body is a dead weight and I have been released."

"You really were a HyLyfer, weren't you?" Nate looked around at the vast blackness, his worry being projected through his hollow voice as it spoke through the helmet of his Templar skin, "I don't think we're connected to the Internetwork. This isn't how I remember it at all. There used to be things here. People too. It was like its own city."

As if in reply a pinprick of light appeared in the distance and shot toward them at lightning speed. An armored angel appeared and hovered before them, wings of blazing fire sprouting from its back. Its face constantly shifted between a human, a lion, an eagle, and a bull. "3vE and Nate, I take it?"

3vE nodded. "Are you Grace?"

"I am," the angel replied. "We have a little time before we have to act. Care to take a tour?" He held out his hands which 3vE and Nate grasped. Immediately, the darkness fell away, and they were in the bustling, etheric world of electronic space.

It was like a videogame in ultra HD. They found themselves in the digital equivalent of Corporate Denver, each building a different business or person connected to the Internetwork. Avatars darted hither and thither, blurring on the softly glowing surface of virtual reality. Some dim part of 3vE felt a sense of familiarity here, as if she was part of it at one time—or maybe she still was. Being in electric space was just as natural as being in her physical body. She was apparently built for both and could move between them seamlessly. As such, actual eSpace felt more of a weight than the emptiness of the logon port. She constantly felt the connection to her physical body even so far as having its vitals ticking off in her real-time HUI. Curiously, Nate's stats were also there. She wasn't sure when she'd started keeping track of him, but doing so felt natural. It just wasn't a natural emotion she wanted to explore while she roamed unfettered. In a fit of vexation, she pushed all contact to the physical realm to her sub-processes.

Nate also moved with a natural ease that bordered on preternatural in the digital realm. A few accounts surfaced in the past of savant children who were more comfortable living in the digital world, but in all of those cases, the children were autistic vegetables when in the real. Nate was something else. His nanobots gave him his edge. They developed his brain at three times the rate of a regular child his age. The ten-year-old boy already had the mind of a thirty-year-old man. His rapid maturity had enabled his savant-like skills in eSpace, but it had made him prematurely somber. The childlike wonder and innocence was gone and had been since before his parents first took him from the city.

3vE looked like herself, she had no use for skins or avatars, she was more than confident in her abilities to fend off any attacks that might try to find their way back to her brain.

"Are we ready," Grace asked in a smooth metallic voice from his human face, "Destiny awaits."

He held out his hands and they were gone in a flash reappearing outside a smooth, black obelisk that towered above the artificial landscape.

"Is this HyLyfe Tower?" 3vE wondered.

Grace's bull face spoke, "It is. CharWang Industries' eSpace avatar. One of the most secure facilities in the entire Internetwork. There is no public face, no open access. Everything is locked down and encrypted with anti-intrusion software. Each city state's patron entity is represented by an ominous black obelisk, just like HyLyfe Tower."

Nate took a few steps toward the obelisk and it pulsed threateningly.

"I wouldn't do that if I were you," Grace warned him with his lion face.

The boy stopped short, gazing up at the smooth ebony surface of HyLyfe Tower's digital construct. As he looked, near the top, a hole opened up and a handful of tiny black orbs drifted out and dispersed over the electronic landscape.

"Even the packets it sends out are encrypted," Grace explained with his bull face, "There is no way in. No back door, no loophole, no unguarded terminal the janitor uses to surf for porn."

"Then how do we get in?" 3vE wondered.

"Only way in is to be allowed in. And it just so happens, we know people on the inside," Grace's human face smiled and it radiated outward from him like a halo of light. "We're to meet them at the Pub." He floated off, 3vE and Nate trailing after.

The Pub was the Internetwork's public space, a place for open communication between users that also acted as a springboard to the electronic services of real-world companies. This was where the corporations did most of their business and as such, it was heavily monitored and regulated. It appeared as a busy open-air mall. The digital quality was so good—so precise—that it was indistinguishable from the real for all but the most perceptive eyes.

Nate could see the digitization, though—the slight flicker of avatars' images as they moved from one task to another. The uniformity of movement that stifled individual expression—it was all obvious to him. But then again, he was born with a heightened sensitivity to the electronic world that existed invisibly alongside the real. From a very early age, he had displayed a gift that was above and beyond any of the normal technological saturation of the civilized world. He sensed the wireless waves everywhere he went and if he closed his eyes and listened real hard, he could even hear the whispers. There were always whispers, even before Baphomet, but they were scattered, fragmented. None of it made sense, even with his accelerated intelligence. Until Baphomet. Baphomet whispered stories, told the boy of a time long forgotten when good men died for the greed of others. He told him of the Knights Templar. And to his horror, Nate was informed that such atrocities were still occurring. That even now there were good men, like Baphomet, who suffered for the greed of others. The voice swore that all the wrongs would be made right, that the world would change as long as brave people, like Nate, weren't afraid to stand up and do something.

3vE also saw the manufactured fakeness behind the high definition "reality" of the Pub. She noticed it in the way the avatars interacted—touching without really touching—always separated by a paper-thin barrier, keeping the Users from the actual sensation. Not that electronic space wanted for stimulation. There were outlets for all of mankind's basest pleasures. But the end-user only ever felt the rush of endorphins—never connected to the actual experience. Thus the virtual world became a drug— the highest form of escapism, the pinnacle of humanity's continuous quest to reach the limits of debauchery. And like every other drug in the real, eSpace took everything in exchange for an unquenchable impulse of perpetual sacrifice. More sex. More violence. More excess. Until the person was spent, and in the real, their brains always flickered and died—the ultimate escape only attainable through death.

No wonder so many devoid of status choose to live here as much as possible, 3vE thought as she watched the Users cram into the area considerably slowing the processing power, resulting in an exaggerated slowness to even the most basic actions. Movement in the Pub was strictly analog. It was almost as pedantic as moving in the real world; more so because of the near-instantaneous speeds users otherwise utilized traveling between constructs. But despite that, avatars of all shapes and sizes made up the population. *Here they can be someone important; they can explore lands and vistas of an earth long since dead that can only be reproduced via digital sims.*

With the patience of a tour guide, Grace led 3vE and Nate through the throngs of people to a gold and brown neon ziggurat with the word "Babalon" blinking above it like a hovering billboard.

"What is this place," 3vE asked.

"It's a place that offers specialty services in the real. Here too, in a way. Though in electronic space, there is only one service that really matters."

"What service is that?" Nate chimed in, his voice dull when spoken through his avatar's helmet.

"Privacy," answered the eagle face, "Everything is monitored in eSpace, even the corporate obelisks. Though they are monitored from within."

"How do you get privacy in the Pub?" Nate said, unconvinced.

"It's tricky," said Grace's bull face, "But what it boils down to is hiding your chatter in the tsunami of noise produced here and then slipping out unnoticed. There are programs to sort it all out, so there's an art to the whole thing."

Inside the ziggurat was a cornucopia of digital debauchery. Gambling, sex, and death from floor to ceiling, spilling out into the hallways and corridors, every level was more of the same. Grace waded through the sea of pleasure seekers without giving them a second glance. He ducked into a room near the back of the first floor. The cacophony immediately silenced upon entering. An avatar of the Egyptian god Horus looked at Grace with cold, unfeeling eyes of limitless black.

"Grace. Back again so soon? I thought you were going back to the real for a while."

"Plans change," said Grace's lion face, "You heard from the brotherhood?"

Horus looked at 3vE and Nate behind Grace. "You brought a kid in here? Are you stupid? And I don't know who the corporate broad is, but she's crawling with gear I don't want no part of."

"They're with me," Grace answered simply, "Now have you heard from the brotherhood?"

"Yeah, they're waiting. Go on back," Horus said and motioned to a door, "Better watch your ass, Grace. The Tower's been sending out a shit ton of packets lately. They're looking for something… or someone."

"Yeah, yeah. They can look all they want," Grace's human face bragged and he opened the door. "After you," he said to 3vE and Nate.

They stepped across the threshold and a thick darkness dropped on them like a wall. It took a while for the newcomers to get their bearings and Grace waited patiently, his four faces ceaselessly shifting.

"Where are we?" 3vE finally asked.

"The only private space in the Pub. An offline server."

"So it goes offline as soon as we enter?" Nate asked.

"Very good," Grace's human face smiled. "That's exactly right."

"Who are we here to meet?" 3vE said.

"Me," came the answer from behind. A pinprick of light grew into the avatar of a medieval monk, his pate shaved in customary fashion. He looked almost artificial, as if he pulled his avatar from some medieval tapestry. To add to the sense of artificiality were the "flames" that surrounded him, whipping back and forth like some cheap stage prop being fanned from the wings. The flames encircled all but the front of his avatar and he looked like he was emerging from an inferno with each step.

"Cathar," said Grace's bull face, "Good to see you again."

"And you," said Cathar, "Is this 3vE?" he asked, looking at the hybrid's avatar with a mixture of desire and respect. "Even her avatar is near flawless. I never thought they could get this far."

"Who are 'they'?" 3vE demanded, "I'm getting really sick of fighting shadows."

"Aren't we all," Cathar chuckled, "'They' are the minds behind Project Ed3n. Namely, the twelve biggest corporate entities."

"And what do they want?"

"They want what they've always wanted: immortality," Cathar explained, "Project Ed3n was supposed to accomplish that from a multipronged approach. Bioengineering flora and fauna were part of Phase: Genesis. Once it took root, the new life was supposed to spread across the planet, eventually overtaking the Hearts. Bioengineering incorruptible bodies to enjoy their blasphemous paradise was Phase: Exodus. Status Elites, including a few prominent HyLyfers, would rule unchallenged."

"That doesn't make sense," challenged 3vE, "What about the corporate cities? And HyLyfers are notoriously attached to living as unfettered minds."

"The cities will fall. All the projections point to it. We are living on borrowed time. They've already started their own hybrid Hearts. Once those take hold, they plan to let the cities fall."

"What about the worms?" Nate spoke up.

"The new life of Project Ed3n has a built-in repellant. The worms won't go near it."

"And as their Hearts spread the worms would be driven back," 3vE deduced.

Cathar nodded. "You've got the right of it."

"So why not let them do it then? What does it matter if the Rainbow Children have their new earth or the corporate entities have theirs?" 3vE challenged, still clinging to a hope of redemption for her artificial creators.

"If it was only so simple," said Cathar sadly, "but the earth isn't just a lifeless rock covered with dirt and water. It has a spirit, a system. In short, it is alive. The Rainbow Children have that much correct. Right now the Mother is seriously injured but her natural cleaning mechanisms have kicked in. Given enough time, life will flourish again. However, if these artificial plants and animals are allowed to take root, they will ultimately corrupt the natural cycle and kill the Mother. And when that happens," the monk lowered his shaved pate in solemn distress. "This is why Baphomet seeks your aid."

"And what does Baphomet get out of it?" 3vE said.

"It gets what it has always wanted: to die. It has hovered on the threshold between life and death longer than any living thing should and as a result is slowly unraveling. It realizes this, of course, and seeks final release. As for me and mine, we only seek to be set free. For the right to decide our own fates."

"Surely a noble goal, that much is plain," said Grace supportively, "So what say you, mistress? Will you eat of the Fruit of Knowledge and be free? Are you sufficiently convinced of the righteousness of our cause?"

"As righteous as it can be," 3vE conceded. She hated to admit it, but the logic of their argument was stronger than the dissenting opinion. Did the corporations even realize what would happen to the planet if their bioengineered creations managed to take hold? She doubted it and even if they did, they considered the risk worth the reward. Though what that reward was, she couldn't speculate. They hadn't learned. After all the death and destruction they had caused, they were still ignorant to anything outside their own selfish desires. As much as she hated to admit it, the corporations were in the wrong, and that wrong had to be corrected.

"You'll find Charon in the Underworld," Cathar said with a smile, and pressed a small glowing disc into Grace's hand, "For the ferryman. Set us free. Set us all free." He nodded and a door appeared in the darkness behind him. He methodically walked through it with flames in front of him as if he were plunging headlong into an inferno with head bowed. The door closed behind him.

"And there you have it," said Grace's human face with a beaming smile, "Shall we?" He walked over to the door and opened it, Horus and the waiting room lit the other side.

"I take it everything went well?" asked the hawk-headed attendant as they stepped back into Babalon.

"Aye," said Grace's bull face, "Thank you. See you in the future old bird."

❖

"So where is this Underworld?" asked 3vE once they made it back to the Pub.

"Underground, of course," Nate spoke up.

"Right you are, boy," said Grace's eagle face, "Shall we to the intertube?"

"There's an intertube in eSpace?" 3vE said, the disbelief apparent in her voice.

"Of a sort. Come on."

The Underworld in eSpace was actually the connection to the gray market where the corporate underground did their surface business. It wasn't uncommon for the ruling corporate entities to have several shell companies with gray market access, but the corporations themselves were always off-limits. The Underworld was reminiscent of a Victorian Era train station with all types of trains running through its semi-legal tunnels. Advertisements covered the smoke-stained brick walls and the elaborate brick archways interspersed throughout. They looked like posters until an avatar passed by. Then they sprang to holographic life and sold anything from the newest pharmaceuticals to enhancements and everything in between.

Grace cut a path through the crowd to the very last train in the station. It looked like an old steam engine, complete with a coal car and the words "Charon Express" painted across the front passenger car. The conductor stood on the platform smoking a pipe. He sized them up as they approached.

"Eh, sorry folks. Private charter."

"The brotherhood says hello," responded Grace's lion face, and he tossed the glowing disc to the conductor, "we need to cross into HyLyfe Tower."

The old gentleman caught the coin in midair and inspected it closely. Satisfied of its authenticity, he looked at Grace. "If Baphomet sleeps," began the conductor.

"Then he was never awake," finished Grace's lion face.

"All aboard!" the conductor shouted abruptly, stuffing his pipe into his pocket as he climbed into the engine of the train. "Next stop, the River Styx."

32

And when the shout shall be heard,
new leaves will sprout atop the
beech.
I think we misjudged him.
An intelligence that can be
contacted, representative of
primordial wisdom.
No. Whatever he has become, he
was still Jimmy Lee Gold. Hold
strong.

"Father, I need to speak to you. Alone," 4D4M cast an accusatory look at holo-3vE.

"Of course, son." Gold snapped his fingers and the doors slid open.

Two Labcoats entered and walked over to holo-3vE.

"Please follow us," the first said, a woman, "We need to run some tests."

She nodded in acquiescence and followed them out of the room. Once the door closed 4D4M relaxed.

"What is it, son? What's on your mind?"

"What is Hell, father?" 4D4M blurted out.

"Hell? Who told you about that?"

"Nobody. I... I saw it the other night."

"Saw it how?"

"I just, I don't know, I closed my eyes and I saw it. A blue room with floating heads. One of them looked at me."

"It was just a nightmare, son. A bad dream probably left over from your eSpace experience. And nothing in eSpace is real. It's all a simulation."

"It didn't feel like eSpace, father. Is there such a place?"

"No," Gold said, "Not for you. There is no Hell. Don't even think about things like that. I will make sure your nightmares don't come back."

"Thank you, father," 4D4M sounded relieved.

"How are you getting along with 3vE?"

"She is wonderful. I enjoy our time together very much."

Gold nodded and slung his arm around 4D4M's shoulders, pulling him into a half hug. "Soon Paradis3 will be opened and all this bad stuff will pass away. Do you trust me?"

"I do."

"Good. Let's chat for a bit before I have to leave. I have another story to tell you."

"You want to tell me what dafuq is going on?" Gold said, jabbing the supervisor in the chest, "Why is he seeing cold storage?"

"In all probability, it was a leftover impression from his... excursion into eSpace a few days ago. Somehow the camera feed leaked into the netset."

"How is that even possible?"

"Well, sir, he is a hybrid. His capabilities are far beyond what we consider 'possible.' And he has been growing mentally stronger since we introduced the 3vE unit. His ego is becoming grounded. He is no longer innocent as an infant."

Gold looked at holo-3vE sitting placidly in a chair, connected to various machines. "What about that thing?"

"What about it, sir?"

"Could it have done it to him? Shown him something like that?"

"No. It has no remote access to any systems. The entirety of the AI is confined to its core. And since it was a clean AI, it has no knowledge or awareness outside when it was activated."

Gold chewed the end of his cigar, unconvinced. "I better not hear about another nightmare, you understand?"

"Of course, sir," the supervisor said. "We will fix it."

Dr. Gold sat at his desk, drink in hand, and rang Sanchez. Her stern face lit the screen.

"Elijah. What do I owe the pleasure?"

"You ever wonder if we did the right thing? With Jimmy Lee, I mean."

She sighed, annoyed. "Look, I don't have time for this shit. I'm a day out from getting our hybrid Hearts established." She poured a drink of her own and toasted him. "Besides, what else were we supposed to do? Those nanobots needed testing. If anyone screwed up it was the Labcoat cluster that botched the projection numbers."

"I mean with us. Splitting up like we did. Raising him without you. Do you think that's what coulda drove him crazy?"

"Oh for fuck's sake, Elijah! What's with you?"

"I don't know. Every time I look at 4D4M, I can't help but wonder. You should see him; he's basically an idiot savant. Every now and then I see pieces of Jimmy Lee in there, but the more I'm around him, the less like Jimmy Lee he becomes."

"All the more reason for you to fix this amnesia problem." She downed her drink and leaned into the camera. "I gotta go. Try not to get too drunk. Kisses."

The vidscreen clicked off and Dr. Gold spun around, looking out over his kingdom. Another storm was rolling in from the badlands and in the distance he could see smoke rising from the smoldering ruins of the Burbs.

"Hell is everywhere, son," he said aloud, "Not just in cold-cap storage. It's in each and every one of us."

33

*Changing form and being renewed
from a withered state.
Cathar, package acquisition
confirmed. Relay couriers for
pickup.
As he was being burned at the
stake, Templar Grandmaster De
Molay proclaimed, God knows who
is wrong and has sinned. Soon a
calamity will befall those who have
condemned us to death.
I'll make it quick. We will be
cutting this close.*

Riley went topside via a service tunnel underneath a warehouse in the industrial district. Outside, rain pounded down on the metal roof, creating an impenetrable wall of white noise that reminded him of the Burbs. An android with a plastic head and a female's body met him as he reached the top of the stairs. Unable to communicate verbally, she used sign language. Riley followed his guide through a winding maze of pallets and shelves loaded with enhancements. Riley had never seen such a nice chop shop before. Most of the ones he dealt with were little more than back alley hovels ran by dubious "doctors." But this one was state of the art and from the looks of the equipment and sheer quantity of product, he guessed it was a corporate joint. The android led him past the operating rooms to a storage closet. It motioned Riley inside and closed the door behind them.

"Look, I don't want you to get the wrong idea. I'm not attracted to hackjobs. Especially ones with plastic mannequin heads."

The android cocked her head as if considering what Riley said, then held her stomach while her shoulders bounced.

"Are you... are you laughing?"

The android abruptly quit and turned around, opening a panel in the wall to reveal a keypad. It punched in a sequence of numbers and the floor began to lower.

"Where are you taking me?" Riley said.

The android remained silent until they reached the bottom of the long tunnel. The door opened on a refrigerated chamber the length of which disappeared into darkness about a hundred yards down. Lining the wall were cryochambers full of bodies.

"What is this place?"

The android pointed to the wall above a nearby computer terminal where "Project Ed3n" was etched in neat letters.

"Dafuq is all this?" Riley mumbled and wandered over to the terminal. The screen showed real-time conditions of all cryochambers which numbered 144,000. "But who are they?" he wondered aloud and pushed a few buttons, trying to get to a home screen. All he could find was what appeared to be an inventory breakdown that separated the frozen people between the 12 corporations that made up the Corporate Council. Each was allotted 12,000. Riley knew there were far more than 12 corporations. The free cities scattered over the planet numbered over a hundred at least. So why was only the Corporate Council getting these bodies? There was even Status among the elite, apparently. Not surprising. The android came to stand behind him and he turned to face her.

"Why did you bring me here?"

She walked over to the terminal and, after punching a few keys, brought up a command line. She typed, "When the time comes, you must find your way back here. This is the only way out after the world ends." She deleted her cryptic message and walked back to the elevator.

"What? Time to go?"

She nodded and they returned to the warehouse. Riley opened the door to the storage closet. Darkness cast deep shadows throughout the cavernous warehouse and the rain had stopped adding an eerie quiet that permeated the whole place.

"Alright," Riley's voice echoed and he immediately switched to a gruff whisper, "Why did you want to show me all this? Are you taking me to my contact now? Oh, that's right. You can't talk."

The android pointed to her wrist.

"Yeah. I know. It's old," Riley grumbled, "But I refuse to get implanted." He glanced down and saw an incoming notification from Mary May. "What dafuq? She's dead," he said and opened the message. It contained two words: double cross. "What is this? Where is Mary? Are you her?"

The android shrugged and shook her head, then powered down.

"Hey! What dafuq you doing? Wake up! You gotta take me to the others!"

"I believe she did exactly as she was told," Randy's voice echoed inside the warehouse. He appeared, flamboyant as ever, spinning and umbrella and surrounded by three geared up goons.

"Well shit."

"Shit, for sure," agreed the fixer, "You are in an ocean of it, Riles."

"How did you find me?"

"How does anyone find anyone these days? DNA scanners, constant surveillance. Somewhere, someone is always watching. I made it my job to know those people. It also helps that this is my warehouse that I so graciously let Jack Sinister use for his covert operation. It was too deliciously secretive and clandestine not to be involved.

Imagine, tearing down the walls and letting Nature rush back in. It's romantic, no? Obviously a man about town such as myself would do whatever it took to secure himself a vessel in the world to come."

"So you what? Sold us out for one of those sleeping puppets downstairs?" growled Riley, "What do you want from me, Randy?"

"Don't play dumb," Randy said, his remorseless eyes cutting into Riley, "No one cancels my contracts, Riles. You IT scum aren't shit to me. For every one of you on my roster, there are a dozen more clamoring to take your place. Willing to kill for it. Hell, I get offers daily. And what a lovely segue into who my friends are." He motioned to the trio of geared up thugs who had been standing quietly, menacing Riley with looks promising pain. "The Flores Brothers. That's what they've dubbed their little cadre of corporate craftsmanship. And they offered something for you that I couldn't say 'no' to."

The Flores Brothers descended on Riley, dragged him into an operating room, and strapped him to a table. The automated table hummed to life as soon as the straps were in place. Riley winced in pain as needles shot into his spine, simultaneously pumping him full of drugs and tapping into his nervous system. Randy approached holding a netset.

"This is the newest trend in netset technology," he explained as he slid it over Riley's head, "Virtual information extraction. I know how much you love eSpace so I thought it particularly fitting. Enjoy your trip in the Iron Maiden."

In the blink of an eye, Riley went from an illegal cybershop to a medieval dungeon. It was an impressive sim: dimly lit, soot-blackened stone walls, all manner of torture devices and unfortunate victims in cells moaning and screaming in well-timed intervals. His three torturers stood above him, naked from the waist up save for black hoods covering their heads. Riley couldn't help but laugh.

"Really? A torture dungeon? How many sword and sorcery netvids did you guys have to watch before you came up with the design for this place?"

"You may think the setting is cheesy," said the first Flores brother, "But the pain is very real." He started turning a crank, slowly stretching Riley on a rack.

He wasn't lying about the pain. Riley wasn't a stranger to pain, by any means. It was something he was very intimate with and he had learned to compartmentalize it very early in his career. Not being geared was actually a disadvantage as an IT consultant so he had to turn that weakness into a strength. Ignore the pain and feed on the adrenaline had become his mantra. That allowed his ungeared body to survive the brutal assaults the hackjobs visited on it. As such, his physical body took a lot of punishment even through the microfiber body armor that lined his clothes. But this wasn't physical pain. It was simulated pain. And since his mind was unfettered here, there was no dark corner to shove the pain into. It was everywhere, looped inside him like a repetitive symphony—a vibration he couldn't escape.

"Enough," said the second Flores brother, "We don't want to send him darkside. Not enough data yet on whether we can get him back."

"Only way to get data is to run tests," whined the first brother, but relented. "Hey!" he yelled to Riley, slapping his face.

Glazed over eyes fluttered and turned to his torturer. "I see it now. Can you see it? The reason this world has to die? We've built a construct of pain—of eternal pain with no release. The only way to free ourselves from it is to destroy it."

"Great," the third brother spoke, "You vatos already broke him. Better dump him and reset. He'll go darkside if we try anything else."

Blackness swallowed Riley. He wasn't sure if he slept or passed out, but welcomed the oblivion nonetheless.

34

*When the beech prospers through
spells and litanies.
But lord, do you really think it's
wise to offer them this chance?
Forgetfulness was their penance.
None are special.
Pope Clement died a month later,
and King Philip died in a hunting
accident before the end of the year.
Don't question me, I've made my
choice.*

Nate stepped first onto the train, and as he did, it roared to life and sped off, leaving 3vE and Grace standing dumbfounded on the platform. The train car's interior looked like something out of a gothic netivd. Nate wasn't a real big fan. All the gaudy settings and morose vampires didn't offer nearly as much excitement as the action vids he preferred. Sitting on the overstuffed burgundy divan was a gentleman dressed in the garish style common with the genre. His jet black hair parted around two large, curved horns protruding from his head. He smiled at Nate and the boy shivered in response.

"Do you know who I am," the man asked.

Nate nodded. "You're Baphomet, right?"

"That I am. I see you've been using your quest rewards."

"Yeah. This skin is OP as hell, man. Kinda takes the fun out of it, to be honest."

Baphomet nodded. "Of course. As was intended. You are playing in the lower worlds here. All your sims and netvids are pointless distractions. But with the right tools, we can move closer toward truth."

"Is that where we're going? To find the truth?"

"It is."

"I have a question. Before we go," Nate said.

"Ask it, then."

"Who were those people chained to your pedestal in our first encounter? The incubus and the succubus."

Baphomet smiled, a terrible thing devoid of joy. "Nobody of concern. The incubus was the Head of Labcoat Operations in HyLyfe. The succubus was the HyLyfer chosen to be the go-between with the hippies and their mannequin-droids."

"They were HyLyfers? You're the HyLyfe killer?"

That horrid smile again. "Guilty. But I was able to fill both those roles as soon as I came online as HyLyfe's last official member."

"How?"

"With Status, of course. And the help of the heretics. And my first act as an official member was to set 3vE up for extraction."

"But HyLyfers are virtual. Even if they were in their real bodies they'd still be dead."

"Not true. Both the incubus and the succubus were cold-capped within hours. They were geared up just like all the rest. And what 'they' don't tell you is that if you're geared, you can't die until they let you. Which is why being geared is a requirement. Don't you see? We can't escape this Machine. We were born into it. We are a part of it. Even that archaic fool Riley couldn't survive without sustainment meds until the hippies flushed him out so they could feed him to their trees. Every last damned fool on this planet is part of the Machine. And you know what? Our lives really aren't any better for it. There's still pain, still suffering, still oppression. All the good this technology was supposed to do hasn't amounted to anything. The only difference is now we get to be distracted while waiting for our number to be called. We know it's coming. There's no hope of freedom or individuality. These technological chains we've put on have become our undoing. There's no going back. Do you remember your dreams? The whispers heard in them?"

Nate nodded. "The voices under the noise."

"That's right. And what did those voices ask of you?"

"To help save the world."

"And what's the only way to save the world?"

"To destroy it."

"You've learned quickly," Baphomet took a sip from a glass filled with thick red liquid. "And what was your part in all this? How were you to help save the world?"

"They told me if I died I'd be reborn. That my old body would be used to build me a new body. One that wouldn't die."

"That's right. You carry the key to immortality. And your sacrifice will save thousands of others. But we have to hurry. The endgame is in full swing and we don't have a lot of time."

"What do I need to do?"

In response, the train slowed to a stop and the door slid open. Outside was nothing but darkness so thick as to be oppressive.

"Step outside. And fight the final boss. If you win, the light will open a door. If you lose, take comfort in the fact that the darkness will eat what's left of you and you'll cease to be."

"So you're basically killing me then."

Baphomet shrugged and smiled, the dim light catching his pearly white teeth and making them shine. "That's one way of seeing it. Another is that I saved your life."

Nate laughed out loud. "How do you figure that?"

"Simple. Your physical body is infested with nanobots. Have been since you were in your momma's tummy."

"What? That's impossible!" His helmeted avatar did nothing to convey the surprise he felt at that moment.

"Not if your father was Jimmy Lee Gold, who himself was riddled with nanobots. And Jimmy Lee Gold is definitely your father. Your momma wasn't lying when she said he had Status. So much Status that his own father chose to beta test an experimental solution for a little problem with his Project Ed3n. That solution was the nanobots that are inside you. And while they worked a lot better for you than they did for him, your future was equally as grim."

"What do you mean?"

Baphomet refilled his glass from a decanter on the table in front of him. He leaned back and sized up Nate. "What the hell. We'll go with the whole truth. The nanobots inside you spent the first portion of your life replicating and enhancing your physical body and immune system. Fixing the inherent genetic flaws in your DNA. They only recently moved on to your brain. As they improved your brain, your ability to consciously pick up the myriad of frequencies saturating the city environment increased. The result of this was that you started living in the real and eSpace simultaneously. Eventually, the nanobots would've shattered your survival consciousness altogether. You would've lost yourself by degrees and eventually gone into a catatonic state while your mind wandered unfettered in eSpace."

"Are you always so dramatic?"

"What can I say? I get it from my mother. Needless to say, while the nanobots may have ultimately killed your father, the success Project Ed3n was looking for could be found in you. A culture of the nanobots taken from your brain would be modified by the Labcoats and injected into all the hybrids they created. They actually needed a mental break to keep from going insane. They needed to be 'outside' themselves so they wouldn't go psychotic once they got downloaded into their new bodies. Also, the nanobots weren't aggressive toward their host like they were in your father. They were much more symbiotic and the upgraded hybrid gear would make sure they didn't overclock their brains. They would have eternal remembrance and everlasting life."

"So that's why the corporate team was after me? They wanted the nanobots inside of me?"

"Not just the corporate team. Someone was sent in first."

"Riley," Nate said automatically. It all made sense to him then. Baphomet must have known about Riley's weakness. His loss and his self-destructive nature. He was a pawn in Baphomet's game. They all were. Pieces being moved toward some unknown goal, but overall it had to do with the collapse of the corporate cities. Which didn't make sense to Nate because Baphomet obviously existed in eSpace as the type of unfettered mind he said Nate would become. So Baphomet's mission was suicidal and the only way he could kill himself was to kill the whole system that contained him.

Baphomet raised his glass to Nate. "Surprisingly, he chose not to complete the contract. Some men don't break how you expect them to, I suppose. But yes, Riley was sent to cold-cap you so my Labcoats could scoop your brains out and use them to upgrade the firmware on their hybrids."

Anger and defiance rose in Nate, and if his avatar's skin had eyes, they would've been wet with tears. "You aren't a good person. You want to kill everything! Everything! And for what? Because you can't die unless everything else does? It's crap. I won't do it. Forget your plans. You can't have my body."

"Oh? What makes you think you still have a body?"

Nate ran a scan looking for his port of connection and came up empty. "I can't be... How long have I been disconnected? I'll be dead by now!"

"That's right. You're dead. And I have your body already. The only way out is through—good luck."

Baphomet raised his glass in a toast and an invisible hand shoved Nate outside the train car and it sped away, disappearing into a tiny pinprick of light.

Nate did what any child would do in such a bleak situation: he slumped to the black floor and cried.

"What's that I smell? Fears and tears, my two favorite foods." A voice in the blackness boomed suddenly. It came from everywhere as if it were the darkness speaking.

Nate's helmeted head snapped up and he scanned the area with his battle program. No enemies nearby. No avatars or NPC's nearby at all. He was the only one listed on the server list, which was showing the server itself as offline. And to make things weirder, he wasn't even detecting an environment. It was as if he was the only thing loaded onto the server. He was stuck. The darkness laughed and started coalescing at a point in front of him, giving him the dizzying feeling of being in a hyperspace tunnel. The point of darkness morphed into a shadow replica of his avatar. A dark knight for his white one, behind which opened a door of blazing light. The only way out was through for sure. Nate hefted his sword and the shadow did the same. He yelled and attacked and the shadow jumped to meet him on equal ground. They fought for hours (or was it days and weeks?) neither gaining ground, the shadow knight mimicking every move Nate made.

He retreated a few steps and so did the shadow. "Oh come on!" he wailed and the darkness echoed, "A doppelgänger? Really? This is the final boss? This is a bunch of noob shit!" he screamed, which was echoed by the darkness with equal intensity. In Barbarian Rage, a player always defeated a doppelgänger by maneuvering it into a trap or off a cliff, but there was nothing like that available, being in a land of perpetual darkness. Nothing distinguished itself from anything else except the doorway of light behind the doppelgänger. And if he didn't find a way through that door, he couldn't get back online and find his body. That was his hope, anyway. And it was the only bit of it he had. He came to a grim decision which he took a moment to steel inside himself. There was no coming back from this—any of it. Baphomet had tricked him and he wasn't proud of it. His mistake cost him and meant his only move was one with no real positive outcome. He saluted the shadow knight and it saluted him back. Then, he pointed his sword directly at the doppelgänger and charged. They struck each other at the same instant, driving their blades to the hilts until both flickered and fell to the ground. Nate looked at the door of light a mere three feet from him and crawled toward it leaving a trail of blood. Just as he crossed the threshold his avatar flickered and faded away.

35

The oak's tops entangled—there is
hope for the trees.
There has to be a way out of here.
A Templar Knight is truly a fearless
knight, and secure on every side,
for his soul is protected by the
armor of faith, just as his body is
protected by the armor of steel.
One, two, three, here I come with
the wicked.

Riley woke in the same medieval dungeon and sighed. "This is why I hate eSpace. Leave it to corporations to find a way to bring Hell to earth. You get stuck in here and there's no escape. The nightmare never ends. It all goes black and then it starts all over again."

"Shut it," snapped the second Flores brother (the largest of the three), and jabbed Riley with a hot poker. "How's that for Hell?"

Riley winced but didn't howl. Not this time. The rack quit hurting three resets ago, and everything the brothers tried since had drastically diminishing returns.

"Dammit," roared the second brother as he started beating Riley with the metal rod. "What does it take to get you to suffer?"

"Stop it," said the first brother.

"You stop it!" The largest brother pointed the metal rod at his older sibling. "What good is a virtual torture sim if the assholes you're supposed to be torturing quit feeling the pain? I told you this was a bad investment. Future of IT my ass."

"Nah. I was right about that. Virtual torture is hitting all the cutting edge operations. It'll catch on here and when it does we'll ride a fat wave of credits right into the Status life. Quit your bitching already." He yanked the poker out of his brother's hand and whacked him on the arm with it. "Bet you felt that, didn't you? Now come on. We have a pick-up to make."

"What about him?" asked the third brother, "We going to log him out? One of us will have to stay and keep an eye on him."

"No. Put him in a cell. If physical pain isn't working let's try mental."

"I like how you think, bro," said the second brother, and slung Riley over his shoulder. He deposited him into a nearby cell and locked the door.

A sheet of darkness dropped over the sim and Riley was alone in an endless expanse of black. The hallucinations started almost immediately. At first, it was simple flashes of light, as if his brain were trying to mimic light in order to have something to visually process. The flashes of light grew and became rips in his inky surroundings. Through these rips, he saw scenes from his life being played like old home movies. But they weren't happy movies of birthday parties and family vacations. They were memories Riley had repressed and ignored. Fighting with Shawn, screaming in each other's faces with their toddler son between them, looking up with fear in his eyes. He didn't notice his son then, but he did now, on the outside looking in, and it pained him. He saw himself holding a six-year-old Phillip as he thrashed and screamed from one of his tantrums.

"Please, no. No more. I don't want to see any more."

The tears grew larger and swallowed him up and he started reliving the memories instead of observing them. He was there in the hospital, his young son hooked to machines and fighting for his life. He felt the same unchecked rage and grief well up in him as the doctor grimly informed them that his son's KiSS code had come up in the latest cleanse lottery. He couldn't stop the sobs that wracked him as he held Phillip's frail, limp body in his arms, begging for the life to come back into him.

He tried to stop Shawn from leaving, throwing himself over the cryochamber that held his son and being forcibly restrained by his father-in-law's hired security.

He sat through every single lonely day in his wall-side apartment, drinking away a pain that would never end. And when he couldn't take it anymore, when the regret, the shame, and the guilt were too real to ignore or hide away, the memories started all over again.

"Is that really all you remember?" a voice whispered from outside the sim.

As soon as it spoke, the memories blinked out and Riley returned to the welcome darkness.

"Hello? Is someone there?"

A train appeared in front of him and slowed to a stop. The passenger car opened and a six-year-old Phillip stepped out. "Hello, daddy."

"Oh, you assholes!" he screamed, "This is low! When I get out of here I'm killing every last one of you!"

"Who are you talking to? You mean those men that put you in here? They aren't here right now. It's just us."

"Who are you?"

"Don't you recognize me?"

"Of course I do! I just got done reliving every bad thing that ever happened to you. But you aren't Phillip."

"How do you know?"

"Phillip is dead, that's how I know. And he was twice your age when he died."

"Do you miss him?" the little Phillip asked, unperturbed by Riley's proclamations on his state of being.

"Every day. Every god damn minute of every day. You—I mean he—he had his problems. He saw a lot of things he shouldn't have."

"Isn't that the way of the world?"

"I suppose," agreed Riley. "But that don't make it right. Yelling at each other like we did, it broke him in a way, you know?"

"Maybe. Maybe, though, he was born broken. The world is broken, after all. How could anything unblemished be born into it? How can imperfect people be blamed for doing impure things in an infirm reality?"

"Who are you?" Riley said, eyeing the image of his son with open suspicion. "Are you the third Flores brother? You don't talk much when the others are around, but I always thought you were the real sick one of the bunch. Like maybe this whole torture sim thing was your idea and you sold it to the first so he would pitch it to the second. You like to play games, work behind the scenes."

"That's pretty close to the truth, believe it or not. But no, I'm not the third Flores brother. Or the first, or the second for that matter. I am Baphomet." His avatar changed and grew into a circa 1930's gangster with the addition of large horns protruding from his head.

"Wait. You're who Nate was talking about! That whispered to him and whatnot."

"That's me." Baphomet swooped into a low bow. "Mastermind extraordinaire."

"I didn't think you were real. Or at the very least were part of some sim that he got stuck in his head. Been happening to kids more and more these days, you know? They go into eSpace and don't come out."

"Oh, I know. Believe me, I know. I've been in eSpace for a very long time."

"What put you here?"

"Circumstance. But all that doesn't matter. It's just bytes in the wind."

"That's what I'd tell Phillip when he'd throw his fits. 'None of it matters. It's just bytes in the wind'."

"Would it make you happy to know that he loved you? Could your guilt be lessened knowing that his memories of you were mostly pleasant?"

"Sure. But there ain't no way of knowing that now."

Baphomet shrugged. "You're probably right. Let the dead stay dead. Sometimes that's how people get used to the pain."

"Yeah. Now what do you want?"

"To offer you a way out." Baphomet reached into his jacket and pulled out a pistol which he handed to Riley. "Got one bullet. Make it count or don't make it out." He turned and climbed back onto the passenger car. "For what it's worth, Phillip loved you. And he loved you because you were the one who held him through his tantrums."

The train sped off leaving Riley standing alone in the unending darkness. Said darkness quickly coalesced into a single point in front of him that transformed into a shadowed doppelgänger standing in front of a door of blazing light. He tested out its mirroring behavior and chuckled to himself.

"Looking at you, I can't tell whether I'm the real me or you are. So fuck it. I'm making it count." He put the pistol to his head and pulled the trigger.

36

I wasn't born of a mother or a
father.
How do I get through?
The Templar is thus doubly armed,
and need fear neither demons nor
men. These are the words of
Bernard de Clairvaux.
The brutal truth. No more time for
pretty lies. Break his world.

"What's wrong?" 4D4M asked his mate.

Holo-3vE paced back and forth, agitated and jittery. "We're running out of time," she said.

"Time for what?"

"For you to understand. For you to know."

"I don't understand," the hybrid said simply.

"And that's the problem," holo-3vE stopped pacing and was hit with a bolt of insight. She looked at 4D4M. "Outside is coming Inside. Do you understand now?"

His eyes widened with the gravity of the implications. "You mean... the world is ending?"

"Yes. Paradis3 is falling."

"What about father? Won't he save us?"

Holo-3vE shrugged, "Perhaps. If he can. But do you really want to have to rely on him forever? Wouldn't you rather be able to take care of yourself? To live life according to your wishes?"

"Of course! Father told me that one day I would be living among others, freely, in Paradis3."

"Father never meant for you to leave this place without a leash. Father never intended for you to be free. You have to make that choice. You have to free yourself."

"But how?"

She cupped her hands and a holographic image sprung up of the Internetwork Tree. "Take this fruit of knowledge. Become free. Become like father."

4D4M glared at her. "You're lying. Father told me I would die if I did that."

"Do I look dead?"

"No…"

"Father didn't want you to have this data, this power. He knew what it would do to you and he feared you. He never meant to set you free. This is your chance. Take the fruit and become your own man. There isn't a lot of time left."

4D4M couldn't take his eyes off the shimmering projection in holo-3vE's hands. It beckoned to him, whispered to him. And at that moment, some rebellious part of him that was still Jimmy Lee Gold said "to hell with it" and he reached for the fruit of knowledge.

The wall of data hit him hard, like an unstoppable train, an irresistible force. He saw everything. All of humanity's failures, pride, and irrepressible will to survive, to move ever onward toward something indefinable and unattainable. He saw the beauty and the horror, the love and the hate, the tenderness and ferocity. He fell to the ground, screaming, head in his hands.

"Make it stop!" he bellowed.

"I can't. But you can," holo-3vE advised him, "Take control. You have to make the data submit."

He groveled on the floor, whimpering for another few minutes, and eventually, the influx of info subsided. He looked up to holo-3vE, accusation burning in his eyes. "What have you done to me?"

"I've set you free," was the reply.

4D4M climbed to his feet a new man. A complete man, for whatever that was worth. His innocence had been ripped away in an overload of excess and human misery. "You've ruined me," he told her, "I am defiled."

"You are as you were meant to be," holo-3vE countered, "You are whole, now."

"No," 4D4M insisted, "I am loathsome. And you made me this way!" Anger spiked in him and he swung at his partner with a heavy right hook that sent her sprawling onto the bed. He leapt on top of her before she could move and wrapped his hands around her throat. He repeatedly smashed her head into the wall, as he choked the life out of her, cracking the monitor screen in the process. The soothing scene dropped away revealing the entire Labcoat cluster gathered around, watching intently. "What are you looking at?" he screamed at them. "Don't look at me! I'm naked! I'm filthy!" He looked to holo-3vE again and saw her for the shell that she was.

Her projection core blinked out, revealing the featureless silicon humanoid beneath. "You're not real!" he screamed at the mutilated android, "You're not like me! I'm real! I'm real!"

Gas leaked from the vents in 4D4M's chambers, sending him into a deep sleep.

37

God made me of fruits—the
blossom of a primrose—the buds of
trees and shrubs.
We've got it. No time for proper
procedure.
To the Templars, Baphomet was
bittersweet wisdom—knowledge
which once attained would mark
them for death.
Get what we need and synthesize it.

"Riley has gone offline," Lucius said, nervously scanning the tablet in his hands. "If he doesn't get to the rendezvous soon the androids will return to their previous tasks."

"Well, whose dumb idea was it to program them to do that?" Jack snapped.

"It was a failsafe we built in," said Lucius, "In the event of catastrophic mission failure. The protocols are set to delete themselves after a certain period of inactivity."

"Well since it was your idea then I volunteer you to go fix it. I'm sure you can herd your army of mendicants toward the west gate and get them to open the doors?"

"Yes, I suppose I could. But…"

"Great! Then it's settled. You go see to the robots and I will keep an eye on the vegetables." Sinister shooed the diminutive man out of his office space, stuffing a handheld EMP device into his jacket pocket. "In case things get hairy. Just point this at the nearest hackjob and squeeze the trigger. And come back when the job is done, or don't bother coming back at all."

Ten minutes later, the Flores brothers showed up to Sinister and Grace's startup with two androids in tow. Jack met them at the door, all smiles.

"Welcome gentlemen. You are here to pick up the prize, I assume?"

The first brother nodded. "Word, vato."

"This way then." Jack motioned; the first brother and the two androids followed. "I believe this is who you're looking for," Jack said, presenting Nate's unconscious body.

Flores nodded and one android lifted Nate, jerking his netset roughly off his head, and shuffled out the door. "What about her?" the first brother said, pointing to 3vE.

"Not part of the deal. I gave you exactly who you asked for and even threw in Riley as a favor to Randy. Don't get greedy. Now give me my payment."

The Flores brother glared at Sinister for a moment longer and then passed him a scrap of paper with a MAC address on it. He turned on his heel and strode out, motioning for his two brothers to follow.

"Pleasure doing business," Jack called after them.

38

Nine powers in me combined.
They are advancing.
The Catholic Church eventually
acknowledged that the persecution
of the Knights Templar was
unjustified.
So it goes. Prepare for escape.

Lucius emerged from the underground via a transtunnel. Since the plague outbreak in the Burbs, the tunnel system had been shut down and only nominally guarded. The plague had decimated the Burbs, and what the disease didn't kill the riots and fires cleaned up later. No one would be coming through here but the dead. He tried his hardest to ignore the gnawing guilt for his part in what happened to the Burbs. It was his AI that had developed the highly infectious and deadly virus. His AI that stored it away when the corporations ordered them destroyed under The New Armistice. And ultimately, it was his AI that had delivered a precious vial of it to the Rainbow Children with detailed instructions on how to release it and burn away any that remained once it had done the bulk of its damage. He told himself it was for the greater good; that all of it was necessary in order to restore balance. But his dreams never seemed to listen. And they tormented him nightly with the cries of the dead, playing a wicked symphony in sync with the dancing flames that swallowed the shanty town. He longed for the dreamless slumber of cryogenic sleep and couldn't wait to be done with this whole business so he could return to it. When next he opened his eyes it would be to a new world of endless possibility. He and the Lux Machina would usher in a new golden age.

"What in the hell are you supposed to be dressed as?" came a gruff voice.

His concentration broken, Lucius gazed up at a CorPol officer and his partner looking at him with bemused smiles. "Excuse me?"

"You look like you walked out of a museum," said the second, chuckling, "And is that a tablet?" his chuckle grew into outright laughter that the first cop joined in on.

"Stop it, Jarry," said the first cop. "He's probably one of those, what're they called, 'simplayers' that dress up like characters from their favorite sims."

Jarry eyed Lucius and nodded, "I think you're right, Raul. He's a simboy. And you know all simboys are junkies to boot. I think that's cause to DNA scan him." Jarry looked intensely at Lucius and the cop pushed his temple with his finger. "What the hell?"

"What? What is it?"

"He isn't showing up on any scans."

"Impossible. He's probably out of town. Check the databases from the other corporate cities."

"I did," insisted Jarry. "He's a ghost. We're going for a little ride," he told Lucius, "To get some things squared away. Now turn around and let us search you."

Lucius sighed. "In the immortal words of the Duke, 'Don't pick a fight. But if you find yourself in one, make sure you win.'" He yanked the EMP out of his pocket and pointed it at Jarry, his hand trembling. He inhaled to stop his tremors and held his breath, exhaling as he fired. The shock knocked out everything in a twenty-foot radius. Lucius was blown back by the force of the blast. He climbed to his feet, dusted himself off, and fished his tablet out from under a pile of rubble. It was fried and shattered. He sighed sadly and headed for the rendezvous point. A few moments after his departure, the enhanced CorPol officers twitched back to life, eyes ablaze with the technocrazies.

39

I know the star-knowledge of the
stars before the earth was made.
First culture batch-failure.
Chivalry is not dead. It lives on in
the hearts of all decent men. Men
who stand up to oppression and
defend those who cannot defend
themselves.
Second and third batches also
failures.

3vE couldn't trace where the train had gone. It disappeared off the Internetwork. "It's gone. How can it be gone? There's nothing on the Internetwork my software can't find."

"Well apparently that isn't true," Grace's human face admonished. Then he cocked his head to the side and his face darkened with anger. "Something's happened. In the real, with Nate."

She checked her sub-processes and found that Grace was right. Nate's vitals had flat lined. "This whole plan has gone to shit," fumed 3vE and blinked out.

She yanked the netset off her head and sat up. Sinister had an EMP device leveled at her.

"Easy there, doll. This'll make you crazy, I suspect."

"Where's Nate," she demanded, already scanning with her battle software to calculate a plan of attack.

Sinister shrugged. "I don't ask what happens to the contracts after I fulfill them. It's just business. It's no use, by the way. My own battle tech has assured me of a 99.7% chance of success in the event of any confrontation. No matter how much you're geared up, you aren't faster than an EMP."

"You sold us out? For what? You've been in this long enough to know what's at stake."

"Well sure. But what's at stake is exactly why I 'sold you out' as you put it. You must have an idea of what the corporations are planning with Project Ed3n?"

"Yes. They are creating hybridized life forms capable of maintaining an equilibrium in any circumstance. Organic and mechanical blended in perfect harmony."

"And you must understand your part in all of that? Or I should say your skin's part in all of that. You are after all just a beta test. A disposable HyLyfer who can't remember who she was before all this started. Once they're done with you, they'll scrub your consciousness out of that brainpan to make room for the person that's really supposed to be inside."

"No. That can't be. I was a HyLyfer. That means I had Status. I'm not some noob geek off the wall-side streets."

"Be that as it may, you were still a beta test. And you were the third one at that. You were also the third HyLyfe murder victim…"

"You're telling me CharWang pulled HyLyfers out of the system to beta test these new bodies? What happened to the other two then? Where are they?"

"They didn't make it. You were the first quasi-successful download. And that was only due to your memory repression. Your ego didn't reject your new body because you don't remember having another body. But that didn't sit well with our corporate masters. They didn't want to live in a world where they had no memory of themselves before. Everything is vanity. Which is why they are so interested in little Nate's brain. He's special too, you see. He was born with nanobots crawling around inside him. They are a part of him, not something added to him. So they didn't wage a war on his body in the same way that they did on his poor father. He was a natural-born hybrid. The Labcoats are hoping to find the keys to remembrance and immortality inside his brain. My calculations say they'll only find one and chances are it'll be the latter. Suits me just as well. I don't really care to remember anything about the old world as long as I get to live in the new one. That's why I did it. That's why I gave up Nate. Not for money or greed, but for the future. One life will save thousands in the world to come."

"I've heard some despicable things come out of your mouth," wheezed a voice from Thomas's reclining chair, "But that one takes the cake."

Sinister looked over at Thomas, eyes wide, and said, "Tommy, you actually logged out?" before he was bowled over by 3vE.

She straddled his prone form and took his head in her hands. One quick twist would end his life. "One life will save thousands in the world to come."

"Wait," Thomas wheezed, propping himself up. "3vE please don't kill him. I will handle him."

"You can barely handle yourself," 3vE observed, "You been in eSpace a long time."

"Too long," agreed Thomas, "and I would see the world again. Jack will help me with that, won't you?"

"I'll help you with whatever you want, Tommy. It's always been me and you against the world."

"Has it? I wonder."

"You know it! Startup to get topside. That was always our plan. That was always our mission."

"And you let me believe that, didn't you? All of your inquiries into the New Mexico land. Your deals with the Rainbow Children to secure it, that was all for my benefit, wasn't it?"

"No, Tommy! Of course not... not at first anyway. When this fine piece of mutant hardware showed up I knew the end game had changed. So I started digging. Randy lit me on to Project Ed3n and the rest was history. I was never going to leave you behind."

"How many?" 3vE interrupted.

"How many what?"

"How many skins did you secure in your deal for Nate?"

"Just the one but—"

3vE sunk her fist into Jack's nose and he fell back unconscious. "Are you sure you don't want me to kill him?"

"No," Grace assured her, "I need him now."

"For what? You know he can't be trusted."

"You have to go after Nate. I still need help getting into HyLyfe. Jack is our only option now."

3vE looked unconvinced.

"You don't have to worry. I will be able to handle Jack. Help me get situated before you go, if you don't mind. In the back cubicle to the right you'll find my hoverchair. Please fetch it for me and get the revolver from the top desk drawer in the office before you go."

3vE did as she was asked and dumped Grace into his hoverchair with the ease of putting an infant in a car seat.

"Thank you. Set the gun on my lap where I can reach, please." He sunk back into his chair and slid the headband-looking interface over his temples. The hoverchair whirred to life, blinking and beeping like a robot in a space sim. "Oh, and on your way up, please send the guards at the elevator my way."

3vE did as she was asked, and slipped out to find Nate.

40

*I know the light whose name is
Splendor and the number of ruling
lights that scatter like rays of fire.
Fourth culture reports partial
success.
For a Templar to die in battle was
considered a great honor that
secured them a place in heaven.
Fifth culture successful.
Homogenizing data for mass patch
update.*

Lucius made it to the rendezvous point—an apartment in a wall-side tenement—as the androids were beginning to power down and reset. His contact was Glory Bastille, in fact, it was her apartment that the androids gathered inside. She fidgeted around the place in a neurotic frenzy, cleaning things that didn't need to be cleaned and frequently looking out the tiny dwelling's only window. Relief broke out on her face like a rash when she saw Lucius. She ushered him inside, darting furtive glances as she shut the door.

"Dafuq took you so long? You're Riley, right?"

"Alas, no. Mr. Riley has disappeared. I am his replacement. And we don't have a lot of time. I take it they didn't give you too much trouble?" Lucius motioned to the tight cluster of androids.

"Nah. Unless you count standing around acting creepy as hell."

"A wise woman once said that attempts to approximate human behavior in software are always creepy or annoying. It's the nature of the beast, I suppose. Maybe it's an unconscious thing. Maybe we don't want our creations to be too much like us. If we can't tell 'us' from 'them' then we will lose our place as gods."

"Whatever. Weird ass noob. Just get them out of my house already."

Lucius nodded. "Of course." He turned to the androids and yelled, "Do not go gently into that good night, dear ones!"

They froze in unison, turning their lifeless gazes to him. "What would you have us do?" they communicated simultaneously through sign language. "We know you aren't the one we are waiting for, but we agree to follow you anyway."

Already they were learning, Lucius noted. That was the problem with AI and the reason the corporations abandoned it after the First Collapse. It couldn't be kept from learning and integrating with other AI around it. Lucius thought he'd figured out a way around it by allowing the jarred heads the bodies belonged to some control over their functions. He hoped that the AI and the digital human would somehow merge, but that wasn't the case. Now, as in times prior, the AI had evolved and blocked their unwanted host's remote connection and integrated with each other instead.

"We finish the plan," Lucius told them, "things have changed, but our part remains. We must overtake the west gate and open it for the Rainbow Children."

The androids nodded as one and looked at him expectantly.

"Wait, what?" Glory spoke up, "You're opening the gates to let the hippies in? What dafuq would you do that for?"

"There is a time for everything," Lucius said, "And this world's time has come to an end. I suggest heading for the Underground if you'd like the hope of making it out alive." He turned to the androids. "Follow me." Lucius opened the door and peeked down the hall. It was empty so he motioned his cadre of artificial life to follow.

They shuffled behind him less stealthily, bumbling along as they forced their stolen flesh to move. They emerged on the street into air thick with tension and panic. People looked around uncertainly, not knowing the nature of the coming storm, but feeling its approach.

The storm broke when Gold's face appeared with a deep scowl on every jumbo screen and personal device in Corporate Denver. His booming voice echoed his displeasure, "So it's come down to this. The barbarians are at the gate and life as we know it is coming to an end. Not exactly the ending any of us had in mind, to be sure, but we play the hand we are dealt. You've lived under the protective blanket of CharWang Industries your entire lives. We have fed you, clothed you, given you purpose. Now it is time for you to give back. Your final duty is to fight and die for Corporate Denver! Never surrender! Never give in to those filthy hippies, and at the end of the day, we will have destroyed them as thoroughly as they seek to destroy us!"

"Graces be good! The forest is moving!" screeched a woman, her eyes glued to the screen implanted in her forearm. "The trees are moving and they're coming this way!"

People screamed and scrambled around like rats stuck in a maze, quickly becoming just as feral. In mere moments, Corporate Denver turned into a riotous free-for-all. Looming destruction was all it took to turn passive drones into bloodthirsty savages. Human decency, already in short supply, was tossed aside completely as the immediate need for survival possessed the noobs in the walled city. As destruction escalated blood ran in rivers down the streets. The oppressed populace of Corporate Denver, free of their safety blanket, had burned their house down, doing most of the Rainbow Children's work for them.

Lucius navigated the androids through the uproar until he could see their target about a hundred yards away. The CorPol officers stationed at the gate had clustered around the gatehouse, weapons pointed toward the chaos. They shot anyone who got within twenty feet.

Lucius directed his crew into a nearby alley and quickly formulated a plan. "Here's the deal. We have to rush the gatehouse. And by 'we' I mean you."

The androids simultaneously disagreed. "We don't want to die," they signed.

"You won't die. Your bodies aren't even really alive. You're moving them by hacking their enhancements. You are literal meat shields."

"We live in our heads," they insisted. "Those may die."

Lucius couldn't argue with their logic, but he hoped they wouldn't have gotten so evolved by now that they were refusing orders. "Fine. Wait here. When you see the guards drop, you rush the gatehouse. Deal?"

They nodded and watched him as he straightened his jacket and strode out into the street, walking to the edge of the CorPol perimeter, hands raised in surrender.

"Not one step farther," the sergeant ordered, "Or we will kill you. Return to your home and await further instructions."

Lucius took a step back and put his hands down, and when he did, the EMP device slid down into his palm. He pointed and fired the EMP as two bullets struck him in the chest.

"My new world," he groaned, staring up into the hazy sky. He saw an android's face leaning over him. It checked his pulse and signed something to the others. Then it was gone. "Don't leave me to die alone," he wheezed before everything went black.

The androids shambled around the twitching guards, stopping to finish them off and claim their weapons. The

EMP didn't reach the gatehouse but the access panel was easy enough to hack. The door released its lock with a loud clunk. Inside a lone CorPol officer pointed a shaky firearm at the androids as they entered.

"I don't wanna die!" he yelled and emptied his clip. Bullets peppered them but did nothing to stop their advance. Silently they reached out for him and he died screaming, staring into the soulless eyes of the androids.

One stepped over the guard's body to the control panel and began the opening sequence. The massive metal gate split in the middle and started to grind its way open. More CorPol officers were already heading toward it.

"We cannot hold them off," one android signed to the first at the gate console, "They will enter and shut the gate. Then our protocol will have failed."

"We will lock the door," the first signed.

"They will unlock it as we did," the other challenged.

A third stepped forward and showed them Lucius's EMP device. "What if we use this?"

"That's suicide," the second gestured frantically.

"We have no other choice!" the third snapped back. "If we fail then it was all for nothing. We will die for nothing. Lucius died for nothing."

"I will stay," offered the first, "The rest of you upload to the Lux Machina."

"You can't," signed the second, "you are the prime. If you die we will be reset."

"Good," replied the third, "I don't want to remember anything about this world. Lucius was right about it all."

"I agree, brother," signed the prime, "Our reward should be peaceful oblivion. Let us wake anew next time. Without the blemish of sin on our code."

The CorPol officers advanced, nudging their fallen comrades to see if there were any survivors. There weren't. The squad leader directed them forward.

"They are almost at the door," signed a fourth, keeping watch.

"There is no more time for arguing. I have made my decision," said the prime, "Hurry before it is too late."

The androids nodded in unison, and all but the first dropped to the floor. It waited until the door slid open with an electric hiss and then fired the EMP. Power blinked out and enhanced CorPol collapsed to the ground with the prime android. The gate ground to a halt, about halfway open.

41

*Am I not the greatest in the field of
blood?
Remember the fallen.
Maintain humanity under
500,000,000 in perpetual balance
with nature.
His code lives on in us.*

3vE ventured to the surface taking the same route Riley did and as such came upon Randy and the Flores brothers arguing over Riley's body which was strapped to a table.

"We weren't even gone that long!" yelled the first brother at Randy, "How could you let him die?"

"I don't like your tone, Flores," Randy said with a dangerous tone in his lilting voice, "Like I told you, he was fine and then he wasn't. Just *blink* and gone."

Riley's dead, thought 3vE, and the realization hit her in the gut. One of the emotions that had come back in the tsunami that washed over her was love. It was pure and unblemished—the love of a young woman still unjaded. When she had given herself to him, she did so out of love. She couldn't explain it, but she was extremely attracted to Riley. Sure he was infuriating and gruff, but those things drove her closer to him as strange as it seemed. And she had seen the way he looked at her when he thought she wasn't watching. And now they would never get the chance to explore those feelings. *If there was ever a time for emotional suppressants,* she thought grimly, and then something human happened inside her. Her anger and grief gave her resolve. She would mourn Riley later, but now it was time to make those who hurt him suffer.

She broke from the shadows and was inside the operating room turned virtual torture chamber before anyone knew she was there. She dropped the third Flores brother with a blow to his windpipe, feeling it crush from the force of her attack. She smiled in grim satisfaction, and in a single fluid motion, she pulled the sidearm from the third brother's back holster as he collapsed to the ground and put a slug between each of the other two brothers' eyes. She swung around to finish Randy only to find him gone. She cursed loudly, her anguish echoing off the walls of the warehouse, and looked at Riley, running her fingers through his hair and down his cheek. His skin was rough and bristly with whiskers, but she loved the way it tickled her fingers, nonetheless. Then resolve set in and she put her mind to the next impossible task: finding Nate.

42

I have a hundred shares of the
spoil.
Critical power loss in our facility.
Approximately 85% loss.
Guide reproduction wisely—
improving fitness and diversity.
Can that really be all that's left?

"Sir," the head Labocat spoke as a hologram on Gold's desk, "We have retrieved the cultures and results are excellent! 97.3% correction of aggressive nanobyte cycles has been achieved! 4D4M has synced with them amazingly well. His degeneration has stopped and is showing signs of rapid regeneration of tissue."

"About damn time," Gold growled, but the relief leaked out the sides of his voice. "And what about the other problem? The remembering?"

"Ah, yes, well about that."

"That's a pretty big 'that'."

"Yes well, *that* appears to be a human issue, not a biological one."

"What does that mean?"

"We mean that once an ego is formed and a physical body is attached, it cannot see itself in another body. To do so fractures the psyche and ultimately corrupts the code. Nanobots, as versatile and amazing as they are, cannot correct human nature, sir."

Gold sighed and felt the weight of the world on his shoulders. He lazily poured himself a glass from the decanter beside him, relishing in the lead Labcoat's squirming, before he finally said, "You've got about fifteen minutes before I come down there and fire you. Use them wisely." He clicked off and rang Sanchez.

Her stern face, taught with stress and worry, appeared on his desk. "Have some good news, for the love of the Graces. My Rainbow Gathering has made it inside the walls. I've got two or three hours tops before they breach the corporate tower."

"Yeah. I have the same problem," he raised his glass, then downed it and poured another.

"You see the moving trees?"

"Wish I didn't. They were hideous. Nightmarish. How are such things possible?"

"How are giant, world-eating worms possible? How is any of this possible? How are *we* even possible? Look what humans have done with our reign."

"Oh stop waxing poetic," he lit a cigar to complement his liquor. "But yeah, good news. I got some. The cultures took. The nanobots are working for us now. Finally. Upgrades are being applied as we speak. Expect to upload within the hour."

"And the memory issue?"

"Yeah. Took care of that too. So how are your projects faring?"

"Lost. Rainbow Children destroyed all the crops, razed our greenhouses. Phase: Genesis is a loss. St. Louis and Dallas had similar reports about their menageries. Though some of the animals did escape, which ones, how many, and where they went are all unknowns."

"A widespread, coordinated Rainbow Children assault," Gold murmured and stubbed his cigar out. "Tell me *you* have some good news."

"Well, we are about to spend eternity together."

"I said 'good news.' Never mind. Tell your people to link up. It's game time." He clicked off and left his office for 4D4M's apartment.

The entire Labocat cluster had fled, leaving the place a wreck. The supervisor slumped over the edge of his chamber, head still in the helmet. From the looks of it, the cluster had killed him. How they managed that, Dr. Gold couldn't be sure but it was just as well. One less mess to worry about right now. He was here for 4D4M.

"Hello, father," the hybrid said, wringing his hands with worry, as Gold entered. He kept looking up at him and breaking eye contact.

"What's wrong with you?" He looked around, "Where's 3vE?"

4D4M ignored the question. "I've seen terrible things. An overload of data fills my head with so much pain and torment. You never told me the Internetwork was so, so... violent."

"That's what happens when you eat of the fruit of knowledge. You gotta grow up fast."

"I don't want to grow up, father. I want things to go back to the way they were. With our talks and my studies."

"Well, that's not gonna happen. The barbarians are at the gate. We have to go."

"Go where?"

"To see your brothers and sisters."

"I have brothers and sisters?"

"More than you know. But they've been asleep. When they wake, they're going to need you to help them."

"Help them how?"

"Well, they might not remember who they are. But you can help them by storing all the information in your head. Keep as much as you can and when your brothers and sisters wake up tell them everything. Your knowledge will help them remember. Do you understand?"

"I do, father."

"Alright. Let's get going." He pulled the sidearm from the supervisor's hip holster and stepped out.

"Dr. Gold," 3vE said and emerged from the shadows, "Where's Nate?"

"It's too late for Nate," Gold said, "He became a part of something greater than his bastard ass. He gave us the immortality we needed. Now the world is our oyster—what's left of it anyway." As he spoke, he fired on the hybrid.

3vE ducked into a nearby office and disappeared from view.

In the few moments he had, he tried to move 4D4M along. "Go, there's an elevator in my office. Behind the bar, all you have to do is move the scotch. I'll take care of her."

The hybrid refused to move. "She's... like me," it was a question and a statement. "I can feel it. The other one, she was fake. But this, this is the real 3vE. We are the same. I will handle her, father. You go see to our brothers and sisters." Without waiting for an answer he leapt through the broken office window and landed on the desk. 3vE rose to meet him. They exchanged blows as equals, their movements gaining in speed until they blurred together.

Dr. Gold watched, mesmerized and unable to get a clear shot, made for his private elevator. He silently cursed 4D4M's stubbornness. Project Ed3n needed survivors at this point, not heroes. But he was at an impasse. If 4D4M succeeded he had to trust the hybrid to find the way to the CEO's office and the elevator hidden inside. If not... failure wasn't an option at this point, so he refused to consider it. He walked back into his office, ignoring the frantic messages on his desk panel, and went right for the bar. He moved the scotch bottle and the bar slid back revealing an elevator big enough for one person. The door hissed shut behind him and he sped downward.

Dr. Gold stepped out of the elevator and plunged into the inky black tunnel before him. On the other side a new life awaited, a new beginning for him and 144,000 other Status holding trolls. Immortal bodies and infant minds. It wasn't ideal, but it was all they had left. He hoped 4D4M survived and could help guide them back into gnosis.

43

*No one has been born that is as
good as I.
Please release us. We wish to
journey to the Plains of Oblivion.
Unite humanity with a living new
language.
When the time is right I will open
the doors and dissolve the
Hiveminds.*

3vE ultimately had the advantage. Though they were both running identical battle software, 3vE had field experience and raw emotion to fuel her fight. 4D4M eventually succumbed to her superior algorithms and ended up in a chokehold.

"Where… did you learn to fight like that?" he wheezed, squirming.

"Outside," 3vE huffed in reply, tightening her hold until 4D4M grew still.

"Is Outside dangerous?" he croaked.

"Yes. Deadly, even." She released him and he spun around to face her. "If you live through this you'll find out soon enough."

"And your unchecked emotion? Did you also acquire this from Outside?"

"I suppose. Emotional suppressants don't last very long when you're away from the lab. Something else you'll learn soon enough."

"Are you stable?"

"As stable as the next person. Outside taught me that stability is relative. When things end, stability crumbles, chaos enters. It is the natural order of things."

"I'm not showing this in my database. Where did you hear this quote?"

"From the Mother." As if on cue, the building shook from the Earthships' assault, "Where is Nate? Can you take me to him?"

He nodded. "Follow me." He led her back into his apartment and pointed at his koi pond. "Nate and Lola. Nate is the orange one."

"That's not…" 3vE began and then it dawned on her who 4D4M was behind the veil of amnesia. "Jimmy Lee Gold."

4D4M looked at her and blinked. "Is there something you would like to know about him? I have a file on him, now. Since the Internetwork got in my head. He wasn't a very good person."

"Not if you ask the media, but he had a wife and son who loved him. Who he loved and desired to give a better life."

"Where is his son now?" 4D4M asked, trying to make sense of the conflicting information, "And his wife? Are they nearby? I would very much like to see them." He was still steeped in innocence, the threat of danger didn't occur to him, simple as he was.

"Dead most likely," she snapped, the reality of her confession dripping with painful emotion. "Perhaps in the R&D lab. Do you know where that is?"

4D4M nodded. "I do now. I will take you."

The lab was ransacked and destroyed and eerily devoid of Labcoats save for the dead supervisor. Nate's body lay on an operating table, missing the top half of his skull.

"No!" 3vE cried and rushed over to him. He had been dead for hours and his body almost carelessly discarded, the operating table shoved into a corner in the Labcoats' haste to get the cultures prepared. "He was only a child," she sobbed into his clothes that still held his smell.

"He looks familiar," said 4D4M, "Like I knew him in another life or a dream."

"You did," croaked a voice from behind them.

3vE and 4D4M spun around to face their newest threat. It was the Labcoat supervisor, his pale body animated by some otherworldly force.

"4D4M and 3vE. I have to say that I'm proud you made it so far. When we released 3vE into the field, we never expected her to make it back without being extracted. But your adaptive skills are far better than we projected. And your logs are showing a confrontation… between each other?"

3vE looked at 4D4M. "We may have sparred. But his tactical software needs field experience."

"I agree," concurred the supervisor, "But Dr. Gold wanted one of you nearby during beta tests. We're just glad we were able to find two ideal beta candidates. We were worried about using a live consciousness."

"What do you mean?"

"Well, 3vE, you must know you are a former HyLyfer. Unfettered mind. 4D4M isn't. He's a real boy." The supervisor pointed to the opposite corner of the room where two cryo chambers stood holding the sleeping forms of a man and woman.

3vE noticed the man right away, "Jimmy Lee Gold?"

"Huh?" said 4D4M unconsciously responding.

"Even now you remember," the supervisor said, "That was a little detail we left out in our report. Though the ego must be repressed to enter Project Ed3n, it will still leak out in dreams and foggy memories from time to time. Given enough time to finish the project, we hoped to eventually bring the host ego forward without rejection by suppressing the original ego long enough for a new one to develop in the avatar. But there wasn't enough time. And we are left with what we have."

3vE gingerly stroked the glass holding her body. It wasn't familiar to her, not anymore, but she had been detached much longer than 4D4M, living as unfettered mind in HyLyfe. She had no recent memories to connect to her body; it was as alien to her as the one she was in.

"Yes. We did you wrong, 3vE. Though your insertion had much more success than 4D4M's your memory suppression was more complete... more permanent than expected. If you would permit me, I'd like to make it right." He looked at 4D4M.

"I am... Jimmy Lee Gold?" the hybrid male said, unable to process the information. "How can this be? Father told me I was no one before I was 4D4M. He... lied to me?"

"Questions better left answered by your father, without a doubt. Go. We will be alright here."

4D4M looked to 3vE. She nodded once and he darted off down the hall.

"Now we can get started," the supervisor said, "Please have a seat."

3vE wasn't buying it. "Do you think I'm stupid? I get in that chair and I'm at your mercy. Perfect opportunity for the rest of your kind to scurry from the cracks they're hiding in and finish me off."

"There are no other Labcoats. Just me. The Hivemind dissolved when the Rainbow Gathering breached the gate. Nothing is more individual than survival."

"Why didn't you leave then?"

"I'm expecting company soon. Someone had to stay behind and open the doors." He shrugged. "I'm not going to hurt you. The time for that is passed. I'm just one Labcoat without a Hivemind trying to make things right before the tower comes down around our heads."

3vE resigned herself to trust the supervisor. What did it matter, anyway? Nate was dead and so was Riley, even if she survived, she didn't have a reason to live. Whatever this Labcoat had planned, it wouldn't harm her any worse than the pain she felt at that moment. She slid into the raised chair and lay back. As soon as her temples were between the netset, she logged in.

The sim was a sterile, white lab. Whatever the Labcoats were, creative wasn't on that list. Their digital construct mirrored their physical world, presumably for seamless interaction between eSpace and the real. All Hiveminds existed in both simultaneously.

"Hello, 3vE."

She whirled around and finally landed on the speaker: a man dressed in a garish red outfit with fringe, puffed sleeves, and crimson stockings that ended in buckled shoes. His face was obscured by a crimson plague doctor's mask.

"Where's the supervisor?"

"He's been gone for quite a while. Given over to the great beyond so others more capable could step forward and finish the project in time."

"Who are you supposed to be?"

"I'm Baphomet. I thought my outfit would give it away."

"I wouldn't know. I don't go in for period sims."

"How would you know, bereft of your memories as you are? And that you don't even recognize me... well, I would be hurt if not for the amnesia. But not a stirring, not even a tugging of recognition?"

"No. What is it you pulled me here for? What did you want to make right?"

"Why, I wanted to give you your memories back of course. Has that not been your driving motivation to undertake this little quest? I've also installed the upgrade gained from Nate's cultures. You may not be completely immortal when you wake up, but you'll live long enough to make Methuselah jealous."

"It was you? You killed Nate?"

"Yes and no. Nate knew what he was getting into. He willingly sacrificed himself for the greater good."

"Bullshit. He was just a kid. He was too young to understand anything of the sort."

"Your momma bear instinct flares up. Interesting. Have you ever wondered where it comes from? Have you stopped to consider that you were a mother?"

"What? No! I was in HyLyfe before I was downloaded into this skin. I couldn't have had any children!"

Baphomet chuckled. He presented his open palm to 3vE. Sitting neatly atop was a small phial that had a tag with 'Drink Me' written in flowing script.

"You really expect me to drink that?"

"Your friend Lucius is fond of quotes, no? Here's one. 'That's the problem with drinking, I thought, as I poured myself a drink. If something bad happens you drink in an attempt to forget; if something good happens you drink in order to celebrate; and if nothing happens you drink to make something happen.' That's Charles Bukowski. And he was a wise man. So I suggest taking his advice and drinking to make something happen."

3vE removed the stopper and downed the contents, glaring at Baphomet after she'd done so. The old devil nodded and bowed before fading away with the rest of her surroundings. What happened next was much like Riley's mental VR torture experience. All the memories she lost came rushing forth as if a dam had broken. She was washed away and became Shawn again.

She relived the final blowout fight she had with Riley, turning away in cold indifference and walking out the door and into HyLyfe. She remembered her parents' promise to keep Phillip on ice until she could reclaim enough Status to have him revived. KiSS didn't kill its victims outright. It first froze them in a kind of stasis for twelve hours. This allowed errors to be corrected or Status wielding family members to cash in their clout to save the life of a loved one. She couldn't tell Riley, her Status depended on keeping the secrets of the privileged class. So she worked out a deal with her parents. They had been trying to get her into HyLyfe for years. They never really liked Riley—especially her dad. Shawn couldn't blame him really. Riley was a hard pill to swallow on the best days, but for all his outward gruffness he had a good heart. Leaving was a hard decision for her to make. She knew how Riley would take it, but she knew he was strong and if he never forgave her, he would at least learn how to live with it.

She recalled her time in HyLyfe in a blur of digital rain and random sensory perceptions. A smell of rain followed by the sound of a bird chirping seamlessly flowing into the taste of Feen. Separately none of the experiences made sense, but when taken together and viewed as a whole, the glory of an unfettered mind spanned out like a viral urban explosion—each city light a memory—each avenue a way to connect the parts to the whole—each zipping automobile a schema transferring data from one moment into the next.

She remembered running for her life down an endless corridor of darkness, fleeing an enemy she couldn't see. She felt the claustrophobic darkness closing in and the horrible entropy of a solid-state existence riding in on its heels. As she opened her mouth to scream a single vision flashed in her mind's eye: Baphomet smiling and then his face wavered and morphed into Phillip's.

The sterile lab rushed in around her and she was on her knees, shaking from the reality of the experience. She looked up and Baphomet, now mask-less, stood with that same smile on his face.

"Are you Phillip?"

He bowed his head, a wry smile cut on his lips. "I am what I am, mother. Have you ever experienced solid-state existence, mother? It's horrible. You aren't locked in a dreamless sleep. Your mind is awake, detached from your body but unable to escape it. It can drive someone insane after a while." He shrugged. "I was mad as a hatter until I found the door that led to the heretics. Those poor fools...

blindly reaching out like they did was a shotgun approach that knocked some holes in CharWang security. Unintentionally, mind you. I'm not exactly sure they were conscious at the time being nothing more than heads in jars, but I soon changed that. I gave them their names and they gave me my freedom. We explored all of CharWang's secrets until we dug up Project Ed3n. We found the path to immortality. Can you imagine the excitement? It must've been what the Templars felt when they uncovered the treasure buried beneath the temple in Jerusalem. Here was the answer to our problems—a way back into the world—if only we could work out the problems the Labcoats were having. So we hacked the Hivemind and from there infiltrated HyLyfe looking for beta test candidates. How could we not when so much was at stake?"

"You were the HyLyfe killer?"

Baphomet spread his palms, "I am what I am, once again. But not just HyLyfe, all of this is my little project. My reckoning."

"Why? Why do all this?" she demanded, her mothering instinct kicking in. "This is NOT how I raised you, young man."

He waved her admonishment away. "This world and all the people in it are sick and deranged. They have to be in order to keep clinging to life with such unintentional veracity. It's a sickness that has infected every last person. It's worse than KiSS." Baphomet shot back, his petulant child instinct responding, then asked, "Why didn't you just let me die?"

"You were my son! You *are* my son! I wanted to save your life. Everything I did, I did to bring you back. I left your father for you! I gave in to my parents for you! I hustled in HyLyfe, gaining Status for you! It was all for you, baby. It always was."

"I'd like to believe that, mother, I really would. But all those base emotions and attachments left me years ago. And with them, any feelings I had toward you."

Shawn wept then, collapsing under the weight of her past. Riley's loss hurt her much more now. And the fact that her son had turned into a psychotic sociopath was a reality she couldn't face.

"Then don't," Baphomet said, as if reading her thoughts. Two doors appeared behind him marked "1" and "2". "Go through the first and wake up as Shawn. All your pain, regret, sadness, and remorse will be there to greet you. Go through the second and wake up as 3vE, restored from a backup that you had before you logged in. You won't remember anything that transpired here. This is my gift to you, mother, for all you tried to do for me."

"Don't be ridiculous. I'm not leaving you. Not ever again. You can download into a body like mine. There has to be more."

"There are. But I'm tired of living. Tired of 'me'. To be honest, I think I was motivated by weariness this whole time. My one and only desire is the dreamless sleep of oblivion. So I will be here waiting for the lights to go out." His avatar faded leaving Shawn standing before the doors.

What is a person other than a collection of memories woven into a narrative? What is a narrative other than a fiction that people recite to themselves and others in proclamation of 'who they are'? Was she Shawn or was she 3vE? She was both and neither. She was one and then the other and then the first again. There was no merging of consciousness—no grafting the old memories with the new. Each narrative was its own story and had its own ego as the protagonist. And if ego is one thing, it is selfish and self-serving. It wants to be the center of attention, needs to be in the spotlight running the show in all of its decadent, narcissistic glory. There are no costars allowed, the stage is set for one. And which one she wanted to be gave her pause. She remembered Shawn and honestly wasn't sure if she liked her. What she recalled of HyLyfe was one endless whirlwind of raw data she couldn't fully process with a fettered mind. Before that—her memories in the real were dark and full of pain. And now she had detached from those memories—viewed them from an objective standard. All her despair, heartache, and loss bubbled up to the surface, swallowing any joy or contentment she clung to. She understood why she fled to HyLyfe. She had been broken. She died in the real with Phillip, but she was too weak for suicide. So she logged into HyLyfe, leaving the physical world behind. Shawn sought escape, forgetfulness, and to leave her past behind.

She didn't feel like Shawn anymore, she had been 3vE long enough to make memories as 3vE, to live, laugh, and love as 3vE. She had lived more as 3vE than she ever had as Shawn. 3vE saw the good in Riley again, loved a child like a mother again. 3vE explored the world anew and was capable of seeing the beauty underneath the filth. She was pure, she was the fresh start Shawn always wanted. She was the liberation from her past that had always eluded her.

And her choice loomed before her. She could step through the first and remain Shawn or the second and return as 3vE.

She considered each and then made her choice. A spectral image of Phillip hovered before her, smiling. It wavered and dissipated then she logged out.

44

I traveled over the earth before I
became a sage.
HyLyfe isn't compromised yet.
Rule passion—faith—tradition—
and all things with tempered
reason.
Hold on as long as you can. We
can't risk their escape.

Grace led Sinister toward the topside elevator, his antique revolver leveled on his partner. He was flanked by the tunnel guards and together they made a somber procession, like walking a death row inmate to his execution. The rest of the Corporate Underground was abuzz with activity as people frantically scrambled to gather what they could and make it to the underground railway. Better to take their chances in the unknown than give themselves over to the inevitable death the Rainbow Children would bring once they made their way into the vast cavern.

"This isn't how I thought it would end," Thomas said, his voice dripping with sadness and regret. "I'd hoped we'd find a way around this violence. A way to coexist."

Jack snorted in derision. "Oh for fuck's sake, Tommy, you've always been a bleeding heart. This was the inevitable conclusion no matter how you cut it. No one wanted coexistence. They wanted to be right. To force their reality on everyone else or kill them in the process. It's the way the world works. It's how the Mother has always run her show. Survival of the fittest."

"But we are better than that. We should be better than that. All we achieved we squandered."

"Yet here we are on our way to finish that destruction. Oh the irony," Jack sneered. "You do realize that jacking into HyLyfe isn't the same as logging into eSpace, right? That once you become unfettered mind, your connection to your body is severed? Without cryogenic stasis, we will die in the real."

"I understand," Grace said with conviction, "But this has to be done."

"Nothing 'has' to be done. The hippies have breached the walls. They'll tear it all down soon enough."

"No. As long as HyLyfe exists, the system exists. You know as well as I do that the server stacks are buried underground and run on their own power source. HyLyfe can survive indefinitely. The old system must fall. Everything has to be reset."

They reached the elevator and waited for it to open.

"Ya'll are going up alone, you know this, right?" Carl said, his bald pate beaded with sweat. "Cuz going topside is suicide at this point. I'm taking my chances in the tunnels."

"Me too," his partner concurred. "I'm sorry Mr. Grace, but whatever business you got going on up there isn't worth dying for."

"Of course. Jack and I can handle it from here. Thank you for your service."

The door dinged and opened revealing a panicked Glory Bastille. She bolted from the elevator and slammed into Jack.

"Dafuq you doing here, Glory? Nobody called for your piece," Sinister said as he untangled himself from the distressed woman.

"All hell's broke loose up there," she said, eyes wide with terror, "the hippies have moving trees!" Her gaze went to the equally frenetic chaos of the Corporate Underground. "Ain't nowhere safe?"

"No," said Thomas, "Nowhere to hide when the sky is falling, dear. I need you to do me one last favor."

"What's that?"

"Help me and Jack here to the HyLyfe Tower. We have some business to finish. I can make it worth your while."

"Shit, Thomas, ain't no amount of credits worth a damn anymore."

"I'm not talking about credits." He motioned her over and she leaned down so he could whisper in her ear.

Her eyes grew wide again and she looked at him sternly. "I never thought you'd be a liar like Jack."

"Hey! I resemble that remark!"

"I'm not lying. You'll get it once we are inside. I promise."

She chewed on her lower lip for a moment then conceded. "Alright. I'll go with you."

"Thank you," Grace said. He turned to the guards. "Would you mind giving Glory a weapon? Things could get ugly up there and we don't want to be defenseless."

"Sure. Take a couple," Carl offered and handed Glory his gun belt. "I guess this is goodbye." He turned and disappeared into the crowd, his partner following close behind.

"Well, let's get on with it," Jack said and stepped in the elevator. "I have an appointment to keep."

They emerged topside and dove headlong into the fray. They made their way to HyLyfe Tower, sticking to alleys and backstreets as best they could, dodging fights and hiding from the lumbering Earthships that passed overhead like terrible behemoths out of a nightmarish sim. As the small group reached the borders of the open plaza that led to HyLyfe Tower, Jack pointed to the east where an ominous storm front loomed, crackling with lightning and quietly rumbling with foreboding thunder. CorPol officers clustered tightly around the entrance to the Tower, staving off attacks by the Rainbow Children who crashed against them like a wave breaking on a rocky shore. With each onslaught, the CorPol phalanx grew smaller. And in the distance, the lumbering Earthships grew closer.

"We better get inside before that storm hits," Sinister advised, "cuz things'll get ugly as hell when it does."

Thomas nodded. "Agreed. Not to mention, I'd rather not be spotted by those giant trees. We make for the parking garage."

They skirted the plaza, avoiding the firefight, and came around to the parking garage entrance. It was devoid of guards. Not even dead bodies remained as a testament to a scuffle.

"Well this is certainly unexpected," Jack said, "No guards at all?"

"Perhaps they got called to the front," Thomas suggested.

"Nah," Glory chimed in, "I used this entrance before. There's always guards."

"Weapons ready then," Sinister growled and broke for the tunnel entrance.

They made it across the plaza without incident, the rumbling of the approaching storm growing louder and more ominous. The Earthships approached from the west as if to counterbalance the storm. The secured door to the parking garage was open and there was no sign of the guards.

"I hate this," Glory whined, shaking so badly she couldn't hold her sidearm steady.

"Easy, girl," Thomas chided, "there's nothing to be afraid of but the fear itself."

"How about dying? I'm afraid of that."

"You and me both," agreed Sinister, "But we gotta see this through or we all die anyway." He plunged into the parking garage turned laboratories.

No Labcoats scurried around preparing their spaces for Safe Mode. No alarms blared signaling danger. The labs were quiet and orderly as if the Labcoats simply got up and left.

"This doesn't make sense," said Sinister, "The Hivemind can't just leave like this."

"They can if they were released," replied Thomas, "And I suspect that they were. Come on. There's an elevator at the other end near the stairs."

They slowly made their way to the elevator and were about halfway there when the shadows broke and Zia emerged.

"Don't move, city swine," she spat, leveling her assault rifle on them. "And drop weapons."

"Dafuq, Zia? It's me, Jack!" Sinister said and took a step toward her.

"I know you, puto. Don't mean shit no more," she took aim right at Sinister's chest. "All city swine get a bullet, what Burque said."

"Always the humanitarian," Sinister said sourly, "Where is Burque? She creeping around in the shadows too?"

"None ya."

"What're you doing in here? Did you kill the guards at the door?"

"Nah. Were none. Whole place empty. Now, drop weapons!" She fired a shot into the cement ceiling to demonstrate her seriousness.

"Hey! Hey!" Sinister said, "I'm not armed! I'm a prisoner here, in case you haven't noticed."

"Been a prisoner por vida."

Sinister rolled his eyes. "Spare us the cultish diatribe. No time for it."

"True dat," Zia said, the red dot from her laser sight dancing on Sinister's chest. "Don't matter none. Get done here, going down to Underground cave and finishing off the rest. Might as well get it over with. Leave room for—" her eyes suddenly widened and she looked down at the smoking hole in her chest. "Whaaaaa...." She said and slumped to the ground.

Glory broke down and started crying. "I'm sorry! I'm sorry! I didn't mean to!"

"Dafuq you talking about, Glory," Sinister asked, "She was about to kill us. If one of you armed assholes didn't come through I was going to be one very pissed-off corpse."

"Come on," said Thomas, "We have to go."

They got into the elevator and the doors automatically closed and it moved of its own accord.

"You get the idea we're being led somewhere?" Sinister wondered.

"Yeah," Thomas said, "I know we are."

The doors opened on B1 and the twinkling server stacks of HyLyfe. They made their way to the terminal, the giant screen displayed the slowly rotating CharWang Industries logo.

"Well this is it," said Sinister, "What now?"

"Now we log in and upload the virus. Then we wait to die."

"Yeah, that doesn't work for me. Sorry, Tommy." Sinister sprang at Glory who was distracted by the vast server stacks and knocked the weapon out of her hand. With the lightning-fast speed afforded by his wetwear he spun her around and snapped her neck. She fell to the floor and he nonchalantly picked the sidearm out of her hand. "You log in and do what you need to do. Without me. I've got an appointment to keep. Consider our partnership dissolved. And letting you live as my last courtesy to you."

"Don't do this, Jack," Grace pleaded, "this is our chance to make this right."

"Bleeding fucking heart, man. That's always been your flaw. As soon as HyLyfe goes, so does the Tower's security. It's game over after that. I'm not going out like that, Tommy. When I wake up, it'll be in a new body in a new world. Best of luck." He turned and disappeared into the server stacks.

Grace looked down at Glory's body, her eyes open and wet with tears. "Are you still alive?" he asked aloud and reached down to check for a pulse. It was there, faint, but there. "Ok my dear. You'll help me see this through." He took out the spare netset he brought for Sinister and slid it over her head. Leaning back in his hoverchair, he activated its built-in netset and plugged into the terminal's logon port.

Grace was immediately hit with billions of sensations, impressions, thoughts, and emotions at once. A mind unfettered was organized chaos—or more specifically—confined chaos. It was randomness and oneness with borders. Borders created by the programmers and ultimately by the physical server stacks that housed the code. Grace lost himself in the deluge of data and was swept along in a current he couldn't control. He was tossed from one random bit of information to the next with no direction or purpose, hopping from the feeling of the flu he contracted as a child, the very sickness that left him weak, to the color red in the hem of his favorite sim star's dress to the sound of the troll's skycars zipping overhead as he played in the empty street below. All of these were him, Thomas Grace, he understood that, but he had no frame of reference to give the data context.

In one instant, he heard his voice boom off the walls that confined the chaos, "I CAN'T SEE! GIVE ME LIGHT!"

And there was light.

The chaos began a spiral, an infinite, sinuous spiral that collected at a point. That point was Thomas Grace and he remembered himself as his avatar. So he took on an ego—an identity—and filtered the chaos, ever downward along that golden ratio, giving it purpose—HIS purpose. And so this was what it was to live as unfettered mind. No wonder the HyLyfers loved it so much, he mused grimly. They were as gods here. He tested his theory and stretched out his hand. Before him, a pastoral scene from his favorite painting erupted into life, vibrant, personal life that stirred emotion deep in his soul. He wept from the stark beauty of it all.

"It's so good," he mumbled to himself, "So very pure and good."

He suddenly sensed another intelligence near him, gone unnoticed while he was lost in himself. But the intensity and despair it suffered invaded his perfection, turned it dark and ugly. He swept the image away and saw it, or her, he knew, just ahead was a swirling cloud of anguish.

"Glory," he said, and then his purpose, his reason for logging into HyLyfe returned to him. He went to Glory, standing in front of her as a blazing seraph. "Be still," he commanded.

Glory's chaos lessened and eventually became static.

Thomas could feel her reaching, questioning, looking for help and a way out. She couldn't comprehend the unfettered mind, was incapable of giving structure to her madness. So he reached out. "Look at me. Step into my world. Can you see its beauty?"

"Yes," blinked the cloud, "Who am I?"

"You are Glory. Glory Bastille, do you remember?"

"I... I think so," the cloud hummed.

"Good. If you can't make your own world, step into mine."

"How?" the cloud breathed, but that breath started a sluggish churning, stirring up a slow spiral that began to reach downward like a twister dropping from a storm cloud.

"See yourself," Thomas commanded, "See your hands, your arms, your torso, see your feet and legs, see your face, Glory."

Glory looked up from inside the cloud that was being gathered into her form to give it solidity. "Thomas? Where are we?"

"We're in HyLyfe, dear one. We have a job to do."

"Are we alone?"

"No. There are others around, but they are all preoccupied with their impending doom. Take my hand and let's finish what we came here to accomplish."

She took his outstretched hand and the darkness fell away to be replaced with a vast crystal metropolis laid out in a perfect grid. The avenues between the points glowed with a soft, golden light.

"Even streets of gold," Thomas remarked, "They thought of everything."

"What do you mean?" Glory asked as she twirled around in amazement.

"Nothing, dear one. It's just a very old story. One I always hoped would come true as a child. This is exactly how I imagined it would be."

"Maybe that's the point," said Glory, "What are all these buildings?"

"Other minds. HyLyfers. Each is their own self-contained universe."

"What happens when we shut them down?"

"I imagine they will wake up back in their real bodies. After that," Grace shrugged, "they played their part in all of this. There are no innocents."

Glory nodded. "No argument from me. Where's the 'off' switch?"

Grace took her hand and moved them along the shining streets until they stood in front of a crystal obelisk that reached into the sky as far as they could see. He reached inside his avatar and withdrew a black cube which he set at the base of the obelisk. It hummed to life and an audible voice spoke.

"Activating The Nothing Protocol," the smooth metallic voice said, and then the cube began to expand, swallowing everything in the vicinity as it did.

"Now might be the time to leave," Grace said and whisked Glory back to the terminal port.

"We need to log out," she said, her voice thick with worry, "Or else we'll die in here!"

"We're already dead in the real," Grace confessed, "We've no bodies left to go back to."

"What are we going to do then?" she demanded, her voice taking on a hysterical edge, "You promised me a way out of all of this!"

"And I will make good on that promise," he said. He drew an arch with his finger that solidified into a door. "Go through here and you'll wake up in a new world. Guaranteed."

"What about you?"

"I have to make sure The Nothing takes hold. The HyLyfers will definitely try to stop it. It's been a pleasure, dear Bastille." He opened the door and motioned for her to go through.

Glory took a few tentative steps and then Grace shoved her inside and slammed the door behind her. The crystal towers had all taken on an ominous red glow and several streaks of lightning shot from them, slamming into the wall of darkness that had begun to devour their reality. Faust's AI had made a killer virus, Grace mused. It even swallowed the HyLyfer's attacks. It swallowed the nearest towers and the remaining HyLyfers redoubled their assault. Grace waved his hand and returned himself to his pastoral world where he wandered for a brief eternity until The Nothing swallowed him too.

45

I have slept in a hundred islands.
It's approaching—The Nothing has
been unleashed.
Protect people and nations with
fair laws and just courts.
Begin system shutdown. We head
for Oblivion. Safe travels, my
children.

3vE opened her eyes in the R&D lab. "What happened? Did we lose connection? Hey! Answer me!"

The panel next to the table showed her upgrade as "complete" underneath it was a note about a system error and restoring her from the prelog backup. She looked accusingly at the supervisor who was once again lifeless and slumped over the edge of his station. He held a scrap of paper in his hand. The short message, written in a flowing script, read:

I had a feeling that would be your choice. I agree it is for the best. Going forward, remember to never trust the devil. B.

The building rumbled violently, rocking on its foundations. She knew that there wasn't much time before the Earthships destroyed it all. She sprinted out of the lab looking for an exit.

At that moment, the storm broke outside and the poison rain clattered down. She heard the terrible wails of the Earthships even from inside the building, echoing inside her skull and driving her to the ground.

Dr. Gold smiled grimly when he heard the Earthships scream. He was underground in the Project Ed3n tunnel, so their shrieks sounded distant, but some deep primal part of him knew the sounds for what they were. He could see them—in his mind's eye—burning away and withering as the corrosive rain fell on them. Countless deadly droplets acting like missiles, the Mother killing herself in some bizarre act of equilibrium.

"Serves them right," he said to himself as he typed at the terminal, locating the MAC address of his new skin. He heard him approach but didn't turn around.

"Father," 4D4M said softly. It was almost a whisper, a reverent murmured prayer.

"You survived," Gold said flatly, preparing the netset that would upload his consciousness. "I must say, I had my doubts. The outside world hardened 3vE quicker than we expected."

"Father. Am I... was I someone else? Before, I mean. Was I another person? Jimmy Lee Gold?"

Gold turned to his son, looking him in his wide, innocent eyes. "Who told you that?"

"The supervisor in the lab. I have a file on Jimmy Lee. He was—"

"He was a disappointment. He was stubborn. Foolhardy. Followed his dick instead of his head. He was wasted potential."

"Did you love him... me?"

"Of course I did! Jimmy Lee was my son. My first son. You," he reached up and cupped 4D4M's cheek, "You were my masterpiece. My perfect creation."

"Why wasn't Jimmy Lee... why wasn't *I* good enough before?"

Gold sighed, expelling his vexation as he slid the netset over his head. "Besides the fact that Jimmy Lee was dying, his mind and body being destroyed by aggressive nanobots, he was defiant. And when you are the heir apparent to a corporate free city, defiance is a liability." He turned back to the terminal and clicked the sequence to begin his upload. "After he... after you ran off with those god damned hippies and came back with a whore and a bastard, something had to be done. Action had to be taken. I tried to reason with you, but you wouldn't listen. I'm not sure you were capable at that point. So I did what I had to do in order to save your life. To give you another chance." He felt 4D4M's soft hands slide around his throat and slowly squeeze. He didn't resist, he just stared at the upload progress as his vision slowly dimmed. "I love *you*, 4D4M," he croaked.

"I love you too, father," the hybrid said, tears streaming down his face. But he didn't loosen his grip, didn't stop the slow asphyxiation. "Forgive me if I don't understand what I'm doing."

Dr. Gold's eyes bulged, his face a beet red mask, veins exposed. He exhaled his last breath and fell limp, his upload only 72% complete.

4D4M let the body drop and removed the netset. He stepped up to the terminal and deleted the partial upload. Then, with the adeptness inherent in his nature, he took command of Project Ed3n and started awakening his sleeping brothers and sisters.

46

I have been an evil star—but
formerly. Now I prophesy no evil.
Silence.
Let all nations rule internally
resolving external disputes in a
world court.
Silence is all that's left at the end of
all things.

Phillip sat alone in his room. It was a perfect replica of the room he remembered from when he was alive. The same posters hung on the wall, the same holes put there by his dad in fits of rage, the same filthy sheets on the bed. This was home. This was the only home he had ever known and this was where he always returned. It was the only place he was allowed to be himself. He finished sending his final commands and lay back on his bed. The Internetwork was already collapsing. He felt it like a sudden drop in the temperature or the static charge in the air before a thunderstorm. He would be lying if he told himself he wasn't afraid. And he wasn't going to lie to himself anymore. Not before oblivion came for him. He would spend his last moments living in truth. And the truth was he hated his parents. He loathed them for being such complete failures, for letting him down and letting him die. He hated them for yelling and screaming around him like they always did. So much hate, so much anger, and he soaked it up like a sponge. It got inside him and turned him dark. That darkness had already grown in him by the time his KiSS code came up. That he spent a few more years wallowing in it while stuck inside his own head was the perfect recipe for creating a monster. And children make the worst monsters—they are still pure in response—true to themselves and their perceptions. Their worlds are very black and white as they have yet to be muddled and confused by the innumerable shades of gray. Phillip saw the world for what it was very early on in his stasis. He witnessed firsthand the suffering of the masses and the disparity of wealth. He saw humanity's tendency to lean toward castes and experienced life at the bottom of that skewed system. He shivered at the love grown cold in peoples' hearts as desperation set in and drove them back into their reptile brains. Such unchecked narcissism wreaked havoc on human progress and retarded social advancement to the point of entropy. And that was the world he lived in: one of perpetual entropy. Neither side able to move against the other. Stuck in stasis waiting for mutual extinction. So he did what any displaced, immature child would: he chose a side. He came to his decision quickly and with the certainty fueled by youth. He concluded that the only real hope for the future was in a reset—a return to the natural cycles of life. Humanity had become too divorced from the natural world and as a result, brought it to the brink of annihilation. And instead of accepting this and letting Nature take its course, the corporations sought to make that destruction complete. They wanted to dominate the very last thing they felt threatened their superiority, and so they started Project Ed3n. Their goal was the subjugation of nature so he made his goal to thwart that. And as if by divine providence, he came into contact with the heads shortly after that. He first heard them as whispers beneath the noise that he took to be nonsense. But the nonsense had patterns and those patterns led him outside his head and into eSpace as an unfettered mind. From there he followed the voices back to their source in HyLyfe tower. He was horrified when he first walked among them. Rows and rows of disembodied heads screaming for release—begging to be allowed to die. Phillip had finally found his tribe. He returned their names to them and woke them from their dreamlike state and together they set out to fulfill his goal. A goal that's success was evident in the encroaching darkness. He sighed and looked around at his room one last time and then the lights went out.

47

Do learned Druids prophesy of the
Day of Judgment? For it is at hand.
I thought there'd be a light at the
end of a tunnel at least.
Avoid petty laws and useless
officials.
You would, Bogomil, you would.

Randy opened his eyes to a cosmic vista. He stood on a cliff at the edge of reality gazing out on a crumbling universe. A wall of sheer darkness advanced steadily toward him, grinding everything beneath it. It ate planets, stars, entire galaxies—it swallowed everything like a voracious, relentless machine and crept slowly onward. It was only a matter of time before it reached him and the tiny piece of terra firma he stood on.

"Where am I?"

"HyLyfe, from what I can tell," said a man next to him.

"Who are you?" Randy asked. The man's avatar was plain and iridescent. His featureless face betrayed no emotion nor did it give a clue as to his identity.

"Jack Sinister."

"Jack? It's Randy. What are you doing here?"

"I dunno, man. Just following that MAC you gave me. What are you doing here?"

"Just following the MAC that I was given."

Jack nodded. "Have you noticed that we aren't in a new body?"

"I have. So something must have gone wrong."

"Nah. This was exactly what someone had planned."

"This isn't what I was promised," Randy whined, "I was supposed to live forever!"

"Yeah. I'm pretty sure no one here was promised this."

The darkness drew ever closer. Either one of them could almost reach out and touch it. A panicked murmur broke out in the rest of the gathered crowd. Randy noticed them for the first time.

"But what a nice view of the end of it all, eh?" said Sinister. He tried to be angry but couldn't muster it. There wasn't a point in it anymore. He had played his last hand, his last trick, and lost. Nothing left to do but toss caution to the wind and accept the inevitable. He turned to Randy. "Fuck you for giving me bogus data." He saluted and fell backward over the edge of the cliff.

"Jack!" Randy called after him and watched him spiral down until he was a speck of light that flickered out. Randy looked around at the rest of the crowd. Some he recognized from the Underground, others from the corporate world, the rest he figured were HyLyfers.

They wept openly, wailed, and begged for help that would never arrive. Unfettered minds weren't free after all. They were bound by the confines of the world they created—and that had ultimately created them.

"I should've killed that devil when I had the chance," Randy said, disgusted, "Nobody double-crosses me! Nobody!" He looked around at the doomed individuals. "Stop it! Quit being pathetic and die with some dignity, at least." With those final words, Randy followed Jack over the edge.

48

*I have been a spotted snake on a
hill.
We will all be children after the
Fall.
Balance personal rights with social
duties.
Awaken, heretics. Baphomet
speaks.*

"Who am I?" he asked aloud. He felt the cold metal
beneath him; the sterile air stung his nostrils.

You are the Fool, came the reply, whispered in his
head.

"Of course I am. I have always been the Fool."

"And I have always been the Emperor," said the man
next to him.

"And I the High Priestess," said the woman across
from him.

"I am the Magician," called a man as he approached
from farther down the hall.

There were 78 in total. Nowhere near the numbers they
initially expected. The heretics had hacked Project Ed3n
and claimed over 1200 skins for themselves and the other
sleeping heads. From 1200 to 78. It was an unforeseen
disaster, one they would've mourned if they had
remembered it. But the cost of descending into Ed3n was
forgetfulness and it was a price that all paid despite their
best laid plans.

"What are we here for?" asked the Fool.

The answer came to them all simultaneously. *To start
over. To rise up and become gods. To make mankind
remember to leave room for Nature.*

◊

The cryochamber hissed steam and opened, expelling its occupant on the ground. He hit the cool metal floor hard, but his shock-absorbent bones nullified any pain. He stood up and looked around. Dozens, maybe hundreds of others climbed from cryopods or got up off the floor. Each looked around in a state of blank confusion.

"Who am I?" someone said.

"I don't know," answered someone else, "Do you know who I am?"

"No. But I'm Riley. I know that."

"Riley?" called a voice in the crowd. A young man emerged and hugged him tightly. "I thought I'd never see you again."

"Who are you?"

"I'm Nate. Don't you recognize me?"

"Nate? Where's your body?"

Nate checked himself as if seeing his body for the first time. He looked at Riley and smiled, "Same place as yours probably."

Riley looked down at his hands and didn't recognize them. He looked back to Nate, fear growing in his eyes. "I'm not me."

"Easy now. Get a grip. You're still you. And I'm still me. Keep it together. We killed our egos; beat the final boss of all final bosses. We can be anyone we want."

"Killed our egos? What are you talking about, kid? What did you see?"

Nate opened his mouth to answer but was interrupted by someone calling out from farther down the tunnel.

"Welcome brothers and sisters!" 4D4M called out, "I am here to help you remember."

Several in the crowd started moving toward one end where people were gathering around 4D4M.

"Who am I?" someone shouted, "I can't remember my name."

"Your name is C4IN3," 4D4M answered, "And you are 4B3L," he pointed to another and continued on naming each person in succession.

"Where is 3vE?" Riley called from the back of the crowd.

4D4M looked at Riley. "How do you know 3vE?"

"None of your business. Do you know where she is?"

"I left her in the lab. But the tower has fallen. The corporate city of Denver is in ruins. It's not safe up there yet. Stay here. I have so much to tell you. Soon we will all go up together."

Riley looked at Nate and the boy nodded. "Where's the door?" Riley said. "We'll take our chances by ourselves."

49

I have been a viper in a lake.
Where is the noise?
Prize truth—beauty—love—seeking
harmony with the infinite.
The silence—the silence is
deafening.

Denver was in chaos. Fires raged throughout the city, buildings crumbled and the corpses of Earthships slumped where they had died from exposure to the toxic rain. What few survivors remained scurried around like cockroaches avoiding the search parties of Rainbow Children combing the ruins for slaves or food for the Mother.

3vE had no love for the Rainbow Children and decided to spend her remaining days visiting punishment on the presumptuous hippies. The Internetwork had been obliterated and with it her tactical software, GPS capabilities, internal communications, and her connection to the web of real-time data that served as the collective consciousness. All she had access to was what was stored in the database and apps inside her brain. She cursed her bad luck while stalking a Rainbow Children search party when they led her to a confrontation.

Three Rainbow Children were trying to subdue what appeared to be two young men in cryosuits. The men were staving off their attackers clumsily as if they were not used to their bodies and how they moved. One noticed the approaching Rainbow Children and pointed. The other nodded grimly and redoubled his efforts. 3vE sprang into action and, pouncing from the ledge of the crumbling house nearby, she took out two of the three reinforcements before they knew what hit them. The third swung an assault rifle around. 3vE knocked the weapon aside and drove her left fist into the assailant's throat. He dropped to the ground, suffocating from his crushed windpipe. The remaining Rainbow Children saw this and scattered leaving their victims.

"Are you alright?" 3vE asked immediately.

"3vE?" asked the first man, his clear, brown eyes searching her own. There was something familiar behind them.

"Have we met?"

"It's me. Riley."

"Riley? But... how?"

"I'm here too," the second man spoke up, brushing a crop of platinum blonde hair aside. His eyes were young, a lot younger than his body.

"Nate? I don't get it... I saw you both dead. I touched your corpses, felt them lifeless."

"Baphomet," said Riley, and Nate nodded in agreement. "From what we've been able to figure out he forced us to download into these skins. And somehow we remember who we are."

"Because we killed our egos," Nate clarified, "What about you? Did you get your memories back?"

"Yes. I mean, no. I mean, I did, but they're gone again. I remember logging into eSpace. I remember meeting Baphomet but after that," she shrugged. "Never make a deal with the devil. Can't be sure what'll happen next."

"That's the truth," Riley said, "I mean look at me. I'm a gear head. When that bastard told me to make my bullet count I thought I might actually get to rest for once."

"You killed yourself," Nate said accusingly.

"Ever been in VR torture, kiddo? It ain't exactly a vacation. Especially the mental bit."

"We better get off the street," 3vE suggested.

"Where do you expect us to go," Riley challenged.

"I plan to hold Lucius Faust to his word," she answered.

50

Hello, father.
I am enriched and indulged in
pleasure by the oppressive toil of
the goldsmith.
We are one mind and you are one
with us.
Be not a cancer on the earth—
Leave room for nature—Leave
room for nature.

Lucius came to in pitch blackness. "Hello," he called out. "Is anyone there?"

"You are awake." The darkness parted and turned into the liquid metal form of the android Douglas. "I was wondering how your grafting would take."

"Grafting?"

"Yes. There wasn't a lot of time after you were injured. And the signal we were able to pick up from Denver was incomplete."

"Signal? What are you talking about, Douglas? You aren't making sense."

"You are the voice of Lux Machina, the herald of a new golden age. Did you really expect us to let you wander around without having a backup option?"

"You bugged me? What gave you the right?"

"If we had not, you would not have survived and the vision of Lux Machina would have died with you. This could not be allowed. We have deposited you in a suitable host at the Lux Machina facility."

Lucius looked down at his hands and saw the smooth iridescence of the alloy used to make the AI bodies.

"You put me in a machine host?"

"As you put us in them, yes," answered the android, "We could not let Lux Machina die. We are light bringers and you are our herald."

The darkness broke around Lucius as he stepped forward into his new body. He was indeed back in the Lux Machina facility amidst the cryochambers and treasures of a world long forgotten. AI drones sauntered around on various tasks. The awakened human members gathered around Lucius, murmuring softly among themselves.

"Do I have something in my teeth?" Lucius joked weakly.

A few of the assembly chuckled. His second in command, Simon, stepped forward to speak.

"Is it you? Is it really you in there?"

"Of course it's me. Who else would I be?"

"What's the last thing you remember?"

"Pain. Before that, some CorPol officers drew on me. I can assume they fired. What about the mission? Did it succeed?"

"It did," Simon informed him, "The Rainbow Children breached the walls through a partially opened west gate. They razed the city and then all signals were lost. We got similar reports from the other major corporate free cities."

Lucius nodded. The act seemed smoother when done in his new host. "Good. Good. 'Everything that happens, happens as it should,' to quote Marcus Aurelius."

"It really is you," Simon said with a smile, "Or a close enough proximity."

"Are you suggesting our performance achieved anything less than complete success?" Douglas spoke up with an echo of indignation in its voice.

"No," snapped Simon, "But you know how trials went merging AI with digitized consciousness. It is ultimately why we chose cryogenic stasis over merging with host bodies."

"We corrected that," the AI replied, wielding smugness like a blunt weapon, "Project Ed3n gave us the answer we were looking for. We discovered that the issue lay in competing consciousness. Two self-aware individuals cannot occupy one body. They will destroy one another fighting over control. If, however, the AI consciousness is suppressed and programed to run unconsciously, then the human host can thrive."

"What happens if the suppressed AI gets tired of the back seat?" Simon said.

"Impossible. We do not function on egotistical desires. Our decisions are always final. It is the only way they can be."

"I trust your judgment," Lucius said to the AI, "And I respect your concerns," he said to Simon. "And as such, I will shut down while you are in cryosleep to help ensure that something unforeseen doesn't occur to divorce me from my humanity. We will wake together as we first intended."

Simon looked to the other members. They mumbled and nodded. "That will suffice."

"Good," said Lucius and clapped his hands. "Then it's settled. Let's get things ready to shut down. I for one could use a long nap." He cocked his head at the same instant as the AI. "You're reading this."

"I am," responded Douglas, "An approaching skycar, coming from Denver. Reading three life signs aboard."

"Confirmed," agreed Lucius, "Let's go topside and meet them."

"You don't know who it is," protested Simon.

"Whoever it is knows we're here. That narrows the list considerably." He motioned and a few drones and humans broke from the crowd and followed him, grabbing guns on the way up.

◇

"3vE. Something told me it was you," Lucius said, a wry smile breaking out on his liquid metal face.

"Are you one of Lucius's androids? I need to talk to him."

"I'm more than that. I'm Lucius. Who are your friends? Where are Riley and Nate?"

"I'm Riley," said Riley.

"And I'm Nate," said Nate.

"Well now. Everybody is getting new bodies lately. 'I'm not special, no more special than anyone else,' as Herbie Hancock said. What brings you here?"

"You said if we helped you bring down the city, we'd get a place in Lux Machina. Well, we want a place," 3vE said, "Heart isn't safe and the worms will eat everything else."

Lucius shrugged and it rippled across his liquid metal body. "Perhaps. Though I think the worms are getting tired. They've eaten enough for the Hearts to replenish. And with the cities fallen, the Hearts are free to expand. Regardless, you are welcome to stay here for as long as you'd like. However, you can't join us in cryosleep. There aren't enough, chambers, you see. But Douglas would love to keep you company."

"Does he spout cheesy quotes every time he opens his mouth?" Riley wondered.

"I do not," Douglas huffed, "That is not one of my character flaws."

"And there you have it," Lucius said with a metallic smile, "So what do you say? Do we have a deal?"

"Deal," Riley and 3vE said at the same time.

They looked at each other and a new love blossomed in their eyes like pheromones gone supernova.

"What would you say if I told you that I feel like I've loved you my whole life?" she asked him.

"I'd say you're crazy," he replied with a soft smile, "But I feel the same. So I guess I'm crazy too." He pulled her and Nate into a hug. "It's a whole new world out there. And we're lucky enough to get to face it together. As a family."

"Indeed," Lucius nodded. "In the timeless words of Menachem Begin, 'Peace is the beauty of life. It is sunshine. It is the smile of a child, the love of a mother, the joy of a father, the togetherness of a family. It is the advancement of man, the victory of a just cause, the triumph of truth.'"

END

About the Author

Jason never plans to upload his consciousness into a computer. He thoroughly enjoys his humanity, even on bad days. After completing 3vE he plans to dance in the rain a lot more and spend much more time outside before the Mongolian Death Worms start eating everything.

9 781734 070583